COACH IN COTTAGE C

Coach In
COTTAGE C

by Rosemary Ryan Imregi & J.R. Minard

*A story inspired by events
in the life of Victor C. Prinzi*

Disclaimers: *Coach in Cottage C,* created by R.R. Imregi and J.R. Minard, is a work of fiction inspired by recorded memories of Florida State University star quarterback Victor C. Prinzi. Characters are not real, and when events and places are real, they are used fictitiously, without intent to relate to any specific individual or group.

The language of the day in 1961 is distinct, and the authors attempted to reflect the Southern accent and teenage vernacular of that time. They struggled with the use of expressions such as "colored," but in the end left them, not with any derogatory intention, but rather to adhere to historical authenticity.

Cover Photo: Triplex housing units completed by the school's construction forces, *Yellow Jacket Newsletter,* Florida School for Boys, 1958.

Produced by Sea Hill Press Inc.

ISBN: 978-0-578-55571-3

Printed in the United States of America

PREFACE

"One period of time in my life affected me more than any other," said Victor C Prinzi, a Florida State University star quarterback in the late 1950s. "It's the time I spent teaching physical education and coaching at the Florida School for Boys, today known as the Dozier School for Boys."

Thus the authors, Rosemary R. Imregi and J. R. Minard, inspired by events in Coach Prinzi's life in 1961, created *Coach in Cottage C*. The story follows lead character, Matt Grazi, as he struggles as a first time football coach at Colby Hill School for Boys where he battles school policies, defends the rights of teenage inmates, and motivates a rebellious delinquent and his followers to succeed through football.

CHAPTER 1

From across the dusty field, he faced a daunting opponent, not a mighty rival, but rather a rag-tag group of delinquent teenage boys who most likely didn't even want to play. Matteo Franco Grazi, the newest addition to the faculty, crossed his arms and stood erect, starting his first early morning as Colby Hill School for Boys' physical education teacher and football coach. Located in the Florida Panhandle, in 1961, CHB claimed to be one of the largest state-operated boys' correctional facilities in the nation.

The lingering hint of smoked breakfast ham in the damp air of the rural campus reached Matt's nostrils, a stark contrast to the sumptuous smells of the overpriced food vendors surrounding football fields in the past.

The distant platoon of boys shuffled among themselves until, "Atten . . . shun!" reverberated between the longleaf pines, and the adolescents fell into lines. An older boy appeared to be in charge.

"Hup . . . , Hup . . . , Hup two three four." The commanded call set the rhythm of the boys' impending march across the dry ground to their destination, the athletic field where Matt now stood.

The hairs on Matt's arms bristled as he listened to the repeated cadence. Something about a marching group evoked a sense of pride or a feeling of dread, depending on the circumstance. The unfamiliar teens brought neither, but rather a rapid pulse indicating his increased anxiety.

He stole a glance over the shoulder of Coach Tom Faber. Matt's eyes moved past the baseball diamond to the group on the turf.

" . . . the first day I arrived at Colby Hill five years ago," Tom said, interrupting his thoughts, "I had never been a P.E. teacher or a coach either. Relax."

"Easier said than done."

"Hup . . . , Hup . . . , Hup two three four."

"Halt!" the leader ordered. "At ease!"

"Listen up," Tom shouted to the boys as he pointed his finger at Matt. "This is our new coach, Coach Grazi. He'll be teaching P.E. and scouting out talent for the upcoming football team, so straighten up."

Hearing his new title prompted a pump of fresh blood to rush through Matt's body. Yes, he had taken this job because he needed one, but looking at these boys, he knew his decision to coach at Colby Hill was about more than an income.

Matt could not accept that his years spent as an athlete were a waste. Everything he had poured into football had to have a meaning, a worth. Success would provide a way for football to remain an integral, active part of his life.

He licked the sweat from his upper lip and gave a quick nod to Tom. The boys, clad in their state-issued white CHB T-shirts and black shorts, maneuvered themselves either onto the benches or ground. The rough language underneath their breaths as they hammered at each other, suggested the hard life that had led them here.

"Today we concentrate on baseball. One ball for every two players!" Coach Faber ordered. "Pair up! Spread out!" He leaned toward Matt. "You ready, Coach?"

Ready? Baseball? For his entire life, Matt had been geared up for the day he would play professional football. Although he knew "pro" teams cut star players from their rosters before a players' twenty-sixth birthday, he hadn't been prepared when it happened to him.

With that option taken away, he had to make a life-changing adjustment. Today he was as ready as he could be. Matt gave Tom a nod, grabbed a mitt, and positioned himself in front of two boys.

"Heads up!" yelled one teen to his cohort. The ball flew, sailing within inches of his receiver's mitt. Instead of reaching to make the catch, the boy let the ball pass. He glanced at Matt, shrugged his shoulders, and turned his back.

"What the . . . ?" Matt strode toward the boy. "A problem here?" he asked. "Why didn't you try?" The boy shrugged his shoulders again.

Determined to crack the boy's apathetic veneer, Matt ordered both teenagers to face each other. "Back away," he said, moving his hands as if he were parting the Red Sea. Connect three balls in a row."

I remember what a piss-ant I was at his age.

"That's better," Matt said after increased throwing distances resulted in partial success. "Work on it."

He looked for a sign that he had made headway with the boy. Instead, the hooded look of the catcher's eyes flashed a warning, taking him off guard.

As quickly as the boy's anger surfaced, it disappeared. The boy looked right and then left, as if reconsidering his response.

Is he watching for someone? Matt looked about the field but saw no one approaching. The teen stepped backward to join his classmates, but not before he lifted his eyebrows asking permission.

Matt nodded. "Move on."

The boy's behavior confused him, and yet it was not totally unexpected.

Am I handling this kid the right way?

He needed to learn the rules at CHB so he could better respond to a boy who didn't obey. He now regretted cutting his early adolescent psychology classes after late evenings of Florida State football victory celebrations.

Matt picked up a ball and headed toward a different batch of teens, determined to try again.

***

Matt breathed a sigh of relief when his first morning classes were over and caught up with Tom.

"How'd you do?" asked Tom.

"Good," Matt said with a forced, confident air. Time to talk football. "How's the competition this year?"

"Better start recruiting soon. The local high schools, they're tough."

Matt turned with a jerk. "Wait a minute. I thought CHB played teams from other institutions."

"We do. Our boys are competing in the final set of basketball conference games against other reform schools next week." Tom thumped his chest in pride. "But for the bulk of the season, regardless of the sport, we're part of the Panhandle High School League."

Shit.

The thought of limited competition from other institutions evaporated, replaced with the knowledge that CHB would go against established high school teams who had proper facilities. Even more than that, the local schools no doubt had more experienced coaches. Competition outside the penal system made winning more difficult.

Matt bit down on his bottom lip. The coin tossed, a new kind of game was about to begin.

***

After scarfing down a Spam sandwich and an RC Cola and donning a quick change of clothes, Matt walked across the campus toward Assistant Director John Santo's office. The hands on his Timex watch told him he had a few extra minutes before the upcoming meeting with his new boss.

A gnawing at his gut made him look upward and he blinked back a memory of the sun's first rays reaching toward him on the FSU gridiron in 1958, three short years ago. Days in the football limelight were gone, kaput, finished. The crowds of fans that had urged him forward now cheered for a new hero.

He searched the sky for a possible heavenly sign to indicate he had made the right decision to come to Colby Hill. Not forthcoming, he stopped, dropped to one knee, and extended his hand across the warm, scrawny tufts of grass. The hard ground and green scratchiness reminded him that even though he no longer starred as a quarterback, he had an important new role to play.

Matt inhaled a long, deep breath of crisp air and held it in his lungs for four controlled seconds, and then exhaled at the same rate. The long-established ritual released tension from his hands and shoulders. His phone interview had gone well. Now his only thought was how to make a good first impression in person.

After passing through clusters of modest brick and cement buildings, he crossed onto a narrow lane. Arching, twisting limbs of live oak trees draped in Spanish moss formed a canopy so thick, the temperature dropped as if entering a hidden cave. The narrow road opened up along the side of grassy areas, the distance for what seemed like the length of three, or maybe four, football fields.

This place looks more like a country village than a reform school.

"Wait a minute," he said aloud.

Where are the guards, the fences, the walls?

No barriers were in sight, anywhere—no gates, no barbed wire, nothing to keep the boys in, and nothing to keep people out.

Are these boys that well behaved?

The administration building, artfully tucked in at the end of the slightly curved lane, wore green-striped awnings on every window. Matt moved his hands up and down his khaki pants in an attempt to smooth out any wrinkles. He ascended four steps into a darkened foyer and moved into the reception area, striding past the one lone couch pressed against the wallpapered wall.

Approaching an oversized antique oak desk, he focused on the smiling, attractive, young brunette behind it. He spotted the nameplate with "Mary Jo Armstrong" prominently etched in black on a gold background. Her first words let Matt know she held the title of "Southern belle."

"Hey there," she said with a twang. Matt returned the smile, and the effort lifted his spirits.

One thing Matt had learned during his college years was that a girl's slow Southern speech might take a while to get used to, but five will get you ten, the voice will come from a gorgeous gal. Mary Jo proved the point.

"Mr. Grazi, I presume," the word "I" pronounced "Ah." "Please have a seat, and I'll go fetch Mr. Santo directly. The keys to your room and the paperwork will be ready for you when you git finished."

She leaned across the desk toward Matt and continued in her delightful drawl.

"I don't know much when it comes to football, but I surely do understand we're *lucky* to have a big celebrity like you joinin' us."

Matt nodded his thanks. *A big celebrity?* At the moment he didn't feel that way.

Matt knew his football record had played a major part in securing the coaching job. But he also was aware that success as a quarterback didn't automatically translate into a dynamite teaching or coaching career.

He had heard the saying that athletes who couldn't play well became good coaches. He couldn't remember if a saying existed about so-called football heroes doing the same. He sure couldn't think of one.

Sitting on the once blue sofa, he poked at the sagging cushions in an effort to be comfortable. Lifting his hand toward his neck to loosen his tie, he realized he wasn't wearing one.

A moment later, John Santo charged out of his office with excitement, his hand extended.

"Mr. Grazi!"

"Yes, sir!"

"No need for the 'sir' stuff. Folks call me Director Santo," he said with a smile. "Santo, to you, Matt."

"Indeed a pleasure, Santo."

"All mine. Welcome to CHB. Can't believe we've landed a young man with your expertise to coach our Ospreys!"

Matt's misgivings shrank away, and his confidence surged. He easily kept pace with Santo's long strides as they moved down the hallway into his office. Topped with a prematurely receding hairline, Santo's tall, hefty frame and loose-fitting shirt didn't fit Matt's vision of a top administrator. Matt had expected a formal tie and jacket, but relaxed at seeing evidence of the more casual dress code.

With Matt finally in his office, Santo appeared to scan his new coach's close-cropped, and yet wavy, dark hair. His gaze slowly turned downward to Matt's newly polished leather wingtips. After a quick nod, the supervisor's eyes moved upward, seeming to take in Matt's muscular frame, his sinewy arms, and his angular face. Six-foot-tall Matt weighed in lighter than other players his same height. Yet, strength showed as one of his obvious assets.

Matt shuffled from one foot to the other, questioning how he had scored on the unspoken test. "So, do I pass?" he asked in his distinctive, gravelly voice.

"Sorry. Guess I didn't expect a quarterback like you to be such a tall, lanky fellow. Tell you what, you sure have a strong, accurate arm on that football field."

"*Had* some arm," Matt countered, "although it still works quite well."

"Our gain, Matt."

"Sure hope so."

Santo gestured toward a chair facing his desk. "So, heard Tom showed you the ropes." The director moved to the opposite side, sat, and faced the new coach.

"Yeah, gym classes went okay. Learned a lot. I had no idea Colby Hill's been around for over fifty years and was originally a home for wayward boys *and* girls. Kinda like FSU, which started off as a women's college."

"Opened up to men in the late forties, right? Well, like Florida State, CHB had girls until just a few years ago. Small at the beginning, today we have nearly one hundred buildings and over two hundred employees. I'm proud to say, we teach over six hundred boys everything from animal husbandry to advanced English. Only thing we need now is a winning football team."

Santo winked at Matt and rose from his chair. He pointed upward to the side wall toward a portrait of a formidable, stern man wearing a starched shirt, tie, and jacket.

"Dr. Adam Strickland, our superintendent, is in charge of the program. His vision is to rehabilitate troubled youths in an environment of beauty and peacefulness, and he's done just that." Santo moved to the window. "How about those stunning redbud trees?" he asked, gazing toward the splashes of purplish flowers. "I tell you, the maintenance staff and their inmates do a fantastic job."

Inmates. Matt flinched. The term was at odds with the lush surroundings. Was this more a school or a prison?

"Hey," Santo said as he reached out and grabbed his sunglasses from the top of the inbox, "Let's get outta here. I want to show you the campus before you go to your cottage."

Matt calmed his instinct to bypass the nature walk and address the team. The tour could come later, and yet, it seemed it couldn't. He knotted his brow, not from disinterest, but from impatience.

"Big place," he said.

"Fourteen hundred acres. Nature provides the fence for most of the grounds and lights keep the open areas illuminated."

"I'll be honest," Matt ventured, as he shifted uneasily. "I don't understand the lack of tighter security."

"We don't want the boys to feel locked up."

"Boys walk around without supervision?"

"Definitely not. The inmates understand that we expect them to be in a pre-approved location every minute of the day. And of course, we make clear the penalties for not meeting that expectation.

"Look over there, on the other side of the road," Santo continued.

"As you know, we have two sides of campus. You'll be here on the South Side, of course. The North Side has its own colored coaches and team."

Matt hadn't considered it any other way. The same segregation policy had existed at Florida State.

"Yes, sir. Can't wait to meet the players." Matt knew that both his comfort level and adrenaline would increase once he met with the football team.

"Players? What players?"

Matt shot a glance at Santo. "What do you mean, 'What players'?"

"Most boys who played last year aren't here anymore. I thought I made it clear you're to create a team, then coach it. The constant turnover of boys requires us to recruit new players every season."

Matt's open mouth hung speechless.

His experience as a quarterback never included working with only freshmen. Returning upperclassmen provided the backbone of high school and college teams, imparting leadership and stability.

"Average length of stay here is about a year," Santo said, "and we automatically lose last year's seventeen year olds, regardless of their sentence. Before their eighteenth birthday, inmates either go home or move on to state prison."

Santo appeared to read the pessimism in Matt's demeanor and hesitated before he spoke again. "I realize the extent of recruiting and training new players presents an added challenge."

Damn right.

"I expected to create a new team by organizing existing and future players," Matt said, "not to start the entire process from scratch."

"Sorry about that. Was I clear that we *not only* want you to create a new team, but we also expect a winning record?"

"That part I got."

"You must understand, Matt." Santo took a long breath. "A lot depends on the score, not just for a record or a trophy. A winning football season generates better funding, positive media attention, and increased support from the community. The more sports that trophy, the larger our budget. A successful state athletic program means increased opportunities and more supplies for our boys."

"I understand. I'm as anxious to win as you are."

They continued their walk in silence. Santo pointed out the hospital, upholstery shop and sewing center, dental office, and newly constructed guidance building. When they circled back toward the administration building, Santo brought Matt's attention to the white church steeple poking up through the large shrubs.

"Church every Sunday."

Matt's mind was still on the nonexistent team.

"And one more thing, about the importance of overcoming the odds," Santo said, "a winning team helps a boy feel accepted and proud, which goes a long way when the young man returns home. It shows we're able to foster school spirit and provide meaningful activity. Success makes the inmates seem like normal teenagers to outsiders. That's important."

"Feeling accepted and being proud happens whenever a team comes together," Matt said, "regardless if they win." He let his point sink in. "But I admit, comradery and pride increase with every victory. It's the nature of any sport."

"Okay, then. Let's get started. You were a winner in high school and college. We need a winner. You'll figure out how to do it."

Santo raised his index finger toward the rear of the campus where a row of wooden cottages lined the chalky road. "Your place is down there. After you pick up the key and other materials from Mary Jo, feel free to walk around. Settle in." The assistant director gave a parting wave, and Matt watched him disappear.

He connected with Santo regarding the man's concern for the boys, and he appreciated his boss's welcome. Matt accepted the urging that his life as a successful quarterback prepared him for this job, but his plans had been derailed. No return of veteran players made victory on the field difficult.

After a few seconds, he turned his head, and then his entire body in a complete circle, taking it all in. The expectations were evident, and the map to reach them was Matt's to draw and follow.

***

Moments later Matt found Mary Jo sitting at her desk in the office. "You gittin' along all right?" she asked, as she smiled and reached for a dangling cluster of labeled keys. Explaining the detailed function of each at a slow, Southern pace, she plopped what seemed like an unending stack of papers in front of him.

"This here's a map of the place, sugar. We're right here, admin," she said, pointing to a square on the diagram. "And thar's your new home, catty-corner to the dentist office. You'll be parkin' in this here lot." She smiled again, circling another area on the map with a freshly sharpened pencil.

"Muchchablige," Matt said. It was easy to slide into the Southern lingo.

"You come by now," she added, "if you need any hep at all."

Matt found his colonial white Ford Fairlane in the front parking area and drove to the lot designated for cottage living. Taking a deep breath, he leaned across the red vinyl front seat to straighten the papers and placed them inside his satchel. Throwing the smaller bag over his shoulder, he grabbed a larger one, which together held everything he needed for the night. He would unpack his stereo and other things tomorrow. About to head for his new residence, Matt turned back when he remembered one other possession. Reaching down to the floor of the front seat, he tucked a precious game ball under his arm.

Crossing a gravel road, Matt noted wooden arrow signs, Washington Cottage, Jackson Cottage, and Madison Cottage, pointing toward what he presumed was the boys' housing. Polk, Wilson, and Monroe signs stood on the opposite side. Something about a name was so much more personal than a number.

"Hey, there," called a salt-and-pepper-haired man shuffling around the corner. Matt observed his brisk but uneven gait, until it slowed on approach. "You the new coach?"

"Yeah, guess I am."

"Bart, Bart Rourk," the man said as he extended his arm and gripped Matt's hand. "I'm a cottage father."

"Cottage father?"

"Yep. My wife and I live upstairs at Monroe," he said, pointing to the dwelling behind him. "Another father lives at the opposite end, and about thirty boys reside below."

"You live with these guys?" Matt asked, failing to conceal his alarm.

"I do. I work a shift, and then switch off with my cohort. We're pretty good at spotting trouble."

"You're upstairs and they're down? Can you trust them around your family?"

"Don't need to trust 'em. My job is to supervise 'em."

"You like your job?"

"The inmates and I get along fine for the most part, and although the pay may not be great, the cost of rent is excellent."

"Aha," Matt said, relaxing his jaw a notch.

"Have you met our night watchman?" Bart asked. "He's a cranky son of a gun who counts heads all night long, and logs numbers into a watch clock he carries on his hip. He sounds the alarm whenever numbers don't add up, or something seems amiss."

"Oh, I feel safer now."

"Heard that." Both men cracked a smile.

"The watchman does his job at night, and I'm on these boys' asses every minute of the day. In the dining hall, the hospital, off campus with a parent, or anywhere else, they always check in with me. Oh, except in the gym and on the field. That's when they're your job."

Matt had been told the importance of knowing who was in class, but he hadn't considered the repercussions if he missed somebody.

"Accountability is number one around here. But no worry, you'll find a way to keep count, get the scoop on every boy, and do your job. All of us do."

A memory of Matt's high school homeroom teacher rose up in his mind. During roll call, Matt's best friend had often responded to the call of his name and vice versa. It had taken the teacher days to figure out who was who. The two of them had hidden their smirks and laughter well.

Now the stakes were higher. A missing boy at Colby Hill could result in much more than laughter. It wasn't far-fetched to imagine a boy falling from a building, or attacking someone. Matt's shoulders straightened up, as if he already knew constant vigilance was an unspoken prerequisite for the job. An accurate roll call moved up his list of priorities.

"Hey, look. Come by for a cottage tour. You'll be fine. It all falls into place, believe me. They're not all bad kids, ya know." Before turning to limp away, he leaned toward Matt. "In fact, I've become quite attached. You will, too."

Matt appreciated Bart's cordial information and encouragement, but the implication that guarding these boys was as important as coaching them was difficult to digest. *Nothing* could be more important than coaching a football team, except of course, playing on one.

Moving down the lane, Matt arrived at a wooden triplex, Cottages A–C. He took a step up between two thin white boards serving as columns supporting a triangular roof and crossed the meager cement platform toward the door of Cottage C. His fingers found the right key, and he repositioned it several times in the steel lock before it turned. Pleased with the sturdy click, he entered the cramped but private living quarters. The twin bed and bare desk caught the late afternoon rays of the sun beaming down through an ancient wooden window.

He plopped down on the squeaky bed. He had shared similar sparse areas during his college days at FSU, but here, at least he had no room-mates to consider. This space belonged to him. No coach yelled, "Lights out!" tonight.

He pulled a stack of papers from his satchel and, deciding to skip dinner, he rifled through a snack bag for beef jerky and Twinkies. He spent time reading over the Resident Rulebook and reviewed his faculty paperwork. Colby Hill School for Boys had chosen him. How many other candidates had applied for the job?

His minor in adolescent criminal psychology at FSU had undoubt-edly helped him land the position, but his conversation with Santo confirmed it was his football notoriety that had clinched the deal.

He pulled out a draft of the pep talk he had prepared for the team, his words designed to make an impact. He crumpled the pages and tossed them into the plastic wastebasket.

What if he wasn't up to the challenge? Would he have to sacri-fice coaching time for safety? He let go of the questions and gravitated toward one concept, "get to know these boys." The more he learned, the easier to keep track, the better to train.

It would be fine.

Sunlight fading, Matt was about to unpack when, instead, he moved toward the window. He rubbed his finger over the rusted, broken lock, thick with paint. The frame lifted with ease, and he felt the cool February air hit his face.

So much for security. Being a light sleeper would have to be enough for now.

He reached for his garnet-and-gold toiletry bag and gray Big Ben alarm clock. After pulling out the metal probe to set his wake-up time, he placed both items on the stained nightstand.

Within minutes, a distinctive *hoo, hoo, too-HOO; hoo, hoo, too-HOO, ooo* of an owl echoed into the air.

"A noisy fella," Matt said, as he moved back toward the window and stared into the dusky woods. The cool evening temperature allowed him the luxury of closing the window, but the thin glass and warped frame didn't diminish the serenade.

After a bar of Ivory soap and Colgate toothpaste had done their jobs, Matt moved to the bed and stretched out his six-foot frame. He ignored the antiseptic smell of Clorox lingering in the air.

The military sound of *Taps* from a lone bugler across campus echoed through the trees. About to doze off, instead, he pushed himself upward and stepped over his shoes toward the desk. He retrieved the wrinkled papers from the wastepaper basket and smoothed them out with his palm.

Falling back on the bed, he closed his eyes. The enormity of the task in front of Matteo Franco Grazi rose up like a three-hundred-pound linebacker. He couldn't run from it, nor did he want to.

The imagined sheep that folks count to combat wakefulness never worked for him. Instead, he visualized an unending line of boys jumping over a fence onto an open football field. He tallied each boy, one by one, until his body settled in and he let go.

Chapter 2

Matt woke with a start and slapped at the blaring alarm, taking a few seconds to recall where he was. Morning's light tossed dust motes about its beam, and *Reveille* sounded from the boys' bugle corps.

He turned on his AM\FM radio to hear the news of the day. As he spun the tuning dial to eliminate the interfering static, highlights of last month's inaugural address carried across the air. President Kennedy's voice filled the room's interior. "My fellow Americans, ask not what your country can do for you; ask what you can do for your country." His arms felt a prickle of pride.

His hand turned the radio's dial away from the news to the local music station, and with the lyrics blaring, he tried to relax by humming along with Del Shannon as he sang "Runaway," a song climbing toward number two on the 1961 *Top 40 Record Chart*. It helped a little.

A quick shower and shave cleared his head, and he pulled on his athletic gear. Santo greeted him outside as he locked his cottage.

"Sleep okay?" Santo asked.

"Slept well." He silently cursed the owl's early repetitions outside his window.

Damn owl.

As the two walked across the grounds, lines of boys emerged from every cottage, slipping on light jackets and rubbing the crust from their eyes.

"Wow," Matt said. "Is this a fire drill?"

Santo laughed. "Nope, just three hundred hungry boys headed for the chow line. Another three hundred on the other side doing the same."

He explained that inmates on both sides of the road had different career objectives. The white boys were required to make progress in school and worked in South Side facilities like the hospital, dental office, store, admin and gym. For the most part, colored inmates grew the crops, logged the land, and learned trades in brick, mortar, and woodwork. The only time coloreds crossed over from one side to another was to labor in the kitchen, laundry or maintenance crews.

"Every employee is responsible to help the boys succeed in education and job training. You'll play your part by keeping the boys fit, teaching gym classes, maintaining the gym, and of course, building up the football team."

"Sounds like you've got everything figured out. I imagine these guys need all the help they can get to stay ahead in school and perform well during their work hours. It's got to be hard when they arrive home, once this stay becomes part of their record."

"Indeed. Did you meet the crew of inmates assigned to the gym?"

"Not yet," Matt said, as the dining hall doors swung wide. "Today."

"Breakfast!" Santo shouted.

The aroma of sizzling sage sausage wafted past them as they moved through the spacious, but unadorned, clapboard building.

They weaved their way between thirty to forty tables, each seating four to eight boys and topped with a simple vase holding a single azalea branch. Santo confirmed the inmates had cut the flowers from the surrounding campus bushes.

"A homey touch, don't you think?" he asked with a slight smile. "A new experience for some."

Inmates shuffled into serving lines wearing the standard uniform that included the state-issued white shirts and black pants. They wore black leather brogans on their feet. Most sported identical D.A. (duck's ass) haircuts, greased back on the sides, coming to a point below the nape of the neck.

The boys appeared sloppy and disheveled, their shirts wrinkled, shoes unpolished. Matt thought it strange that the school didn't require a tighter dress code, but he kept his observations to himself.

The boys lined up at two buffet stations where a kitchen crew of colored inmates plopped oatmeal and other hot breakfast foods onto their plates. Staff members paced between each area of tables, watching the boys as they ate.

"Someone I'd like you to meet," Santo said. He waved toward a heavyset man patrolling the room's middle section. He extended his arm into the air toward the man, tapped his watch, splayed five fingers, and flashed them twice to indicate the man needed to come over in ten minutes.

"Andrews is my right-hand man," Santo said. "He's on the rotating schedule for dining hall duty. Every faculty member has an extracurricular responsibility."

"Me, too?"

"Yep, you're on the emergency call roster. On occasion, you'll help us lead fire drills, break up fights, and assist in locating students. Things like that."

Other tasks to take away time from coaching.

They had almost finished their meals of heaped sausage patties, bright-yellow scrambled eggs, and grits, when Santo motioned for Matt to join him on the side of the staff serving area. After an obligatory welcome and rigid handshake, Santo introduced Carl Andrews.

"This guy maintains order, without him, chaos," he said to Matt.

Andrews acknowledged the compliment with a smile. "Thanks, John." He grunted Santo's first name, implying that the two were close. "We run a tight ship here. Inmates are my charge, and I take that task seriously."

Don't we all?

"Round here, I ensure these plebes follow the rules and behave," Andrews said, pointing to his chest. He craned his muscular, square neck inches closer to Matt.

Matt was tempted to step away, but instead held his ground. He drew his arm high across his chest in a blocking position.

Andrews seemed to sense Matt's resistance and stepped back. "If a boy does what he's supposed to do," he said, "rewards come his way. When he doesn't, well . . . then it's my job to set him straight. If these boys received discipline at home, we wouldn't need places like CHB. But let me tell you," Andrews said, inflating his chest and patting it, "once they've screwed up, it's our *duty* to provide the structure they need. Hell, it works the same way here as it does in the Marines. I know what I'm talking about; I used to be in the Corps."

Matt made a mental note to never tangle with this guy. He visualized a clear picture of the overbearing drill instructor barking out rules on orientation day.

"Each inmate *will* toe the line," Andrews continued, pointing to the hard ground, "even if I have to personally break every bone in his body." An ear-to-ear grin covered the disciplinarian's face.

Break every bone in his body?

"Is Andrews for real?" Matt asked, as he and Santo returned to their table to finish their coffee.

Santo gave a dismissive wave. "You'll come to understand Andrews. He's been here a long time. He keeps things running smoothly." He cocked his head toward Matt as if he were about to tell a secret. "He takes care of the everyday issues with the inmates, and his methods are effective. These boys aren't sent here because they're nice fellows, if you know what I mean."

"But . . ."

"But what?"

Matt considered the timing of confiding doubts to his new boss and held his tongue. He certainly didn't want to be viewed as confrontational, or even worse, have his job over before it started.

Don't rock the boat.

"Nothing," Matt said.

"You'll see Andrews all over campus. Get to know him. He can handle any situation and make your life easier."

Although Matt accepted corporal punishment as an accepted means of discipline, his impression of Andrews' enthusiastic, head-cracking approach left him with more questions than answers.

Santo has to know what he's talking about.

Perhaps the blustering Andrews was just that . . . bluster. He accepted that premise for now, despite his instant dislike for the man.

***

Matt joined Coach Tom Faber on the field for a gym class, leaning down to help lift an extra equipment bag.

"What'd you think of Santo?" Tom asked.

"Went okay. He told me about the team, or lack of one."

"Oh, yeah. A year's stay is about right. Think you'll last that long?"

"Count on it."

"Then come on. Time for introductions."

"Didn't we cover that yesterday?"

"Oh, today's classes are a different group of boys. Inmates don't go to school five days a week like kids in a normal school. They attend class every other day."

Tom explained that the five-day school and work week alternated. "A boy who has school on Monday, Wednesday, and Friday the first week has school on Tuesday and Thursday the following week. On a work crew every other day."

"How the hell does this schedule affect practice?" Matt asked.

"It works out. You'll see. The regime keeps the boys with short attention spans on their toes. And think of it this way, today's gym classes may hold the football team recruits you're looking for, except for the younger elementary and middle school kids."

"Kids are *that* young?"

"Most of our younger classes are made up of ten- to fourteen-year-olds. Got one inmate who's only seven."

"Is that even legal?"

"Guess so."

"Seven years old?"

"The kid's a pro at stealing money out of telephone booths. He's a slugger when it comes to smashing telephones, and he won't stay in school. Been caught over a dozen times."

"So you got any older football prospects picked out for me, in the classes we're not babysitting?"

"Ha. One you might like is Richard Bern, a big, burly guy who *loves* rough-necking. Another real athlete is Harry Beauregard. The inmates call him Bo for short. He arrived in January, a month before you."

"What's he in for?" Matt asked.

"This time? Breaking and entering. Last time, auto theft. That boy knows how to work the system. But if he isn't careful, he'll get more days added to his sentence. With little effort, he guarantees himself a future accommodation at Apalachee State. It's the correctional institute down the road a piece."

Tom turned toward the incoming gym class. "Look, as usual, the boys need help quieting down."

"Who's the tall kid with each class?" Matt asked.

"A higher ranked inmate with a good record at CHB. He's usually a boy close to discharge." Tom reiterated yesterday's procedure of throwing baseballs. "See who stands out for you."

"Which one's Bo?"

"Not here."

"What do you mean?"

"In the next class, with the younger inmates."

"That doesn't make sense."

"Flunked his placement test, I bet."

Matt had learned that a placement test determined which classes a boy attended. But despite a poor grade, it was inconceivable a sixteen year old would end up in a class of elementary or middle school boys.

"It doesn't happen often, but it happens," Tom said.

After fifty minutes the bell's clang signaled gym class was over and the first group moved on to their next class. The younger group appeared within minutes.

Matt recognized Bo immediately. Although only five feet ten inches or so in height, he towered over the younger boys. As the inmates moved toward their assigned positions, Bo separated himself from the others and sauntered onto the field's fringe.

Crossing his arms, Matt watched. About one hundred seventy pounds, Bo's muscular body and narrow waist appeared as if chiseled from stone. With sandy colored hair atop his broad forehead, he had a square, determined jaw.

When Bo raised his arm or finger, four or five boys fell over themselves trying to accommodate him by scrambling to be the one to toss him a ball or move out for a catch. The teenage athlete appeared to garner respect from every boy around him. Matt observed the result of secret commands given by word or hand, the boys nodding and scattering into designated positions.

Even the older inmate who escorted the group kept Bo in sight. Whenever signaled, he moved closer for further direction from the kingpin.

Matt took slow steps toward the boy. *If Bo has this type of influence, he could be the ticket to getting others on board.*

A tattoo on Bo's forearm became visible. Common in the military, Matt had never seen one on a teen. The unidentifiable dark symbol beside a smashing inked hammer, spoke loud and clear, *I am a warrior. I am a bad-ass. Stay away from me.*

Matt caught the questioning look on Bo's face and returned the stare. Standing tall, he held the boy's gaze. The new coach's stature and determined eye contact gave out a message of his own.

I'm the new leader in this pack.

Bo turned away.

Good.

Class continued, and even though Bo obeyed all requests, he did so in the slowest way possible. Matt sensed resistance, but he also felt an inner strength emanate from the boy, strength that could carry a team.

His mind wandered. *If this street-smart offender would follow my lead . . .*

After class, Tom joined Matt, and they walked across the field.

"Spot anyone?" Tom asked.

"Bern is one massive kid who still thinks he's back on the streets. With proper direction, he could be some blocker. Bo is in incredible physical shape, but I sense a strong reluctance to participate. It's obvious a pecking order exists here."

"It adjusts with every new arrival."

"And Bo seems to have risen to the top, fast."

"Probably has to do with him being a known repeat customer at CHB, or his reputation as a competitive boxer."

Inmates listened to their instincts. In order to survive up against an inmate like Bo, who demanded respect, they either succumbed, stayed away, or confronted him.

"Noted a few other possibilities too," Matt added.

"That's a start. I've watched you play, you know," Tom said. "You were good. Very good."

"Thanks. Appreciate that."

"So, how come you're not playing football with the pros?"

Matt inhaled and bit down on his lower lip, drawing back from the uncomfortable question. It seemed just yesterday he had been a college quarterback with bigger and better things to come. Drafted by the New York Giants, he had endless possibilities, before it fell apart.

"Graduating ended the college game," Matt said, "then dropped from the Giants' roster early in the season."

"That stinks. But didn't you get picked up by the Denver Broncos?"

"Yup."

The newly founded 1959 American Football League, which included the Broncos, was looking to stock their team with quality players.

They included NFL castoffs like Matt.

"Yeah, thought I was lucky when that happened. Didn't turn out that way. After three games, their budget demanded a decrease in size. Never got a chance to prove myself."

Embarrassed, Matt wished he'd gone out with a life-changing injury. Folks could understand and admire that. He'd been just a player who didn't cut it. He pressed his lips together and took a breath.

"You're a pro," Tom said. "Your talent is wasted here."

"Tom, I . . ."

"You're too good for this place."

Matt didn't speak for several seconds. "Tom," he said in a lowered, gravelly voice, "nobody . . . is too good for *any* place."

Tom squinted at Matt as if studying him, or contemplating the words he had spoken.

"Look," Matt continued, "I've committed myself to recruit and coach boys to play football for CHB, and that's what I intend to do."

"Okay," Tom said, "I'm glad. Let's circle the bleachers before we head back to the gym, and I'll point out the worn area around the football field they call a track."

"So how about last year's team? How'd they do?"

"Recently, it's been sad. Haven't won in seven years. That's why we're so thrilled to have a pro like you. "

"Seven years?" Matt blurted. "Not one game in seven years?"

A twinkle appeared in Tom's eye. "Okay, okay," he laughed. "That may be a bit of an exaggeration. Thought it might motivate you to jump right in."

Motivation to jump right out, Matt thought, not amused.

"Look, I'm kidding. Like most years, they lost more than they won." The two coaches rounded the bleacher area and moved on to the pool area.

"An Olympic size pool?"

"The boys compete in swimming and diving. Hey, did Santo tell you about the conference basketball games next weekend? You'll probably be required to go. You can check out our best kids in action."

"And the boys who aren't our best kids?"

"The tougher boys have potential," Tom said. "But most don't want to exert themselves unless it instantly benefits them. But, hell, maybe with a little investigation and lots of charm, you could round them up."

Matt's palm moved to his forehead in frustration. Eyeing Tom, he shook his head.

"Oh, and I'd skip the chorus class if I were you," Tom added. "Not really a recruitment area for the macho types you'll need on the field, if you know what I mean." He looked up into the sky's incoming grayness and focused downward on their disappearing shadows. The air spun in mixed directions. "Damn, a storm brewing. Inside."

"Wait, I . . ." Matt began, but Tom had already upped his pace to beat the heavy raindrops.

"And a warning, knowing Santo, after the basketball game he might ask a college guy like you to write an article about the players for the CHB newsletter, *The Flying Osprey.*" Tom took a breath before adding, "My writing stinks."

Matt hadn't considered writing newspaper articles as one of his duties, but he was learning fast that requests or mandatory assignments could come from any angle.

Within minutes the boys gathered inside under the basketball hoops. A buzz of conversations emerged. The inmates' voices grew louder.

"Lower the noise level!" Tom boomed from across the court.

"Hey, this is our free time, man!" one of the boys responded.

"Not anymore, pal," Tom yelled as he excused himself and ran across the floor toward the ruckus. "Be right back, Matt," he shouted over his head.

Matt watched from afar as Tom cornered the culprits and leaned toward them. Within moments the boys lowered their heads, and a hushed silence replaced the bawdy outbursts.

Control. Absolutely necessary.

Despite Tom's quirky sense of humor, his display of authority climbed him up a notch in Matt's estimation.

***

Classes over, Matt grabbed the wad of keys from his jacket and walked to his car. He retrieved his stereo and remaining personal items and entered his room. Having limited living space, he placed the speakers so he could achieve the best sound.

With a click, "My Prayer" a song by The Platters, crooned at his discretion. The rhythm from the record player eased his mind and reminded him of home. He stacked his albums on the flat board of pine

above the desk as a librarian shelved books, putting each artist in al-
phabetical order, Bill Haley and the Comets, Carl Perkins, and Little
Richard. Satisfied, Matt took out a weathered framed photograph of
his parents and placed it on the nightstand.

*How easily I could have ended up in a place like this. Hey, I am in
a place like this.*

At this moment Matt appreciated, more than ever, his parents'
sacrifice for him. The second of five boys, Matt had grown up on
Staten Island, one of the five boroughs of New York City. When
World War II raged from 1939 through 1945, local folks neither accepted nor trusted the minority populations of Italian or German
descent. Matt's middle school classmates seldom let him forget the
European lineage of his father, a baker who had emigrated from Italy.
Even ten years later, the word "wop" stung. The slur from his teenage
peers implied Italians were second-rate citizens.

Matt's experience with teens who enjoyed breaking the law first
prompted him to retreat, but not long after, he realized no satisfaction in backing off. Instead, to shut up the petty hoodlums, he joined
in their games of vandalism and shoplifting, determined to show he
could be one of them.

When he came home one night, bragging about street signs he
and his fourteen-year-old friends had stolen, his father's demeanor
flattened.

"*Vieni con me.* Come with me."

Tools in hand, he escorted Matt back to every crime site. As they
replaced the signs, his father laced into him.

"You want to prove you're better than those boys who call you
names? Then do it with your brain. Make something of yourself.
Mamma and I have dreams for you, and jail is not one of them.

"This is America. You have a choice. Either use your body and
brain to become a success, or follow the code of these thugs and end
up facing time. If you choose the later, you may never see us again. We
love you. Don't you know that?"

Matt had gone forward to become a decent student and good athlete. His FSU coaches trained and supported him, and together with
his teammates, they had become his second family.

That's it.

The same blend of ingredients that saved him from going down
the wrong road could work for these boys. He would convince these

delinquents that the team needed to go forward as a family. And of course, he wanted to make his folks proud. Yes, that went without saying.

CHAPTER 3

On his third day at Colby Hill, Matt devoured a scrumptious breakfast in the dining hall and looked at his watch. He jumped up, threw his tray onto the conveyor belt circling into the kitchen, and sprinted toward the gym.

"You sleep last night?" Tom asked as he poked his head around Matt's office door.

"Mostly. But what's with the owl? I'm big on nature, but this fella makes a racket."

"Now don't pick on our nighttime mascot. The barred owl keeps our rodent population down. He's been here a long time. You actually saw him? Wow."

"I actually heard him."

"You'll get used to him."

"When?"

Tom laughed. "Like your new digs?"

Matt's office consisted of one of three small rooms to the side of the gym. It held a standard desk, two file cabinets, and an extra chair where a boy could sit. His coaches during his playing days had occupied similar sparse settings at FSU.

He gave Tom the obligatory, "Nice," and pushed aside debris

sprawled across his wooden desk, presumably left by the previous occupant.

Tom turned toward the over-flowing metal monster in the corner. "How about I give you a little assistance and introduce you to the always present paperwork?" For thirty minutes they reviewed state forms requiring completion on a daily, weekly, and monthly basis.

"I was the first to enter the dining hall this morning, Tom, and couldn't help noticing the beefy arms on the colored kid serving the grits. Bet that kid could be some lineman."

"What?"

"Wish I could recruit . . ."

"Are you nuts? You know where you are?"

"Yeah, but Jackie Robinson . . ."

"Stop. Not another word."

"Listen . . ."

"No, you listen. No coloreds on the FSU team, right?"

"Well right, but that was a few years ago and . . ."

"And things are still the same. White boys compete at white schools, colored boys compete at colored schools. Things aren't any different here than anywhere else in the Panhandle, or for that matter, any different from the rest of the South."

"It's just that I saw the massive arms on this kid and thought . . ."

"Enough. Keep your scouting on this side of campus. One of our chief crew members is ready to meet you next door in the equipment room. Concentrate on that."

Feeling like a kid who touched a hot plate to test the temperature, Matt drew back. He moved from his office to the nearby open doorway of the storage area where a red-haired boy sat in a chair, beating an imaginary drum. Amused by the solo, he stood in place until the boy became aware of his presence and jumped to attention.

"Sir? Oh, eh, hello, Mr. Grazi. I'm Mulany." He shifted his gaze downward, fidgeting with his hands.

"Hey, it's okay," Matt gave the boy a reassuring pat on the back. "I hear you're responsible for keeping this place in tip-top shape. I'm on my way to take a closer look at the gym and showers. Join me. Oh, and let's drop that 'Mr. Grazi.' It makes me feel old. 'Coach' will do."

They moved down the hallway, and Matt eased into small talk about campus life. They entered the boys' locker room.

"Pretty disgusting," Matt wrinkled his nose at the shower area. "And just what is that dark, cottony ooze near the drain?"

Mulany stepped back. "Sir?"

"You didn't hear me?"

"Yeah, but . . . Mr. . . . I mean, Coach, we clean the showers almost every time we use 'em."

"Ah, that might be the problem. If you clean almost every day, the way this looks is not surprising. You may wipe things down, but it doesn't appear that you really clean."

"I dunno how much cleaner we can get 'em. Hell, we do our best."

"Watch your mouth. No place for that here."

"Yes, sir."

Matt ran a finger across the shower tiles. He raised his brown, scum-covered digit toward the boy.

"Your best will have to be better." Seeing the frown deepen on the boy's face, he slowed. "Crewing here isn't easy. Not only do you have to keep things sparkling, you must distribute and collect equipment, assist Coach Faber and me, and handle any task set before you. That right?"

Mulany nodded.

"And I understand you do it better than any other crew member. That right, too?"

Mulany cocked his head toward Matt, as if questioning whether he had really received a compliment. "Yes, Coach."

Matt grabbed the sudsy bucket and plunged his hand deep into the bottom for the sponge and brush. "Okay then, here, let me show you, sponge first, brush second, clear rinse. Repeat if necessary. Got it?"

"Yeah, I got it."

"Look," Matt faced the boy. "There's a chance someday you'll go into the service, where a sergeant will perform what's called a 'white glove' inspection. He'll wipe his gloved fingers over a surface like I'm doing, and if there's the tiniest smudge, he'll order a re-scrubbing, with a toothbrush if necessary. I won't go the toothbrush route, but you need to clean the shower area again. Come to my office when it's ready for re-inspection."

Mulany scrunched his face and grabbed the dripping, soapy cloth. He disappeared into the shower, mumbling a barely audible, "Son of a bitch!"

Although Matt felt he had succeeded in showing Mulany who was in charge, the boy's parting comment indicated he was not on board. For the next thirty minutes, Matt agonized over what his next response needed to be, based on either a negative or positive re-inspection.

When the boy reported back to Matt, he spoke in a more reserved manner. "Coach, wanna take another look at everything?"

Matt followed the boy to the shower area. "Ah, you're getting the idea." His shoulders relaxed with relief. "Not bad. Not bad at all."

Mulany's response indicated he expected more. "You're really a hard-ass, ain't you, Coach?"

Stunned, Matt held off answering. He knew he had pushed the boy, but certainly not as hard as he could have.

"No, I'm not a hard-ass." Matt's voice was firm. "But there are things I want done, and I want them done well." When Mulany didn't reply, he started again.

"Listen, I want you to handle what I dish out, to deal with anything I throw at you, not just because that's what I want, but because that's what somebody else will demand of you when you return to the outside. If you learn how to cope with conditions here, you'll be able to better handle the crummy things that will come down the line. Does that make any sense to you?"

Mulany took a step back and eyed Matt. "Okay," he mumbled.

"You're damn right, 'okay'."

A hush fell on the room. Mulany shuffled from one foot to another before raising his head.

Matt lowered his voice again. "You'll learn I'm on your side, but right now, if you want to remain on this crew, I've got to see you're on mine."

"All right. All right, Coach." Matt nodded and threw the dirty rags into the hamper.

"Let's talk about shiny floors and clean showers another time," Matt said. They moved down the hallway toward his office. "You play basketball or baseball?"

"Baseball, sometimes. I like sports. I figure it's a good way to pass time, and it helps to keep my nose clean."

"And how does one keep his nose clean around here?"

Mulany thought for a moment and then shrugged. "You stay away from trouble, you don't get near the edge or gray areas, and you make yourself real visible to anybody who's gonna be marking you."

Make yourself visible to somebody marking you. Now that's a concept.

"Anything else?" Matt asked.

"Yeah, most of all, you pick your friends, real careful like."

"Yeah, bet that's right."

"Coach? I did okay?"

"You did well, Mulany, real well."

***

Thirty boys in each class, five classes a day, times two. The thought of facing three hundred boys in the next two days' classes prompted Matt to work overtime with Tom to finalize his lesson plan. He repeatedly reviewed what he would say to the boys in the gym. When he took his turn leading the class, he was determined to be in control from the first moment he spoke.

"Okay, they're here," Tom said. "Let's find out who wants to play, and who wants to sit on his duff."

"You don't make them all play?"

"Only when I have extra energy and extra time, which is never. Forcing a boy to play takes attention away from class and creates hassles like grab-ass, fights, or worse."

"I see," Matt said, although he didn't see at all.

"All set to take over?"

"You bet." Matt threw his notes aside.

Taking his turn in front of the group caused the anticipated increase in pulse, but other than the boys squabbling with each other, Matt was pleased with the responses. Three classes came and went with no major altercations, and he looked forward to the first of the afternoon classes, which included his most promising football recruit, Harry Beauregard.

As with the earlier classes, both coaches burst into the gym, getting immediate attention. Boys seated on the floor looked up simultaneously, and those leaning against the gym wall straightened their stance.

Tom motioned with his arm extended, indicating the boys should seat themselves in a wide semicircle. Some whispered to each other, their arms crossed in front of their chests, while others shuffled in place. Several purposely tripped and laughed as they stepped up and sat down.

He signaled Matt to move front and center. "The ball's in your hands. Got your back," he said low.

Matt walked among the young audience. He caught Bo's stare and watched the boy nod his head and shift his eyes upward as if he already knew what this new coach was about to say.

Of course, he thinks he knows everything.

"As you know, I'm Coach Grazi, and my job is to make each of you a better athlete. That means improving your physical condition from whatever it is at this moment. To do that, no more relaxed game times or half-assed exercise periods."

The boys appeared to listen half-heartedly, mumbling among themselves. When Matt turned his focus away, one lowered his head to the side, stuffed a small bit of paper into his mouth, and started chewing.

Bo sat with the others, his legs extended and crossed in front of him. On the fringe of the group, he leaned back, bracing his arms on the floor behind him.

"Together we will accomplish two things," Matt said in an even voice, "One, increasing your physical strength and coordination." He looked from face to face. "I think you have a good idea of what that means."

With no warning, the reckless, chewing inmate fired off a spitball. It smacked into the side of another boy's face, dropping onto his shirt, leaving a wet, sticky imprint behind.

"Damn it," the spitball recipient shouted to the room. He wiped his cheek with the back of his hand and started to rise. A sheepish grin and chuckle came from the source of the attack.

Both coaches jumped into action. "Back off!" Matt yelled, and he and Tom separated the two boys as they lunged toward each other. The coaches interrupted the assault before it had a chance to elevate into a verbal squabble or physical battle.

Matt's gaze flicked from the spitter to the recipient. "It's over!" he shouted. "I'll see you both after classes end this afternoon. Let your cottage fathers know."

He returned his attention to the group and his commands carried into the air. "Those in the back, move up! You! And you! Closer!"

The boys moved as ordered, their grumbles lowering until quiet settled in.

"As I was saying, your physical strength and coordination will improve in this class and, even more important, you'll learn how to build a connection to every boy around you. You may not understand that concept yet, but as of today, you're part of something you've never been part of before. In this class, you are no longer alone."

"I don't get it," one boy said aloud.

"My point. But that's okay," Matt said. "You'll understand as we move forward."

Matt moved toward Bo and looked down at the teen. Bo exhibited no visible reaction.

"Did you understand everything I said, young man?" Matt asked in a subdued and steady voice. Bo smirked and answered with a muffled grunt.

"When I speak to you," Matt stated calmly, "I expect a response." Bo turned his head and snickered.

Matt had hoped to start off with a clean slate with Bo, but it appeared the boy was determined to push him as far as he could.

"Stand up," Matt said in a steadfast manner, "now."

Bo groaned as he rose, shooting a quick glance to his audience as if confirming their attention to his unhurried movement.

"You will address me as Coach, or Mr. Grazi," Matt said, his voice controlled.

"Yeah, I know who you are."

"Really?"

"I know you're a Yank who used to be some kind of college football hero. Know you got axed from the pros, and . . . know you couldn't get a job anywhere 'cept here."

What? How the hell did . . . ?

Matt's instinct ordered his fists to clench by his sides, but instead, he crossed his arms and shifted his weight.

"And how, young man, do you know that?"

"I make it my business to know *everything* around here."

Matt thought for a few short seconds before changing his tactic.

"I may be looking for a knowledgeable athlete like yourself to work on my crew. Think you could handle something like that?"

Bo looked him up and down. The action didn't go unnoticed. Matt didn't blink, and his body remained tight.

Is he wondering if I'd be a match for him?

"Fuck off," Bo said.

A gasp swept from one boy to another, the kind heard at a game when a favorite player was hurt.

"Move!" Matt ordered, pointing toward the basketball hoop area across the floor. "We settle this now."

A nod to Tom let him know he wanted to handle this alone. Tom moved the class to the far end of the gym, out of hearing distance.

Matt stared at the boy in front of him. "Mr. Beauregard," he said in a voice one notch above a whisper, emphasizing every syllable. "Don't you *ever, and I mean ever*, swear at me again. A remark like that guarantees suspension from all areas of the gym, field, and pool. And you look like a guy who thrives on stuff like that."

Bo shrugged his shoulders.

"It only takes a word to confine you to your bed, or make solitary your new home."

"Like that crap hasn't been done before? I've been shit on a thousand times. You're just another asshole who's gonna do it."

Bingo. This kid is angry.

"Watch your mouth, Mr. Tough Guy," Matt said, "or do we end this talk right now, and escort you to your cottage?"

Bo looked down at the floor and kicked his foot outward, scuffing the wooden surface. He looked back up at Matt.

"You done?" Matt asked. "Cause I'm the tough guy here, the top athlete, not you."

Bo's pressed tight lips said he was considering his options. Matt waited to confirm the boy had no comeback. After seconds of silence, he continued.

"I've played on teams made up of the most tenacious players in the world, guys who banged heads like they were cantaloupes. I've dodged hitters with bodies of bricks. I've been protected by the best defense in the country, but I've also been tackled so hard I wondered if I would ever stand up."

"I'm still tougher than you."

Matt sensed Bo's weak response and took the advantage. "You have potential, but you aren't even close. But if you want to be a tough-ass, I can make that happen. I can put you on a field where everyone can see what you're made of."

"Yeah, how 'bout in the boxing ring?" Bo asked. "Then we'd see how quick you are on your feet." Word had spread about Bo's successful boxing bouts in an athletic after-school program.

"Oh, I've heard you're one mean boxer. If, or when, the time comes, and we have to do it, we'll do it. Until then, I've changed my mind."

"What do ya mean?"

Matt waited a short minute. "Do you play baseball?"

"What?" Bo asked.

Again Matt waited, not repeating the question.

"Yeah, I play baseball."

"Going out for the team?"

"Maybe, maybe not."

"Bo," Matt said, "You *do* realize I'm one of the baseball coaches."

No response.

"How about football? Ever play in Pensacola?" Bo's raised eyebrows told Matt the mention of his hometown sparked a new interest.

"Never mind," Matt said, interrupting the moment. "I don't think you're conditioned enough to play football, and I'm not sure you have the stamina to work your ass off. For either, you'd have to be a *real* athlete."

As if his reflexes had kicked in, Bo took a deep breath, flared his nostrils, and blew out a rush of air. He clenched his muscles and inflated his lungs. Pushing his chest forward, he held his breath and took a small step forward.

"Calm down," Matt said with a wave of his hand. "I don't mean just physically strong. You can't huff and puff toughness! You have to prove it."

Bo hesitated.

"When I say tough, I mean solid up here," Matt said, pointing to his sweaty head.

Bo exhaled, raised his eyebrows, slightly tilting his head in question.

A final thought crossed Matt's mind. "I'm here, when you change your mind, when you want to be part of a real team." His pulse was racing. "Now, control your mouth and get back to the others."

Bo obeyed but gave no sign Coach Grazi had made any kind of impression.

Matt's recruitment effort appeared to have backfired, big time. He was no closer to his goal of winning this boy over. In fact, he might have alienated him.

He maintained control for the remaining time in class. The boys mumbled obscenities under their breaths, but no inmate challenged him directly. That was something. One thing for sure, appearing strong and confident in this tough crowd took more effort than he had ever anticipated.

CHAPTER 4

Being "on-call" in case of an emergency could mean anything. Since no security guards patrolled the premises, staff provided the manpower for arising crises.

Matt's extracurricular duty routinely ran from 7:00 p.m. to 7:00 a.m., one night every two weeks. Not scheduled for another week, he received the afternoon duty roster and saw his name listed. A hand-written memo explained the school was temporarily short-staffed.

Once in his room, he reviewed the resident manual and found the campus map showing the outside assembly area where he would report if needed. Rubbing his hands together, he stared at the black rotary phone on the end table. He had not heard it ring since his arrival last week. He picked up the receiver. Good, a dial tone. He wished he had asked Tom to make a practice call earlier. He hoped the ring would be loud enough to wake him.

Matt donned an oversized FSU tee shirt and plopped down on the squeaky twin bed. Expecting to be unable to sleep, he instead fell into a deep slumber.

The high-pitched jangle of the telephone broke into Matt's dreams at 2:07 a.m. He fumbled for the handle before answering, separating himself from a blurry mirage of outlandish football games.

"Grazi," Matt said, half-awake.

"Code R," a voice bellowed, followed by a loud click. Matt read the list of codes before him.

A runaway. Hurry.

He pushed the receiver back so hard onto the phone's cradle, it slid across and dangled from the nightstand. After slipping on his pants, he shoved his sock-less feet into his shoes, and grabbed his long-sleeved shirt before stumbling out the door. Outside, he pushed his arms through his sleeves and raced toward the pre-assigned assembly point. He prayed they would find this kid quick.

Like most folks, Matt was acquainted with stories about the peril of the Southern Florida Everglades and their associated swamps, but having attended FSU he had become aware of the dangers associated with the woods and rivers running throughout North Florida. A boy could easily encounter a hungry gator able to lunge into a run faster than a deer for the first twenty feet. Cottonmouths swam in drainage ditches and at the edges of ponds, lakes, and streams and often ventured overland far from permanent water.

Panting, Matt arrived at the meeting area and swiped at the sweat accumulating above his upper lip. He stared at the idling staff-filled cars and trucks.

I can do this, he thought to himself. *Whatever 'this' is.*

He turned toward emphatic commands coming from along the forest line and followed the booming voice of Andrews, who strode forward like an oversized General Patton. The disciplinarian carried a pistol on his hip as if it were a coveted prize he had won.

"Everyone," he bellowed, "into your cars!"

"What's the gun for?" Matt asked.

Andrews' expression soured. "Mr. Grazi, . . ."

Matt felt like he was ten again.

"You'll soon learn you can't trust these little bastards. If one of them ever puts me in a corner, well, I could be forced to use this."

The thought of Andrews drawing a gun on an unarmed boy made Matt's stomach churn.

Andrews turned his back on Matt as if dismissing him. The former marine continued his stomp down the line of cars, patting his weapon with his head held high, continuing to blast directives to the drivers of the waiting vehicles.

"Over here," an unfamiliar voice shouted from a dust-covered, army-green truck. Turning toward the sound, Matt pointed to himself in question.

"Yes, you!"

Matt raced to the running vehicle and slid into the split vinyl front seat.

"Time to round up this kid and bring him back," the driver announced as the truck's oversized wheels spun dust into the air.

With one hand clenching the armrest, Matt braced his other hand on the dashboard. The vehicle jostled down the gravel lane and minutes later slowed, resulting in a smoother ride. He exhaled and leaned back onto the headrest.

"So you've piloted a drag racer before?"

The driver laughed. "Don't worry. Things slow down later. So *you're* the new coach we've heard so much about?"

"Yeah," Matt mumbled, not facing the man, but instead, focused on the ragged sharpness of foliage illuminated by the truck's headlights.

"Gary Lissitar, English teacher. Not the best circumstance to welcome a new colleague, huh?"

Matt tilted his head at the absurdity of the question. "Grazi," he said with a long breath. "Matt Grazi."

"Ready for tonight's hunt?"

Hunt? Matt cringed. "Isn't that a term used for wild animals?"

"You know what I mean. An eleven-year-old to bring back to CHB."

"Eleven years old? To retrieve with a gun?"

"Andrews must have his reasons," Lissitar said with a shrug. "Can't say I've ever seen him fire it, though."

The teacher swerved onto a narrow side road. High-beam headlights from other vehicles flared into the columns of pines and jagged underbrush, crisscrossing through the dark.

"Open your window," Lissitar ordered as the truck came to a crawl. He readjusted his thick, black-rimmed glasses. "Quiet."

"What should I do?" Matt asked in a lowered voice.

"Listen for thrashing sounds. Keep your eyes open for any movement in the brush."

"A boy must be desperate to run through this."

"Or stupid. Our constant reminder about the dangers and penalties of running results in most inmates respecting the boundaries, but there's always a few who feel the need to test the limits. And oddly enough, the challenge of running presents an incentive for some. Running is costly, and it earns respect, regardless of the outcome."

With the safety of the quiet campus far behind, night sounds in the woods magnified. Lissitar identified the snorting of wild pigs and the aggressive rising trill of competing spring peeper frogs. The overwhelming vibrations jarred Matt, and he suspected the unfamiliar sounds would shake up even the most hardened inmate.

The earthy aroma of the gray mist swept into the truck. It took only minutes before the invisible night insects began their silent attack on the exposed part of Matt's face and lean arms. He slapped them away and scratched at his skin, all the while thinking about the number of red welts that must be rising on the unprotected skin of the runaway.

"These boys believe if they run on an overcast or dark night like tonight, they can hide better," Lissitar said.

"And?"

"And instead, it means no light to guide them."

After ten minutes, Lissitar yelled, "Hang on!" and pressed his foot to the gas pedal. Matt again clawed at the door's slick armrest, as they bounced over the rutted, overgrown road.

"Slow down! You're hitting all sorts of crap!"

"Sorry," he answered. "But if I drive fast enough, the bugs should blow out. You can close your window on this next stretch."

As the car lumbered down the jungle-like dirt lane, Matt spied fallen trees along the border which seemed laid out to trip any boy who dared cross their path. The constant but irregular rhythm of the vehicle's engine caused him to lose track of time.

"Got him," the sudden loud crackle of a walkie-talkie scratched through the air. "Return to campus."

"Do you usually find a boy this quick?" Matt asked, glancing at his watch. It had been only forty minutes since his phone rang.

"With the younger ones, yes. It's a little different with the older boys. They move faster. We sometimes need to call in a team from ACI to round 'em up."

"The adult prison?"

"Yeah."

Lissitar told Matt that Apalachee Correctional Institute's staff, inmates, and dogs mobilized on any request from CHB. Referred to as "the goon squad" by the inmates, the ACI guards brought their animals, beating sticks, guns, and a few of their prisoners to help in the search.

"What? A goon squad? Beating sticks and dogs?"

"Last resort, but those animals locate boys we can't find."

"So they're always caught?"

"Since I've been here, yep."

"And before your time at Colby Hill?"

"Heard one died on the run, fell off a train trestle, but I never heard of anyone getting away to tell about it."

"Oh, shit," Matt cursed between his clenched teeth. He had thought of tonight as a retrieval process, necessary to protect a boy from the dangerous animals and harsh environment. Now it seemed much more. Running could be a deadly mission.

"At least it's over," Matt said with a sigh, "and he's not hurt."

"For tonight," Lissitar said. "But these kids are predictable. It's just a matter of time before another brilliant inmate thinks he has somehow increased his odds for an escape."

Fatigue etched its way into Matt's face, his four hours of deep sleep a distant blur.

As their truck pulled into the parking area, Andrews emerged from the haze, striding toward a parked sedan. He gripped a crying child under his bulky arm. With one hand, he set the young boy's feet on the sandy ground, while the other hand pushed the boy's head down into the open door of the rear seat.

Only after the boy squirmed onto the back cushion and the door slammed did the youngster raise his head. As if his fear had a weight of its own, the boy's forehead dropped onto the window and his face pressed against the glass. Matt caught the wide, haunted eyes.

"God . . . ," Matt pleaded. He continued to stare. *I'm on the side with the gun.*

Transfixed on the tear-stained face of the trapped boy, Matt wiped a round of surfacing sweat from his brow.

"Want a lift back?" the driver asked.

"No thanks." Matt stepped from the vehicle. "I'll walk."

Cars disappeared one by one as he stood in the clearing. A shiver of distrust ran down his back when he thought of Andrews.

He trudged toward his room. His life as a teenage delinquent had not prepared him for tonight's lesson in institutional living. His past close calls with jail were miles from the real thing.

Regaining a sense of composure once he entered his room, Matt closed the door with his back and leaned against it for several seconds.

There has to be a better way.

***

Amid the muddled lightness of dawn, Matt ran, clenching his fingers into fists, holding last night's turmoil tight inside. He jogged underneath the towering pines to calm his nerves before heading for his gym office. The previous evening's pursuit prompted him to take a new interest in the lower woods. Tangled vines and branches wove between the emerald walls of sharp saw palmetto. The palm's name reflected its protective mechanism, the razor-like edges of the stems threatened to slash any intruder.

Without warning, a broad owl swooped down and landed on a branch twenty feet above. Matt ducked as the bird's shadow passed over him. He stopped to gaze upward at the vertical black-and-tan plumage of the almost round creature perched like the top part of a feathered fence post. The bird's talons gripped the twisted branch, and it returned his focused stare. Powerful.

"So, you're the wise one. What do *you* know, that I don't know?"

The owl responded with a quizzical expression and a tilt of his head just seconds before his rhythmical, flapping, wings lifted him into the dark green space of the woods. The experience somehow eased Matt's tension, and he continued toward the red brick gym.

After a quick shower, he sat at his office desk, staring at the phone and wanting answers.

"Hey," Santo said, as he stuck his head into the small work space. Matt's body jerked to attention as his boss entered.

"Thought I'd find you here. You okay?"

Matt pursed his lips toward one side of his face as they exchanged glances.

"Why, Santo? Why did he try to escape?"

"Figured you might have questions."

Santo spotted the single metal chair, repositioned it, and took a seat. He ran his fingers through his hair as if something he would say might cause Matt discomfort.

"A number of reasons why boys run away. Some are homesick, others bolt because they're frightened, scared to stay. A greater flight risk exists right after a boy's arrival because he thinks his sentence to Colby Hill means he's sunk as low as he can go and things couldn't get any worse. He's wrong of course." Santo took a breath. "Institutional life is an adjustment."

"For everyone. But last night . . . It's just . . . just that the boy was so young."

"You've got younger boys in your gym classes."

"I know, but to hunt down a kid . . . "

"Look," Santo interrupted with a stiffened demeanor. "We stop most boys before they run. Last night's new arrival went off on a 'toot' as we call it, after counselors had spent hours with him. Despite our efforts, he chose to ignore everyone and play the game his way." The strength of Santo's response caused Matt to remain silent.

"The boy knew trying to escape was a severe offense," Santo added. "He was quite aware the school has no tolerance for anyone who doesn't listen or makes his own rules."

Matt fumbled for a way to re-enter the conversation. "The boy last night . . . is he from a broken family?"

"I don't know this kid's entire history, but most inmates have family issues. Society and this economy play a big part too. These boys are from every walk of life. A boy could come from a shack across the tracks or a private boarding school. Breaking the law puts them all in the same predicament."

"A long list of types of offenses, I hear."

"Everything from disturbing the peace to aggravated assault. We even process a handful of felons every year. Have two in for murder."

Matt's eyes widened and his muscles tensed. *Murder?*

"But still, this kid, well he's just a kid."

"Don't be fooled," Santo said, pulling the chair closer to the front of Matt's desk. "Regardless of how old an inmate is, I can guarantee you he's misbehaved more than once to end up here. It takes an unusual circumstance for a judge to send any boy to CHB on a first, or even second, offense. I know I sound hard when it comes to controlling run-aways, but breaking out of a state reform school is a third-degree felony and warrants a strong hand."

"Andrews looked like he was enjoying his job way too much."

"The man may be intimidating, but he operates by the book. He's been here two years longer than I have, so he knows every trick the inmates try to play."

"So, what happens to this boy? Does Andrews determine his punishment?"

"No, the higher ups make that call. Andrews carries out the recommended procedure."

Matt looked down at his shoes, and then upward toward Santo.

"Coach, are you able . .?" Santo asked, "I mean, do you need . . . ?" Santo shook his head. "Never mind." As if expecting no response, he waved his hand, palm side in the air, and rose to leave.

Matt realized he had only seconds to buy in or opt out. "I need more towels and gym shorts," he said, stopping Santo's exit.

Santo turned. "The laundry truck delivers clean towels to the cottages and the gym," he said, facing Matt. "I'll tell the driver to drop off as many as you need. Let me check on the shorts situation."

"The boys need PF Flyers too."

"Okay, okay, message received. Work with Tom to put them in the budget."

"Well then, I guess those leather state shoes will have to do for now."

"Brogans," Santo said, reminding him with a feeble smile.

"What?"

"The shoes, they're called brogans."

***

"Murder? Really, Tom? How do I work with a kid like that?" The two coaches moved about the gym cleaning up anything left behind.

"Do yourself a favor, Matt. Assess these boys as you get to know 'em, whether an inmate's in for drug pushing or incorrigibility."

"Incorrigibility? Am I supposed to know what that means?"

"It's a misbehavior that disrupts the school or the community, even though technically, the law hasn't been broken. A boy could have skipped school too many times, got into an umpteen number of fights, or ran away from home. The court just has to demonstrate to a judge that parents aren't in control and that somebody is at risk. "

"Let me get this straight. Some boys are committed felons, others haven't broken any laws at all?"

"Where else should these kids go when they get into fights and refuse to go home or to school? Gonna let them roam the streets?"

"What does it say about a judge who sentences an unmanageable boy to a place like CHB? Surely, these types of offenses could be resolved by the school or parents."

"Apparently not." Tom said. He and Matt moved down the narrow hallway. "Heard you were on the search last night."

"Yeah, a real learning experience. I'm trying hard to hold my tongue when I discuss our revered disciplinarian and his prized weapon of choice."

"Our home-town marine is from Colby Hill and he knows how to relate to these boys. We need him."

"Yeah, so I hear. But there's something about him. He gives me the creeps."

"So, what? His job requires scare tactics, and they work."

"If that's the case, he did a bang-up job last night. That kid was scared shitless. Are you telling me it was all a big show? That Andrews won't lay a hand on the boy?"

"Oh, I didn't say that, Matt. He'll be the one to give the kid a few swats."

"Swats?"

"Spanking, paddling, whatever you want to call it. Lots of schools operate that way. It doesn't hurt them. My dad spanked me when I found trouble or endangered myself. Didn't yours?"

Spare the rod and spoil the child.

Matt remembered the proverb stating that children needed to be physically reminded when they did wrong, or their personal development would suffer. He also recalled his dad spanking him when he misbehaved, but never hurting him.

"You don't seem to know much about how reform schools work, Matt. Tell me something, just how did you pick CHB as the place to land?"

Matt took a sip of his cold four-hour-old coffee before answering. "My friend Larry from college worked here before he took a job as a sports writer, and he thought the boys' school might be a logical career step into coaching."

Tom repositioned an equipment bag on his shoulder. "You mean Larry Farnsworth?"

"You know him?"

"Enjoyed coaching with the guy. But why not a regular high school?"

"The boys," Matt said. "I minored in adolescent criminal psychology at FSU, and I have a soft spot for kids who can't avoid trouble."

"Really, now. And what made you study teenage delinquents?"

Matt lowered his voice, "I *was* one of them."

"Sorry, didn't mean to pry."

"Don't be. I guess I didn't appreciate how lucky I was until last night. I never served time for my antics."

Matt didn't know Tom well enough to tell him another reason CHB had become his final destination. The truth was that he hadn't been able to find another school that required no coaching experience. CHB appreciated his college degree, had an opening in the middle of the season, and was impressed with his brief pro-ball career.

"It's okay, Tom."

"I'm glad. The boys need a coach who has the talent to bring them together. That's you, right?"

Matt smiled for the first time since his emergency call had re-introduced him to CHB. "Join me for a fine dinner in our spacious dining hall?"

"Another night. My wife and I live off campus, and it takes me a while to drive home. And by the way, we call it "supper," not dinner. Dinner is served at holidays like Christmas or Thanksgiving." With both a grin and a wave, he headed for the exit.

Supper, not dinner. Another thing to know.

Local language undoubtedly increased the comfort level. Familiar expressions could help Matt slide into a conversation. Despite his misgivings about the school's policies, he was anxious to improve his next verbal approach with the boys, and yes, with Bo too.

CHAPTER 5

"I need to get out of here," Matt said as he locked his cottage and headed for the gym for his weekend workout.

He wanted a place where he could forget the school for a while. He hadn't forgotten the verbal attack delivered by Bo in the gym or the disturbing night pursuit. His escape options consisted of driving to Tallahassee or exploring the town of Colby Hill.

"Hey," Santo yelled as he approached from behind. "Want to retreat and regroup by driving off campus and joining me for lunch in town?"

"Now how the heck did you . . . ?"

"Tom's a good friend to have, Matt. Okay to pick you up in the cottage parking lot at noon? I'll drive."

Santo drove ten minutes north before turning onto Franklin, the main street in Colby Hill.

"Don't blink, Matt," Santo said, "or you'll miss the town completely."

Matt scanned the four blocks of natural and white brick build-ings dominating the center of town. Storefronts boasted the standard awnings. A whoosh of warm air rushed through the triangular vent windows, and the tension Matt had unconsciously held in his muscles released. He was grateful for the break in routine.

"Colby Hill is basically an agricultural community," Santo said.

"Did I tell you the Cotton County Cattlemen's Association is coming out to CHB to view our fescue and Bahia grasses soon?"

"Really? Wow."

"I know. I know. Not impressive to a city slicker, but important to us. So, what do you like? Interested in going to the Ritz Theater to see a movie for a dollar? I hear Spartacus is coming soon."

"Might do in a pinch."

"How about a drive to the Piggly Wiggly market for a moon pie?"

"You're getting warmer, but still a far cry from what I had in mind," Matt said with a forced grin.

"You know, of course, there's no public place in town to order a drink."

"Too bad. Sure might enjoy a beer once in a while."

Matt was familiar with the blue laws of the county and had a plan in mind to escape back to his usual haunts in Tallahassee.

"But don't worry, Matt, we have private bottle clubs, like The Country Club."

Matt's face lit up. "All right!

"We're headed for great food, good service, a pool, tennis courts, pool tables, ladies, and a bar."

"Sounds like my kind of place. What's the name of the country club?"

"The Country Club. That is the name of the bottle club." Santo laughed at the absurdity and Matt joined in.

"I want you to meet some genuine people, Matt. I'm hoping a few will be at lunch."

"Folks who work at CHB?"

"No, no. People who live and work in the community. Like the ladies in the garden club. They're really supportive of our boys, and are already planning for next Christmas."

Santo went on to tell Matt that women from town wrapped hundreds of presents over the year for boys on both campuses who didn't have a family to send them holiday gifts.

"Close to Christmas, our staff informs the ladies which boys are predicted to have no gifts coming in. Then voila! Wrapped packages appear under every designated cottage Christmas tree."

"Does that cause problems?" Matt asked. "I mean, kids who have parents who can't afford to buy or send gifts versus those who have families who give everything?"

"We try to even things out when we can. Hey, look," Santo said pointing to the elongated driveway on the left side of the dusty two-lane road, "there's the club." He pulled into an unpaved parking area with space for about two dozen cars.

"This is The Country Club?" Matt asked. "It looks like somebody's house."

"It matches the size of the town," Santo said with a grin.

The two-story brick-and-cement block building stood on the west side of a hill, a dramatic drop-off in the back to tennis courts below. A slightly curved walkway led to a center wooden door. As Matt and Santo entered, and their pupils expanded to take in the new darkness, the glass eyes of a mounted twelve-point buck stared back at them.

Turning right they moved into a small wood-paneled dining area where sunshine filtered through three large square windows on the side wall. The smell of beef sizzling over a wood grill wafted into the air as patrons devoured their steaks, burgers, and ribs.

"Sit anywhere you like, boys," called a soft Southern voice from the open kitchen.

The rustic room seated close to fifty people sitting at thick, wooden, hand-made tables. The interspersed flannel shirts and blue jeans among the suits and jackets brought a sense of comfort to Matt as they merged into the low hum of conversations.

A neatly dressed blonde waitress approached the table, her natural sway and shapely figure complementing the fringed green-and-white western outfit. She had pushed the felt western hat off her head so that it, and her swaying ponytail, hung down her back.

"Why hey, y'all," she greeted them. Touching her finger to her cheek, she tucked a wisp of hair behind her ear. "Sweet tea?" Her eyes met Matt's.

Intended words of greeting remained in Matt's throat. He nodded a greeting.

"Here ya go," she said, reaching her slim arm between Matt and Santo to place the menus on the table. Matt smelled the splash of honeysuckle and felt his heart rate quicken. He didn't even like sweet tea, but swallowed any words of protest.

"Be right back," she said.

Matt stared at the slight sway of her shorter-than-normal green skirt. He imagined the shape of her bosom, waist, and hips beneath the cotton fabric. She seemed to have an envelope of air between her body and the garment as she disappeared into the kitchen.

"Now isn't she a lovely diversion from campus life?" Santo asked.

"Think she's a college student?"

"Might be. Junior college is nearby."

"Did you see the shade of those baby blues?" Matt whispered as his head followed the girl around the room.

"Might be a little young for you, Buddy," Santo teased.

"What?" Matt pouted. "Twenty-five's not *that* old."

"Ha-ha. Maybe, maybe not."

Matt leaned back in his chair, absorbing the relaxed atmosphere of laughter and Southern banter.

"What brought you to Colby Hill, Santo?"

"The good ol' Florida Board of Commissioners charmed me into it."

"The Board of Commissioners?"

"The group of folks above my boss, Dr. Strickland. They promised me freer rein and more responsibility than I had as principal of a private boys' school. They vowed there'd be fewer politics and minimum red tape. Most of all, they convinced me I could make a difference in these boys' lives."

"A hard decision?" Matt asked, reflecting on his own indecision before focusing on CHB.

"Change is always hard. But the bottom line is I believe good words and deeds set the right tone, and I wanted to be the example in leadership these boys needed."

"I've met most of the boys in gym class, and one kid stands out to me. Harry Beauregard. You know him?"

"Our boxer," Santo said. "Quite the fighter."

Matt explained that Bo was not just an athletic opponent. He described the boy's snitching network and repeated the conversation concerning the exposure of his personal information. He skipped details of the boy's defying outburst.

Santo's jaw dropped. "So how do you think he got it?"

"Hard to say, but the only place those facts exist are in your office, right."

"Nothing in your room or office?"

"Nope."

"Damn. I'll find out more about this. We'll monitor crew activity a little closer next week, and lock a few more file drawers." Santo paused.

"But what do you say we deal with this on Monday? For now, let's turn to the question of how old you really are." He raised his hand and waved the waitress over to the table.

"I'll be done with my studies in December," the attractive food server said, answering Santo's inquiry about her ambitions to land a job in the med-tech field. "And how about you, mister?" She gazed at Matt. "Haven't seen you before."

"Just arrived," Matt said with a wide grin. "A coach at CHB. Matt, Matt Grazi."

"You look like a coach," she said softly, flattering his ego just enough to maximize her tip. "I'm Bettiann Carter. Folks call me Betty." She had a natural magnetic charm. Instead of lowering her eyes in a traditional way, she tossed her head with confidence, like a sexy Sandra Dee, and sauntered away from the table.

"Helloooo?" Santo's voice intruded into Matt's imagination.

"She's a beauty," Matt said. "Probably has a steady. And with my work schedule, when could I squeeze her in?"

Santo shook his head. "You're kidding, right?"

"Does that mean you'll give me time off if I need it?"

"You wish. But I'm sure you could figure something out."

"Heard that phrase before."

Matt perused the menu as he covertly watched Betty's every move. She sat with an elderly couple, engrossed in conversation for a few minutes before patting the older woman's hand and resuming her duties.

Yes, this was a place he could unwind. Maybe more.

On the ride back to campus, Matt took a deep breath and the lightness of the outing remained with him. The trip to The Country Club had offered him the opportunity to relax and know Santo better. Thoughts of Christmas bounced through his mind in synchrony with the rhythm of the car's motor, and he was back with his brother, wrestling on his family's living room floor in front of a decorated tree in snowy New York.

"Matt?"

"Sorry, reminiscing. I look forward to seeing CHB at Christmas."

"Seeing it? You'll be part of it! It's our time to give back to the community," Santo said as he brightened. "Two weeks before Christmas, we turn on our holiday lights, and thousands of cars begin streaming through this place, and I mean thousands! Folks come from all over, mostly from the Florida Panhandle, Georgia, and Alabama. The inmates and staff build and assemble the best damn light display and carnival in the region. It's a really a big deal."

By Christmas, the football season would be over. Hopefully, Matt not only would have achieved a winning season but also would be recruiting early for the following season. That was his idea of a really big deal.

***

Lifting his head from his desk Monday morning, Matt signaled Mulany through the office doorway. He summoned the boy with one sole purpose, to gather more information on Bo. Probing didn't sit right with him, and yet he had to know more.

"You friends with Harry Beauregard?"

"Nah, but I done been around him for the last month or so. He's pretty much taken over."

"Any issues?"

"No problems. I let Bo have his space, so I can have mine. Heard tell he's got a kid a-working every part of campus."

"Does that include here?"

Mulany hesitated and looked away.

"What's wrong?"

"Not sure I should be talking 'bout this stuff."

"Everything said in my office stays in my office."

Mulany shuffled in place before speaking. "Just saying, I don't puke on nobody."

"Puke?"

"Snitch on someone who gets in trouble."

"Nobody's in trouble. Tell me what's going on."

Mulany appeared cautious as he spoke of the tight-lipped communication system between the boys. "Our code is to keep our mouth shut," he warned, "'bout everything. You want privacy, you need to hide things and keep quiet."

"So you can't offer any assistance regarding who reported my personal information to Bo?"

"Might be somebody who thinks he's a big shot because he's a Pilot."

"Pilot?"

"One level below the highest rank of Ace. You know, the boys who lead the classes around. They get extra privileges, like a later curfew or traveling on their own into town to run errands."

Matt couldn't imagine a boy leaving campus unescorted. "No problem when a boy goes into Colby Hill on his own?"

"Not usually. By the time they're that kind of big shot, they're close
to going home and don't want any trouble."

"What rank are you?"

"Pioneer, a step above Rookie, the rank everyone gets at check in."

"Like me."

"Yeah," Mulany said with a smile. "Like you."

"So, there's a head guy in every gym class?"

"Could be any high rank. Like Jeff Argot, for instance. He's a Pilot
with a mouth like a post office, takin' in messages and passin' them
along."

Argot . . .

"I see. I'll keep my eyes open." Mulany seemed to relax, his shoulders dropping. "One more thing, Mulany. Think Bo could fit in around
here?"

Mulany shot Matt a quick glance.

"Come on, Mulany, don't stop now. It's just you and me."

"Okay, dunno, probably not. As I said, you'd have a tough time
getting Bo to leave the print shop. When he does the printing, he learns
everything before anyone else. He's their runner too, delivering the
papers, so he gits to go everywhere. He's got it all figured out."

Mulany reminded Matt that a crazy Mr. Clean episode, like the one
he had experienced their first day scouring the shower area, would no
doubt cause Bo to bolt.

"But not 'fore he let a fist fly in your direction, if you get my 'drift'."

"I get your drift. Has Bo ever let a fist fly in *your* direction?"

The question was apparently all Mulany needed to plunge into
an animated boxing demonstration. He appeared eager to mimic Bo's
boxing talents.

"No fist ever near me, but I hear it only took a left," Mulany said
as he tucked his head and threw a left punch into the air, "and then
a right," he swung again, "to bust an older inmate flat out the other
night."

Quick and fast in a fight could mean quick and fast on a football field.

Mulany smiled at the little show he was putting on. "Yes, sir, Bo
had them boys put that hoodlum in his bed, and the cottage father
never even knew 'bout it." Matt heard respect in the boy's voice.

"Sounds like Bo's good at ducking a punch, and even more talented at delivering one. Know what caused the fight?"

"A jerk pushed a little kid around 'cause he refused to cop cigarettes for him. Bo don't like bullies. He comes off as a bad dude, but he looks out for the younger boys. He don't want nobody coming on to these kids. He looks real mean at anybody who goes after them."

Matt stared ahead and tapped his pencil on the desk while he processed the information. Bo didn't like bullies, and neither did he.

Seconds passed before he realized Mulany, still standing in front of him, was waiting.

"How old are you, son?"

"Me? Fifteen, almost sixteen."

"Going out for baseball?"

"Thinking about it."

"How about football?"

"Never played."

"Bet you'd be good at it."

"Think so?" Mulany asked with a wide grin.

***

"Bo's grades on the placement test are what landed him in the younger class. I checked, Matt."

"It doesn't make sense, Tom."

"Why not? He's been to CHB before. Bo knows all about completing contract books, and how to move up to the next grade, *if he wants to.* There's talk he's a slow learner, but I don't buy it."

"Couldn't teachers figure out if a boy intentionally performed badly?"

Tom shrugged his shoulders. "Ask them."

"But why would Bo want to fail a placement test?"

"My bet is that he blew off the test to stay with the youngsters, or doesn't see any advantage to moving up. The younger boys do simpler tasks, and they have less-rigid rules. That might play right into his game plan, to serve his time and do as little as possible."

"I want to light a fire under that boy. He's got potential."

"Yeah, okay. But uncovering talent takes effort, something we don't have time for. After five classes a day, we're lucky to have the energy for afternoon team activities."

"How can I entice him to participate?"

Bo was not pro-active in class, but he devoted an untold number of hours working out. His athletic prowess was his strength, but it could also be his weakness.

"How about a physical challenge? A workout and exercise competition?"

"With who? The other boys? You, Matt?"

"I don't know."

"What would it prove? Why would Bo buy off on it? Sounds like too many 'ifs' in that scenario, don't you think? I mean, what if Bo won't compete? Or even worse, what if he *wins*? Then where are you?"

"I could design drills to give me control. Bo's a cocky kid. He won't be able to resist, and each minute spent with him will give me the advantage in recruiting and training. I've just got to figure out a way to beat the boy without him having hard feelings. I don't want to come across as an arrogant jock."

"Hmm. Not so sure how you're going to do that."

CHAPTER 6

The unusually quiet CHB basketball team stared through the moisture build-up covering the bus windows as they rumbled their way toward the Apalachicola Valley Conference tournament. The last games of the season were to be held at Anhinga Bay High School, a school southward, near the Ochlockonee River.

Both coaches sat near the front discussing the accuracy of Tom's earlier prediction.

"So, hear that Santo requested you write a piece for the school newsletter following the tournament. Glad you've got this one," Tom said. "Both Santo and his boss, Dr. Strickland, will read *every* word."

"Oh, thanks," Matt said. "No pressure then."

"Ha. So what are you gonna write?"

"No idea. Played basketball, but sure don't know it like I do football. Luckily, I have an in with the CHB head basketball coach, who will undoubtedly give me the scoop on each player before and during this bus trip. Might even give me his autograph. Right into my scrapbook."

"Cool. Get me one too." They laughed.

Two hours later Tom and Matt watched with excitement as CHB beat two Panhandle high schools in the first rounds. Disappointment surged in the last round when an under-rated Miccosukee team surprised everyone by beating the Ospreys 53–51.

Weary, Matt sat at his desk late that night, replaying the hard-fought game in his mind. After a ragged regular season, the Ospreys had come within three points of winning the basketball championship. He admired the strength and courage of the opposing Miccosukee Mullets. What could he write to inspire?

The loss in the final minutes of a University of Florida football game flashed in his mind. He had interpreted the disappointing results as his personal failure. His coach had convinced him otherwise.

"It doesn't matter that we lost the game if you gave it your all. Did you, Matt? Did you give it your all?" The coach's repeated word, "courage," had taken on a whole different meaning that day.

The blank paper stared at him. Then, almost on its own, the pen began leaving a trail of letters. His scribbled thoughts did not describe the significance of physical attributes, but rather stressed the importance of mental stamina. Before he knew it, his heavy head dropped onto his trusty gray-green notepad, his cheek pressed against the written words.

The willingness to realize odds are against you and be man enough to accept the challenge, to do the best you can and then some . . . so goes the story of the Osprey basketball team.

The article "Young Men with Courage" appeared the end of March in the *Flying Osprey* newsletter. Following his short dissertation on mental strength, Matt introduced the top players on the team and summarized their attributes on the court. When the newsletter hit the campus, he reviewed the piece and pictured the same boys dressed out in football uniforms.

"Nice job," Santo said as he and Matt walked across the field. "Have you really experienced the agony of defeat at the end of a great season?"

"Thanks, and yes," Matt shifted his gaze downward. "Times when I didn't handle losing as well as I should have." He ran his hand across the top of his head before adding, "It's hard to lose."

"Tell me about it. Easier now?"

"Never."

***

"Straighten up!" Matt yelled to his gym class. "Got your shorts under your pants?"

Stripping off the first layer of clothing made it quicker for the boys to change clothes and resulted in a shorter time getting their butts onto the field.

Matt watched the boys scramble. The pushing, bumping, and slapping brought up images of a TV comedy, *The Three Stooges*.

A lot of Larry, Curly, and Moes around here.

"Today we jog!" Matt shouted, and turned toward the door. "Up!" he yelled, his arm rising above his head in a charge.

With no time to consider an alternative, the boys fell into line behind Matt, jogging the quarter mile past the field. Tom ran at the end, pushing the stragglers.

Complaining and moaning, the boys tried to keep pace, the grunts and heavy breathing music to Matt's ears. He led them to a flat area, where he ordered ten boys to form a line across, and then arranged three boys eight feet apart to step behind each of the ten. He demonstrated how to do an exercise and then watched each boy attempt twenty repetitions. He scribbled in his spiral notepad, who could keep up the intense pace and who couldn't.

Constant prodding encouraged the boys to succeed at the hard-ass drills he had designed. As they pushed themselves, he recognized a rise of determination.

When Bo's class arrived and they had completed the jog, Tom gave an order to march farther down the ridge.

"Not you, Bo," Matt instructed. "Let's you and I do a few drills together, on our own. Up for it?"

"What do *you* think?"

When Matt explained the exercises and told the teen he would have to perform in an exact way, Bo was quick to agree.

"You could be a good athlete if you keep up with me," Matt taunted.

Bo responded with a smirk. "Yeah? You could be a decent coach if you keep up with me."

"Able to handle a demanding set of calisthenics?"

"Watch me." Bo had taken the gauntlet and agreed to compete.

Almost three inches taller than Bo, Matt looked slightly down toward his opponent. He repositioned himself to better observe the boy and began a round of jumping jacks. When Bo responded with irregular repetitions, Matt called him on it.

"Come on, Bo. Look at me. Do them right! Feet land three feet apart. Hands touch at the top."

Bo adjusted and performed the jumping jacks with precision.

Afterward, both coach and boy bent over to get their breaths.

"How long can you hold a push-up?" Matt asked seconds later.

"As long as you can," Bo said and positioned himself on the ground opposite Matt.

"Stay relaxed. Let your mind wander," Matt instructed. On his lead, they held their push-ups in place, their muscles rigid as they eyeballed each other.

Matt whispered, "So, who's going to fall first?" Bo bit down, the clenched jaw signaling he planned to win. Drops of sweat emerged from every pore of both participants.

Minutes passed before Bo's shaking arms gave way and he collapsed onto the ground. Matt fell immediately behind him. They both lay flat, the pain of lactic acid accumulating in their muscles as they struggled to raise themselves up. Matt grasped his wrists in an effort to calm his trembling arms. Assuming Bo's limbs felt the same way, Matt called for a short recess and water break before continuing.

Across the field, Tom worked on drills with the younger athletes. When he finished a set, the boys began to shuffle toward the demanding coach and the teenage boss man.

"Hold it there, boys," said Tom. "We have more to do here. Two-minute break and back in line!" The boys returned to their places but watched from afar.

Matt had proven to be in excellent shape a few short months ago on the Broncos' team, and he dared Bo to race in a shuttle cone run, a long-standing drill at college. Matt expected to have the advantage.

"In the shuttle cone drill," Matt said, "we run and touch that cone five yards away, then come back and touch the ground behind the yard line. Then we repeat the process, touching the second cone ten yards away and the third one at fifteen. The first to return and correctly touch the ground the third time is the winner."

Bo nodded in agreement.

"Plant your feet and stay low when touching the cone," Matt said.

Bo's stocky frame seemed remarkably light as he bounced back and forth between the cones and the ground. When Matt spotted the final cone, he surged forward just enough for him to touch down at nearly the same moment as Bo. With gasping breaths, the young athlete and coach pressed their hands to their sweaty thighs.

Bo proved to be a stiffer competitor than Matt had calculated. He had not fully appreciated the athletic prowess of the boy, ten years younger, panting beside him. A sudden realization smacked him in the face. If he lost any part of this competition, there would be consequences. He could lose the respect of not only the inmates but the staff as well. He could come out of this looking like a fool.

Should I quit now, while I'm ahead?

He stared at the lines of the final dash. Lightweight and thin legs were assets in the next contest, and he had practiced this run more times than he could remember. His last recorded time on the forty-yard dash had been four and a half seconds, quick by any standards.

Matt had been anxious to best Bo, to gain his respect. So much so, that he had not fully considered another possibility. If he won this competition and Bo lost, would Bo lose the respect of the other boys?

Too late now.

Tom and his group moved from the far end of the field, stopping in a semi-circle around Coach Grazi and Bo. As planned, Tom picked up the stopwatch to clock Bo's speed.

The eyes of the young inmates popped wide in anticipation.

"A four-point stance at start," Matt said, demonstrating the correct position. Bo took his place and copied his coach almost perfectly.

"Ready . . . , Set . . . , Go!" Tom yelled, and Matt and Bo blew away from the starting line. The young inmates began cheering, urging Bo to beat the coach any way he could. Bo appeared oblivious to their rally. His jaw set, he seemed to focus on one thing . . . winning.

Matt's legs stretched to their maximum, and Bo flew at his side, pushing his shorter legs into almost double time. In the last ten yards, Matt edged ahead with Bo less than an arm's length behind him.

"Four point eight seconds," Tom whispered to Matt after the race ended.

Gasping for air, Matt turned to Bo. "Incredible for a first run! With practice, you could easily improve."

The younger boys heard the praise and gathered around Bo, slapping him on the back and yelling words of encouragement. He would surely beat Coach Grazi on a rematch.

Tom ended class yelling, "Heads up! Jog back!"

"Your technique is good," Matt said to Bo as they lagged behind the other boys, "but it needs to get better."

"Yeah, sure."

"So how do you feel about today?"

Without hesitation, Bo responded, "There's always tomorrow." He increased his pace and joined his classmates.

Matt dropped back and a glimmer of hope raced through his mind. Bo had offered to continue the match. Holding Bo's attention by discussing further competition would allow Matt the opportunity to spout the advantages of joining the football team and athletic crew.

"Boy, you ruffled a few feathers today," Tom exclaimed as they followed the boys into the gym. "And don't think I didn't notice that whole setup was based on football drills and exercises."

"Of course," Matt replied. "It's always about football."

"I listened to the boys' chatter about Bo, mostly how he isn't used to anybody beating him, *at anything*."

"Good. I'm hoping Bo will *want* to beat me. And I noticed the boys in class supported him regardless of the outcome, which I'm sure happy about."

"You beat him at every exercise?"

"All but one which we tied, and the other drills only by a slim margin. He seemed to handle it well. I was better than he was, and he knew it, but I'm betting we both know he'll be able to beat me in future competitions if he puts his mind to it."

"You took a big chance."

"Had to. Both Bo and the boys needed to see I'm not only in charge, I'm able to compete too. Have to be strong before I can be soft."

CHAPTER 7

Matt not only observed the pecking order within classes but also, and more interesting, the hierarchy existing underneath Bo. The teen had a cadre of athletic friends who respected and followed him without question. Spending time with Bo's cohorts could be a winning strategy to reach Bo and recruit players.

Matt picked two of Bo's innermost circle to be captains in their gym class. David Bell, a towering, long-legged athlete who talked fast showed himself to be a definite quarterback candidate. Tony Castor, a gregarious boy, athletic and a little on the plump side, could prove to be a future defensive player.

"So, Bell," Matt said, "You can't pick Castor as a teammate since I've chosen him as the captain of the opposing team. You must choose your team based on skill."

Matt's approach resulted in teams being almost even in talent. After a tight game, Bell and Castor gathered the balls with new enthusiasm, patting each other on the back.

"Good effort, boys," Matt said.

Matt enjoyed conversing with the boys, all the while trying to entice Bo to join them. The boy, however, made it clear he wasn't interested. He tilted his head in silence or looked away whenever Matt attempted conversation. Each day Matt watched Bo leave class, dragging one shoe and then the other in the sandy soil, shuffling off the field.

Matt was angry with Bo because of his disinterest, and with himself because he seemed unable to reach the boy.

"Damn it." Matt cursed under his breath as he and Tom ambled toward the gym. "Bo does everything I ask him to do, but continues to move in slow motion."

"He's figured out how to get under your skin."

"Got that right," Matt admitted.

"Don't think he trusts you."

"I'm working on that."

"Better find a way to reach him soon."

"I know. I know."

When Matt left the gym, he spotted Bo entering Polk Cottage, home of the youngest boys on campus. His interest piqued, he followed the boy and watched from afar. Bo clenched what looked like an Osprey newsletter in his hand, and Matt speculated that it was the most recent issue containing his article on the basketball team. Following the teen into the cottage, he stopped behind a corner of the front library area.

Bo rolled the paper into a tube and then twisted it. The boy raised his arm toward the trash can in the corner of the room and let it fly. Missing the can, it landed on the floor. He lifted the tightly wrinkled paper and popped it into the garbage.

The young boxer strode toward a table on a far side of the common space. Three young boys fought each other to be the first to jump up. Each pushed his chair forward toward him in an obvious show of welcome.

Bo tousled one of the young boy's heads and fell limp into his temporary throne. The youngsters scrambled to move their papers and to give him space. The smiles on their faces seemed to be contagious. In a few seconds Bo's frown transformed into a wide grin.

Unseen, Matt backed out the door.

What am I doing that keeps the boy at a distance?

Deciding not to go back to his room, he crossed the lane and entered the older boys' residence. He passed the pool table and overstuffed couches and made his way toward a cluster of teens near the ping pong table.

"Hi, guys," Matt said. "Mr. Rourk around?"

"Upstairs. Want us to go git 'im?"

"No, that's okay. I'm actually here to talk to you guys."

Thirty minutes later, Bo sauntered into the cottage. It took only a moment for him to see Matt with his friends and a scowl deepened on his face. A chair screeched as he yanked it back and sat down at a table across the room.

Visible and within earshot of Bo, Matt eased into casual conversation with Danny Williams, a slight, talented athlete and another member of Bo's hierarchy.

"Why Florida State, Coach?" Williams asked.

Matt turned his head, just enough to catch Bo tapping his fingers on his table. The boy rubbed the back of his neck before looking away.

"Followed my high school coach," Matt said, returning his attention toward the boys.

"Really? I never followed any teacher anywhere." Williams' response prompted surrounding chuckles.

"He was a great coach. I believed in him, and he believed in me. I would have followed him anywhere."

"You sure were a super quarterback, Coach. I watched you win games with my dad when I was a little kid."

Matt grinned. "Not just me. One person never wins the game. The team does. I do admit though, at first I thought the guys in the backfield were the most important players. But it didn't take long to figure out that without the offensive line blocking and opening holes for the running backs, we wouldn't be scoring any points. Every person on a team matters. You never know who will rise to the occasion."

"The Noles went on to win the Sun Bowl, didn't they, Coach?" Williams asked.

"Yeah, we did." Matt smiled at the boy's wide grin that revealed a significant space between his front teeth.

"Let's talk about you guys," Matt said, pleased the boys had opened up to him. "I have to tell you, Coach Faber and I have been watching you. We like the way you jump right in during class. No wasted time. Good job."

Bell, the quarterback prospect, shoved Gonzales, who sat beside him. The athletic Hispanic boy sported a thick head of black hair that refused to cooperate with the brush stroke of the common duck's ass haircut, despite the lavish amount of Brylcreem.

"This guy didn't run fast enough till I pushed in behind and gave him a squeeze in the caboose," Bell teased, "if you know what I mean."

"Sheet, man, you the one who good throw, but no good runner."

A round of laughter echoed in the cottage, interrupted by a book slamming closed. Startled, the boys in Matt's group turned to where the noise had come in time to see Bo marching toward them.

"What are you doing here?" Bo demanded, his foot tapping the floor.

"Slow down, Bo. We're having a little chat."

"Like shit you are."

Matt jumped to attention and stepped toward Bo. "Outside, young man!" he ordered. "Now!"

Matt moved out the door, praying Bo followed behind him. The other boys watched with open mouths as the two left the cottage, and the door closed behind them.

"So, what is the problem?" Matt began.

"You're in my face all the time. It's bad enough when we're out there," Bo said pointing to the campus, "but here where I live? No." Bo looked directly at Matt. "This is my home base, not yours."

"I, I . . ." Matt hesitated. Although he had not considered his visit an invasion of privacy, he sensed he had overstepped his bounds. He had bet that Bo would see how approachable he could be, and participate in their conversation. He had lost on both counts.

"I wish you had joined us," said Matt, in a slow, steady, lowered voice. "But that apparently isn't going to happen."

"No kidding!" Bo said as he crossed his arms. "And remember that race or competition, whatever you called it? I want you to know I faked it. I let you win."

"I'm not sure why you're so angry," Matt said, ignoring his comment. "But I understand you need your space. We all do." He looked directly at Bo and straightened his stance, reaching as much height as possible. "I'll respect your home turf, and will not come back without an invitation."

Bo's eyebrows lifted in surprise.

Matt succeeded in finding a way to make himself visible to the person marking him, but the outcome was disastrous. He turned to leave and, after a few steps, spun back and faced Bo.

"However, I do *not* intend to stop recruiting you. You would be good for the team, and more importantly, the team would be good for you."

***

Matt met cottage father, Bart Rourk, on his front porch the following day during lunch.

"Glad to see you for the tour I promised," Bart said.

"I'm looking for more than a trek around the building. Hoping for conversation."

"About Bo, I suspect." Matt's eyebrows rose in surprise. "But first, a glimpse of CHB cottage life. This way."

Bart led Matt from the front library area into the recreation room on the right. Each cottage had a theme, and Monroe's was obvious. Cowboy hats, riding gear, and other paraphernalia hung on the walls. A western saddle sat on a stand in the corner.

"The cottage across the way is under a redesign, and our boys are assisting with the overhaul from World War II airplanes to African animals. Boys like that sort of stuff," Bart said.

"You heard about my little spat with Bo?"

"Get right to the point, why don't ya? Yeah, not from Bo though. Other versions."

"I'm having a tough time reaching this kid."

"So what's your motive?"

"What?"

"With Bo."

"I don't understand."

"You've got to want something, or you wouldn't be spending so much time on him." The accusation stung hard. Matt took a moment before responding.

"Bo's the most athletic boy I've seen on campus. What I want is for him to be the best he can be, to participate on our teams. The two of us seem to inch toward some kind of progress, but then things backfire. Can't figure out why he's not comfortable around me."

They ambled from the casual air of the rec room into the even larger sleeping area similar to those found in a military boot camp.

"Wow, wall to wall beds," Matt said. Three dozen neatly made beds alternated head to toe in the glossy, terra-cotta-colored room. "Why are the beds arranged like that?"

"To discourage talking after "lights out," Bart answered. "I run a tight ship."

"And that's how I run the gym," Matt said. "Bo seems to respect your rules. Don't understand why he doesn't respect mine."

"He seems agitated whenever he mentions you. His voice has an edge to it. Maybe he thinks his position as kingpin is threatened."

"Threatened?" Matt questioned. "Really?"

"The boys always looked up to him. Now they admire you."

Matt was stunned. "That's not my intent. I'm trying to connect with him so he'll join the team and athletic crew."

"Might want to explain that better," Bart said. "But don't give up. I like the boy. He'll come around."

How does Bart have such a good relationship going?

"See those glass walls on both sides of the cottage?" Bart asked.

Matt turned to see stacks of translucent blocks forming the north and south walls. Upon further inspection, he realized the walls hid two staircases. Small rectangular openings appeared after every few steps.

"I observe these boys from afar without them ever knowing. "I can see the smallest light and hear the softest sound without ever going downstairs. Saves me a lot of steps, especially after lights out."

"So you immediately catch any boy who misbehaves or tries to run away?"

"Most times. Only time I ever missed somebody trying to run, the night watchman reported him after an hourly tally, and we picked him right up."

"Bart," Matt asked, "How does Bo fit in here?"

"Most boys moan about the strict regulations, but Bo keeps his mouth shut and seems to take it all in stride."

"I've never experienced someone with such incredible athletic potential, and yet so resistant to a coach's attention. I'm not sure what to do next."

"Resistance is not an uncommon trait around here. Maybe a counselor in the guidance office can give you advice."

Matt frowned. Guidance counselors didn't fully understand the value of sports. In his way of thinking, they had a limited understanding about the positive impact of football on a boy's morale, stamina, and physical well-being.

He had not considered an outside team approach with a player, but baseball's sign-up date was fast approaching. Since he saw no indication Bo would join the baseball team, and spring football started two weeks into April, it was worth a shot.

CHAPTER 8

Matt rose early and entered the guidance office where a crew member at the front reception desk cradled the phone handle between his shoulder and ear. With his free hand, he signaled to Matt to take a seat.

Alone in the waiting area, Matt listened to the incessant, irritating sound of conversation and laughter pulsating from adjacent cubicles. He stared at the white standard-issue clock on the wall in front of him. *Tick tock.* Encircled by a black rim, the arrows acted as hands clicking off in rigid increments over bold, black numbers. *Tick tock.* Minutes passed. He moved back toward the front desk.

"Excuse me, I'm here to take a look at a student's file."

"Oh, okay, I'll go git somebody," the crew member said as if Matt had first arrived.

"Right."

"I'm sorry," a nearby counselor interrupted. "Is there a problem?" Matt summarized his request, tapping his foot.

"And just what are you looking for?"

"Want to review background information on a boy."

"Please step over to my desk," the counselor said. "Now, who are you, and who are you interested in?"

"Matt Grazi, the new coach. The boy's Harry Beauregard."

"Okay. Let's see, I can make an appointment with . . ."

"Look, I don't need an appointment. I'd just like to read my student's file. I don't want to discuss it, write on it, or publish it, for God's sake."

"I don't care what you want to do with it," the counselor snapped. "Nobody does a chart review without written permission from the director of the counseling department, or the director of the school."

"Okay, okay," Matt said as he waved his hand in front of him. "Never mind."

He turned for the door. The contention in the guidance office had transformed into a battle, and smoke fumed from both sides. Matt's impatience was the only victor.

He crossed the field and entered his office. The pressure was increasing. Players for baseball and football had to be selected and trained for the Osprey teams. The school's baseball schedule against the local schools was already hanging in the gym office. Spring football started in less than a month.

Then he remembered one likable counselor he had met on his second day of orientation.

Now, what was his name?

Finding the resident handbook in a file drawer, he confirmed Wayne Hayden was the person he sought.

"Coach Grazi," he said into the phone. "I'd like to speak with Wayne Hayden, please. Yes, I'll hold."

"Hayden," the counselor answered. "Yeah, I remember you, the FSU football hero, right?"

In one long breath, Matt thanked Hayden, asked if he liked football, and explained about Bo. He skipped the details about his previous visit to the guidance office.

"Beauregard? I'm about to schedule an appointment with the psychiatrist for that boy."

The counselor described a skirmish outside a classroom between Bo and another inmate. A teacher had recommended a referral to Dr. Hemlick, who supervised all medical treatment programs.

"Any chance I could learn more about this kid before he's put on a treatment plan? Perhaps review his file with you first?"

"Possible."

Convincing Hayden of his good intentions, Matt secured an appointment to meet later in the day. This time he approached the reception desk with the politeness of a British prince, and the reception-ist pointed the direction to the counselor's office.

"I may have come on a bit too strong earlier this morning," Matt confessed.

"A bit too strong?"

"Okay, okay. I'm sure you heard about it."

"Everyone heard about it."

"Well, why did they give me such a hard time? They acted like a bunch of prima donnas, like they're the only ones who need to know about these boys."

"Really? I got the impression you may have *told* them, rather than *asked* them, to read Bo's file."

"Guess I was a little pushy."

"Yeah. Privacy of records is a big thing around here."

Matt sighed. "Sorry. May I get a pass on my impatience? My capac-ity for calmness is limited."

"Get a handle on that," Hayden said. "Tell you what. Stay here a minute."

Matt waited. He took in the peeling, pale green walls, and thought that the guidance budget should include a paint job. Where the heck was Hayden?

After another five minutes, the counselor returned, flipping through pages. Approaching Matt, he guarded a file by holding it near his chest.

"The written entry upon Bo's arrival to CHB includes how he learned to fight, how he committed armed robbery, and how breaking and entering became part of his record. Cops caught him stealing a car."

"Oh boy."

Hayden read on. "Mom said she couldn't cope. It appears Bo's real father disappeared when he was young. Might have joined the service."

Aha, no padre in this boy's life.

"Although the older stepbrother spent most of his time away from home, Bo brags about his brother's boxing achievements." Hayden con-tinued to scan the pages. "A few notes on his conversations with his guidance counselor. Mom works full time at the A&P food store, as a meat wrapper. No mention of her work schedule, but it seems Bo's been on his own for a while."

Matt absorbed every word. He extended his hand toward Hayden to receive a picture of a 1920's two-family home.

"Bo's?"

"A rental. Not in the worst part of town, but not in the best either."

"Anything else?" Matt asked.

"At one point, Bo's mother couldn't support him, and he lived at a juvenile home outside Pensacola. Staff members documented that he became a big brother to the younger children, protecting them twenty-four seven."

"So this kid has both a rap sheet and a heart."

"Might be," Hayden said. "And he refuses to watch TV shows like *Father Knows Best* or *Lassie* because families like that 'don't really exist'."

"I'd bet money most of the boys on campus feel the same way. Does he talk about any of his neighborhood friends?"

After another shuffle of papers, Wayne found a conversation about a buddy who was a tough guy and boxing enthusiast with several run-ins with the law.

"The last time this guy was arrested, he went to prison on two counts of assault, one against a police officer no less. Oh, and on multiple firearms violations."

"Yikes." Matt sat back in his chair and drew a breath. The number of reasons for Bo's anger multiplied.

Matt's conviction that he and Bo had much in common weakened. This kid had it worse than he ever did. The biggest difference, his dad wasn't around.

***

"I've figured it out," Matt told Hayden on a return visit the following day. "Bo has to speak with me if I met with him in an official capacity. Do you think I could be present during his next counseling session? Even better, speak with him alone?"

"Why not talk to the kid on your own time?"

"Not willing to sit down with me."

"I see. Well, getting you information about Bo was one thing," Hayden said, "but meeting with him, that's another."

"I've done a couple of interviews like this in my psychology coursework at FSU."

"Not the same. Your limited experience and capacity for patience might cause you to say something that might come back to haunt both you and us."

"Okay, okay," Matt said as he turned to leave.

"Hold on there, Matt," Hayden said as he waved his hand. "With that being said, we want to encourage teachers to take time to talk to the boys, so let me consult with both Bo's social worker and the head of the guidance department."

Two days later, he called Matt.

"Willing to observe a few of our counseling sessions?"

"You bet. Let me know when to be here. I'll be a fly on the wall."

"Not quite so fast. There are a few other things. We'll acquaint you with our report format, and the head counselor will decide where to go from there."

"Agreed."

Matt attended two counseling sessions. Expecting to be more confident, instead his nerves played havoc with his restless stomach. He was learning how much he didn't know.

The next step was a short session with Bo. The regular counselor laid the list of dos and don'ts on the table. He would listen to their conversation through a speaker system and could intervene at any point.

When Bo entered the guidance office at his scheduled time and saw Matt, darts of anger shot across the room.

"Hello, Bo."

"What are *you* doin' here?"

"Glad to see you, too. Now sit down," Matt said, pointing to the empty chair a few feet away. He lowered his voice and added, "Please."

Bo hesitated and then jerked the chair back away from Matt. He plopped down on the hard vinyl seat.

"I spoke with the guidance department who was kind enough to share your history with me. Thought you wouldn't mind, since you already know about me." The memory of the boy's smugness still stung.

Bo clenched his jaw but said nothing. Matt pulled closer.

"I want to talk to you, about you." He spoke in a calm, steady tone, using similar words delivered to him by his high school coach.

"You carry a huge chip on your shoulder, mister," Matt began. Bo leaned back on the chair's two back legs but said nothing.

"Chair on the ground."

Bo inhaled a long, slow breath and then complied.

"You seem to challenge everyone to knock it off. Anyone who tests you takes the chance of finding your fist in their face."

"Is that right?"

"Yeah, that's right. You've got a problem."

"And just what's my problem?"

Matt paused, hoping Bo would volunteer more. Nothing.

"You don't realize your future outside these walls will be determined by what you do inside them. Your ass is on the line."

"I don't see any line."

"Cut the crap." Silence filled the air.

"Look, fighting doesn't always solve the problem, Bo. Until you figure out this game of yours only works for a short time, you're going to keep getting into trouble. People don't respond well to threats. Keep it up and all you'll have after leaving Colby Hill is one prison after another. Is that what you want?"

Bo diverted his attention to the wall, and then back toward Matt. "Talk is cheap. Why should I listen to you?"

"Because it may be hard for you to understand, but I'm one of the good guys. There are a lot of people in this world, which makes it tough to figure out who to trust. You've got to learn how to recognize the decent human beings from the thugs. You appear to be smart. You know what to watch out for. Find folks who give a damn."

Matt waited for a response that didn't come.

"Have faith, Bo. When you find somebody you can put your faith in, an amazing thing can happen. They might turn around and put their faith in you."

Bo's head snapped toward Matt. His eyes took on a glazed appearance, and he blinked before turning away. Perhaps Bo had either heard that phrase before, or it meant something to him. Then the spark disappeared.

Have I hit a nerve?

Bo scanned everything in the room, except his coach. Matt tapped on the open folder, concentrating on giving Bo time to respond.

"What makes you such an authority?" Bo finally blurted out.

Matt took a breath and laid his forms and pen on the desk beside him.

"I considered myself a pro at playing games in high school, on and off the field, just like you do. I've learned a few things since then."

Silence.

"Look, Bo, I've looked at your file. I'm onto your gameplay. Take school, for example. I know you use the print shop to your advantage, and I sure as hell know you've accessed information about me. You're a lot smarter than you pretend to be. Is the dumb routine easier than pulling your weight with boys your own age?"

No response.

"How about you cut the bullshit. Talk to me. There's *something* good inside you. You just have to let it out."

What is he thinking?

"Bo, do you have *anything* you want to say?"

Tilting his head, Bo's intense stare moved toward the door.

"Yeah, are we done?"

Matt's shoulders slumped forward, his erect posture gone. "I guess so," he said. He waited for another second to see if Bo would add to the conversation.

"Okay, Bo, but if you ever want to talk."

Bo's eyes said, "I don't." "Can I go now?"

Matt nodded. The droplets of sweat accumulated underneath his pressed, but now wrinkled, shirt.

The boy stood and pushed his chair away, and without turning back, let the door slam behind him.

"Shit." Matt reached for his pen and the required interview forms, realizing he hadn't made a single comment. He scratched out a summary of the meeting and handed it to Bo's counselor as he exited the small conference room.

"Why don't we try that again in two weeks together?" the counselor said. "Let's talk later."

"Sure," Matt said, already halfway out the door.

He pressed his lips together and took a deep breath. His potential star player had retreated. It was his turn to back off and look for another boy to lead the football team.

CHAPTER 9

"Coach! Coach!" screamed a boy's voice, as he pounded on Matt's cottage door in the middle of the night. "Bo's done tried to run away, and he's in the hospital!"

"What the . . . ?" Matt mumbled as he shook his head and grabbed the piled pair of pants on the floor by his bed. Upon opening the door, crew member Mulany burst in and knocked Matt into the wall behind him.

"He's bad off. The dogs done ripped him open, and he got the shit beat out of him!"

"Oh, my God."

Grabbing a button-down shirt as he slipped his bare feet into penny loafers, Matt ushered Mulany out of his cottage. They sprinted to the nearby campus hospital. Matt's Timex watch read 3:08 a.m.

The two charged through the front door, slowing down long enough to catch their breaths and inquire at the front desk about Bo's location.

"Can I stay, Coach?"

"Better return to your cottage. It's late. They'll be looking for you."

"Okay. You'll tell him I was here?"

"Of course, and I'll tell him you'll visit later. And Mulany . . . thanks."

Matt turned and made his way down the hall. He halted in front of the wing of patient beds. Taking a full breath, he rubbed his hands over his face. Trying to stay calm, he gingerly knocked on the double doors of the ward. After a few seconds with no response, Matt used his shoulder to press against the right side of the swinging doors. As the slit of light widened, he peeked into the long room and stepped forward.

At the end of the rows of mostly empty beds, Bo lay motionless. Matt slowly walked down the center aisle. He gasped when he spied the lacerations covering the boy's face. Black-and-blue bruising surrounded one eye, the other eye swollen shut. He inched closer. Bo's bulging nose indicated it might be broken, and his forehead puckered with a long, jagged cut. Multiple stitches closed savage and oozing wounds on his right arm. A white sheet, blotchy with red stains, covered the boy's battered body.

"Jesus," Matt whispered.

An older, bearded man tended to Bo. The doctor raised his head slightly as Matt approached, but didn't turn.

"Graves, Dr. Graves," the man said, still not lifting his hands from Bo's wounds. "Just about done."

"How bad?"

Glancing at Matt, the doctor shook his head. "Bad." He lifted a clean sheet from the table and shook it out. After removing the stained one, he drew its crisp edge over Bo's stitched, distended abdomen and tucked it under the boy's chin.

Giving the wounds on the puffy face a final check, Dr. Graves moved the vials of medication and bloody gauze strips to one side. He adjusted the I.V. line of fluid and slipped the plastic nasal cannula behind Bo's head to transport the life-giving oxygen into his lungs. He slipped off his gloves, tossing them into the trash.

"I've given him something to make him more comfortable. Antibiotics for the damn dog bites."

The doctor lumbered as if the weight of ten years at CHB weighed him down. He appeared to have patched far too numerous boys for his liking. Moving across the aisle, he placed his hand on another boy's forehead, nodded and left.

Sitting on the nearby empty bed, Matt stared at Bo, unsure of what to say or do. He struggled to maintain control. Until this moment, he and Bo had been testing each other, neither one willing to compromise. It had been a continual contest of wills to see who the tougher man was. Toughness no longer mattered.

Damn it, Bo.

As Matt focused on the pitiful sight before him, Bo peeked through swollen slits and moved his blood-crusted lips. Matt returned a broken smile. The boy's eyes closed, rolling up underneath heavy eyelids.

Arching his back to loosen his tightened muscles, Matt leaned toward the head of the bed. "Bo?" The boy was still.

Touching the sheet that covered Bo's hand, Matt paused for a few moments before whispering. "You ride the crest high, Harry Beauregard, pushing yourself to be top dog at whatever you do. You mustered the guts and fortitude to run but bailed out of the fight to stay. Why?"

Matt saw movement underneath the distended, almost-purple lids, but they didn't open.

"Bo, I know how protective you are when it comes to the younger kids, and how they respond to you. You're their role model."

Bo moaned and attempted to shift in the metal bed.

"There's so much more to this world than what's in front of you. You have a future, and I see the things you could do, the person you could be." Matt bit down hard and gazed at the mangled body in front of him. "I see *me* in you."

And then even softer, "I'm sorry if I . . ." Matt inhaled and lowered his head. Quiet hung in the air.

After several seconds, Matt stood. Starting to turn, he heard a raspy, unrecognizable whisper. Bo's cracked lips moved ever so slightly.

"C . . . Coach?" Bo asked, a slurred voice resulting from a tongue twice its normal size.

"What . . . ?" Matt whispered. He inched closer toward the headboard.

"Bo?" Stillness enclosed the room like a freshly laundered sheet over a lumpy mattress.

"I . . . " Bo began. He winced at the effort. He inched his hand toward Matt. A cough caused a tortuous smile. Crimson fluid eased from the corner of his mouth.

"Bo?" Matt asked again in a panicked, louder voice.

Bo nodded ever so slightly. He blinked back clear fluid in his eyes, and his eyes closed the same time his head dropped to the side.

"Doc!" Matt yelled to the air. "Doc!" he yelled even louder. He bolted through the door and into the hallway. His screams and waving arms alerted a medical crew member, who in turn ran for the doctor.

Matt grabbed the wall for physical and emotional support as Santo approached.

"You okay?" Santo asked.

"I don't understand," Matt whispered. "The boy is barely alive."

"I'm sorry about what happened, Matt. Shit." he cursed under his breath. Santo placed his hand on Matt's shoulder, but Matt jerked his arm away.

"Was Andrews in on this?"

"If you mean was he in charge of retrieving the boy," Santo paused. "Of course."

Matt's jaw hardened and his teeth pressed together. "I want to beat his brains in! This should never have happened."

"Hold it, Matt. You . . ."

Matt pointed to the hospital door behind him and screamed. "Take a look. It's wrong! Terribly wrong!" Matt's stare cut into Santo like a knife. "Go in there and then tell me how you feel!"

"Take a walk, Matt," Santo said. "And return to your cottage. You can see the boy tomorrow. He's in good hands."

"But . . ."

"It's not a suggestion." Santo turned his back on Matt. The doctor ran past them, flinging the ward doors open.

"Now," Santo added.

More drained than he had ever felt on a football field, Matt stood alone in the brightly lit corridor. The scratch of ink on a nearby monitor intermingled with distant moans echoing from behind closed doors.

The night walk across campus resulted in an unsettling mist penetrating Matt's skin, and he shivered. Once inside his cottage, he opened the paned window and viewed the moon sending its shafts of light through the towering pines. It took all his remaining energy to fight back the overwhelming sadness and stifle the increasing anger.

***

Matt sat rigid at his desk early the next morning, expecting to hear something about Bo. After morning classes had come and gone, he took the initiative and made a call to Santo.

"I've never seen such a bloody mess," Matt said after they had shared morning greetings.

"It upset me too."

"What are you going to do? I mean about Bo's injuries?"

"Step back, Matt. I'll do what I need to do."

Matt stiffened at Santo's response. "Which means?"

"Which means that it's my job, not yours. Bo knew the risks and consequences of running. I'll address the extent of the boy's injuries with the ACI staff at the prison. For you, the incident is closed. Concentrate on your classes and your team."

His jaw tight, Matt wanted to slam down the phone. Instead, he mumbled, "Yes, sir," and squeezing the phone handle with all his strength, slowly placed it back on the receiver.

Is this the leadership Santo claims to provide for the boys?

Matt paced down to the workout area and pumped weights. Struggling to focus, he burned every available ounce of his energy. After sweat had soaked his shirt, he gulped down half the bottle of water and poured the remaining liquid over his head. Shaking his head back and forth and toweling off, he inhaled deeply.

Santo's implication that he had overstepped his bounds took him by surprise. And yet, hadn't he done just that? His defiance had alienated his boss.

But at this moment, Santo wasn't his main concern.

Would Bo recover? Why had he run?

CHAPTER 10

Matt drove to The Country Club to find Betty. Just her presence put his mind at ease. On numerous occasions, they had enjoyed conversation paired with a barbecue sandwich and a Pabst Blue Ribbon beer in a frosted mug.

When Betty served his drink, their arms touched, and Matt felt heat spread through his body.

"Gettin' off in an hour," she said. "Like to stay till then?"

Matt's raised eyebrows and wide grin asked, "Are you kidding?"

The swing of Betty's sashay and ponytail captivated him as she moved about the room. He empathized with her struggle to find enough hours in the day to work and fit in her studying, because he had the same time-management dilemma. Each day he taught gym classes and squeezed in a brief visit to Bo, who hadn't opened his eyes. Boys showing potential or interest in football gobbled up the remaining moments until dusk.

Deep in thought, Matt lost all concept of time until a gentle pat on the shoulder returned him to the moment.

"Hey," Betty said, smiling as she slid into the chair opposite him. Despite just finishing a busy shift, she looked refreshed. She had a reserved manner, her delicate and smooth hands calm, as she placed them on the table.

"You look, kinda . . . different," Matt stammered.

"Well, bless your heart. You sure know how to turn a girl's head."

Matt cocked his head in question. Was she serious, or did she mean, "Good Lord, what an idiot!"

"Anything different about my attire?" she hinted. "Absence of the silly western outfit? Hair out of that crazy ponytail?"

Embarrassed, Matt apologized. "Sorry, really. Didn't mean different. I meant, well, great." Sometimes his gift of gab was out of tune.

"Stop talking," she said, mocking him. "I mean, thanks. Wanna hear about my day? Exciting times at The Country Club."

"How's that?"

"A big argument at lunch," Betty began. "A pompous ass spouted off about the nerve of a local colored man's son. Turns out the kid had participated in a sit-in."

"Here?"

"No, at the counter in the Woolworths store in Tallahassee."

"Old ways are hard to change."

"More than that," Betty said. "Folks 'round here don't take kindly to outsiders makin' new rules for them."

"'Difficult to change a man's heart through laws and force,'" Matt recited under his breath.

"Eisenhower say that?" Betty asked.

She caught the look of surprise from Matt after her comeback. "Us Southern girls are smarter than people might imagine," she said with a wink, "I can turn on a radio and unwrap a newspaper too."

Matt grinned. "I bet you can."

"And you? What's new at the school?"

"Big stuff," Matt said. Santo says CHB will sell its extra steers and dairy cows at auction." Betty cocked her head.

"Fun time. You wanna go?" Laughter lightened the mood.

"Anything else, a tad more personal?" she asked.

"One boy on my mind. Don't think you'd want to hear about him."

"But I do," Betty said, appearing to notice the tension in Matt's face. She spoke softer. "I enjoy listenin' to that mesmerizin', gravelly voice of yours."

A partial grin crossed Matt's face but quickly disappeared. "He's . . ." Matt paused. *I better keep Bo to myself.*

"Barry or Bo something?" Betty said as if she had pulled a rabbit from an empty hat. "No, I'm not psychic. You've talked about him before. Isn't he the boy you were pushing to be your athletic machine?"

"What?" Stunned, Matt was embarrassed at how much he had shared. "Damn, did I really say that?"

"Didn't make it up."

"Okay, okay, I may have thought about him like that at first, but I don't think that way anymore."

"So, he doesn't have the potential you thought he did?"

Matt sighed. "It's not that. It would be great if the boy joined the team, but we've gone back and forth at each other, and it hasn't clicked."

"It's been a while. Sounds like that dog won't hunt."

"May be my fault. Pushed too hard."

"Oh, I see."

"Worse than that, Betty. Bo ran away from the school, with terrible consequences. I'm to blame."

Betty reached across the table. She took a long breath, giving him time to speak.

Matt lifted his face and his hand touched hers. He told all.

"I'm so sorry," tumbled from her lips.

"I'll talk more with the boy when he's better."

"So for now, why not wipe the guilt off your face. No sense in wearing it, until you know for sure you deserve it."

Matt reached for her fingers and gently squeezed. "You've got a way . . . Let's take a walk on the golf course. Full moon."

Matt wasn't sure if Betty's face said, "I'm hearing you," or "Bless your heart," but it didn't matter. He gave her his warmest smile, and with his hand pressed against the small of her back, ushered her into the night.

***

He's still alive.

Matt stood beside Bo's bed the following day, not saying a word. Either sleeping or unconscious, the boy didn't move. Each time Bo's chest rose and fell, Matt locked onto the rhythm and relief passed over him.

By the end of the week, Matt watched Bo pull himself up in bed and attempt to adjust the dial on his transistor radio.

"You're looking better."

"A hard time seeing with this eye, and it still hurts to breathe."

"Bruised ribs," Matt stated, repeating Dr. Graves' diagnosis.

"Geez, feel like they're broke. I tell ya, heard lots of stories about them goons at ACI beatin' the livin' crap out of inmates, but, shit, I didn't believe it could be this bad." Bo let out a wheezy chuckle and winced. "Look at me now, I'm living proof it ain't no lie."

"Maybe your mangled body will convince the others that these guys aren't kidding."

"Yeah, maybe," Bo said, lifting his eyes upward. "Coach?"

Matt cocked his head in question.

"Sit down," the boy whispered. Matt hesitated. "Please."

Matt pulled a chair toward the bed.

"You wanna hear 'bout it?" Bo asked. "My run?"

Matt nodded and remained silent. Bo told him about the night watchman shining his light on each bed, counting bodies, punching numbers into the time clock on his hip, and moving on.

"I was worried 'bout the dog upstairs livin' with the Rourks, but guess I done a good job at being quiet. I carried my shoes till I made the woods. My plan was to hit the highway or tracks north of here, but I got all turned around."

Bo asked Matt to hand him his water. Matt bent the straw and passed the cup.

"It was pitch black, and I mean pitch black. All a sudden, I saw a dim light ahead of me, like a clearing, or maybe a road. And then I heard 'em."

"Them?"

"The dogs, howlin', barkin'. I almost shit my pants."

The dogs' sounds meant the guards and inmates from ACI had joined the hunt. Matt heard the bowel-loosening fear in Bo's unsteady voice.

"I couldn't hardly see through the damn bushes and trees. When I saw flickers of light and heard yellin', I panicked." Bo's breathing became more rapid. "I ran in the opposite direction until the weight of those crazy dogs jumpin' up on my back slammed me to the ground." Tears emerged. "I thought I was gonna die."

"Easy, Bo. You're safe now."

"I don't feel safe."

Matt sucked in a deep breath. He had never heard Bo speak like this.

"The stinkin' breath comin' from those damn dogs was . . . well, like rotten meat. I tried to protect myself by rollin' into a ball, but shit. I screamed when those fangs tore into me. When I threw my arms up to protect my face and neck, it didn't do no good. Those hounds went for my arms and my belly."

"Oh Bo, I . . . "

"That's not all," Bo interrupted. "When the guards pulled the dogs off me, I thanked God I was still alive. That's when a whack I ain't never felt before in my life hit my back. It smashed me across the ground. The guards turned me over and kicked me in the balls and the ribs, even worse than the hit to the back. I 'member rolling around in them bushes and hearin' them men laughin'. Not sure what happened next. I must'a taken a good one to the head, 'cause next thing I knew, I done woke in this bed."

Matt grabbed the front of his shirt, hoping the pressure of his hand would calm his racing pulse. Revulsion crawled from his abdomen to the rest of his body. He cringed at the thought of the dogs' rabid-like attack and the following beating.

He reached over toward the bed and covered the boy's sheeted hand with his. With his free hand, he slid the chair closer.

"Why, Bo? Why did you run?" The solitary hum of a fluorescent light filled the room, muffled by voices from outside.

Bo stared through unseeing eyes, his mind another place. He answered in a lowered voice. "I dunno, Coach. All of a sudden like, I jest had to git outta here."

"Did it have anything to do with me?" Matt braced himself for the answer.

"I was pissed at myself, at you, at this place."

Matt shook his head. He faced the agonizing truth of his role in Bo's decision to run.

"Bo, I'm sorry. If I'm to blame, I'm sorry."

Bo nodded, saying nothing.

"Running is a natural instinct when things are too much, but . . ." Matt's throat closed in a knot, and he couldn't speak any further. He pulled his heavy body from the chair.

Bo watched his coach rise and move toward the door.

"Coach, can I ask you somethin' 'fore ya go?"

"Rest up. We'll talk later."

"No, now."

Matt didn't want any more conversation. It was too hard. He shook his head.

"You still want me on your crew?"

The words Matt had been hoping to hear for so long reverberated through his skull. He bit his lip and fought back the guilt of Bo's run.

"Bo, I . . . I can't answer that now."

Shock and disappointment covered Bo's face.

"But when you're better and out of this hospital, ask me again. If you do, I'll say yes."

First down.

***

On Monday morning, with excitement in his voice, Matt revealed his upcoming plan to Tom.

"Santo gave permission for two more inmates to be added to our crew."

Tom shuffled his position throughout the announcement, which seemed to indicate his patience was wearing thin. "What the hell for? We've got two boys to help us. One boy every day. They seem to be handling the job just fine."

"I've mentioned this idea to you before, Tom."

"I know, and I still don't think it's necessary."

"The way I see it, more athletic crew members can help achieve our goal of a winning football team."

Tom straightened his stance. "Your goal." He placed his hands on his hips. "Oh, I see. Even though the baseball season has just started, the football team is much more important."

"No, it's not . . ."

"Football's everything, isn't it?"

"Maybe not *everything* . . ." Matt replied. "Listen, making jocks a part of the crew will help every sport, baseball included. I want these athletes to make the field and gym their home during any season."

The word "baseball" seemed to catch Tom's attention. He leaned backward in his chair, tipping onto the rear legs. "And this play brings Bo on board, doesn't it?"

"He's one of our best prospects, isn't he?"

"I can think of others."

"Okay, you choose the other athlete to add to the crew, but you know *if* Bo decides to work with us, and I do say *if,* we'd be in better shape. No matter which player comes on board, with fresh fighting spirit, we'd have a better chance of building the physical and mental power structure we need to form the nucleus of our teams."

Selecting the right core of key team members promoted comradery. Matt had been part of a tight inner circle in high school and college, and he wanted that between him, Tom, Bo, the crew, and the boys. Comradery was contagious, and a rejuvenated team spirit won games.

"From the start, I saw Bo being the Pied Piper who leads the others in. Bo thinks like the other boys. He knows what makes them tick. He's aware of what makes them happy and what pisses them off. But whether Bo joins in or not, I want to begin a new approach with an added top crew member for both odd and even days."

Tom tilted his head as if considering the change. His chair leaned forward until four legs were flat on the ground.

"We could try it."

"Tom, remember your gung ho in the service? With a little bit of that, you, me, and the new crew can do more than 'try it.'"

"Tough finding something new that hits home, Matt."

"How about we work on a few tempting carrots to dangle in front of these boys? Small rewards make a difference. Together, we'll figure it out. So, you in?"

CHAPTER 11

The following afternoon the phone rang, and Matt held his breath as he listened. "Coach Grazi? Got a transfer request. Sending him over."

Although Matt felt like whooping into the phone, he held on to his composure.

"Fine."

Twenty minutes seemed an hour before he saw Bo shuffling down the hall. He walked with a slight limp, alongside one of the top-ranked students in the school, an Ace. Matt accepted an envelope from the inmate, signed the paperwork, and dismissed the escort.

"So, you're serious about this?" Matt asked, shutting his office door.

"I'm here."

Matt motioned toward the chair.

One step at a time.

"How are you feeling? Nobody's laid another hand on you, have they?"

"No, I was lucky," Bo said as he slid onto the chair's metal surface.

"Lucky?"

"Yup. At the hospital, people were talking when I was supposed to be sleeping. Only I wasn't. I couldn't open my eyes or nothin', but my ears still worked. Anyway, one guy said, 'This kid's a mess. Better skip the strap.' So . . . I'm fine."

"Now wait a minute, they would beat a boy who had already been beaten?"

"The rule is, when you run and git caught, it's down to the lowest rank of Grub, and time to line up for a-beatin'. The rule doesn't depend on what shape you're in. Like I said, guess I'm a lucky guy."

Matt shook his head. "So, how lucky do you feel about being demoted from Rookie to Grub?"

"Been there before. No big deal."

"Wrong. It *is* a big deal. If you want to work with me, you'll never be a Grub again."

Matt could see the question mark on Bo's face. No wise-ass remarks, just a hard stare.

Bo shifted his gaze downward and his foot moved slightly, as if chasing an imaginary bug, or a speck of dust. Moments passed without anyone speaking.

Have I gone to the Twilight Zone or what?

Seconds later, Matt broke the silence. "Okay then. If you're ready for my rules, I'll put you on the crew with Mulany."

"Heard you kicked his ass into shape," Bo spoke with the first hint of a smile.

"And I'll kick yours if I need to, wise guy. Mulany will show you the ropes and I'll give the orders."

Bo waved a hand in front of his face. "Yeah, yeah. I know all that."

He dug his hands into his pockets and rose to leave. Before he could take a step, Matt raised his hand.

"Whoa right there." He pointed to the chair. "We need to discuss a few more things." Bo eyed him before retaking his seat.

"First thing, by Wednesday you need a crew cut."

"What? What's the matter with my hair?"

"Nothing, if that's what you want, but it's not what will work on this crew. Two, those state clothes you're wearing . . . anywhere other than the gym or field, you represent the teams. I want your shirt clean and ironed."

"Ironed? How am I gonna iron the dammed thing?"

"Watch your mouth. I checked out the cottages. Irons and ironing boards are in the closets." He paused before adding, "And those shoes, or 'brogans' as they're called, need to be shined."

"Anything else?" Bo asked in frustration.

"Yeah, arrive showered and on time."

"This sucks."

Matt remembered the result of pushing too hard. He took a deep breath before continuing in a slower, more concerned tone.

"Those are the rules. It's a tough job, and if you can't hack it, don't show up. Make up your mind. For now, find Mulany. First inspection, tomorrow."

Minutes after Bo had departed, Tom entered Matt's office. "What in the world did you say to Bo? He sure looked strange."

"Hope that look is a good thing. I laid it on strong."

Matt had bet that the greater the challenge, the better chance Bo had of not backing down. He related the details of the tense conversation to Tom.

"No shit, and he swallowed that?"

"We'll see. I'm feeling a new sense of energy. This school is on its way to a dynamite football season, and I can't wait."

"Don't get too psyched too soon, Matt. You've got a *long* way to go."

***

The next morning Bo took a quick step to avoid what looked like a crack in the walkway. He headed toward the gym, his limp slightly less noticeable.

Planning for this day, Matt reviewed the series of dos and don'ts he had written and re-written in his mind. Dos: Go easy with the boy, be firm, show excitement. Don'ts: Don't be too critical, don't piss the boy off, don't let the boy piss you off.

The shaved, washed, and pressed Bo arrived on time, sporting a crew cut.

"Man, you look good," Matt said.

"That's your opinion."

Oh, boy.

Matt took a quick breath before pumping up the importance of crew responsibilities and details of the job. "Any questions so far?"

Bo shook his head. Then in what appeared to be an afterthought, spoke. "Yeah," he said. "Am I too late?"

"For what?"

"For getting on the baseball team."

"But you never signed up."

"Yeah, I know. Remember? Was in the hospital on sign-up day. So, am I too late to play?"

"I don't know," Matt admitted. "When can you swing a bat?"

"I'm taped up real good, and my stitches come out soon."

"We'd need approval from Dr. Graves, and Coach Faber will have to speak with you. Let me check it out."

They moved to the locker room. "You know what to do, Mulany," Matt said. "Show this Grub the ropes."

Matt excused himself and returned to his office. Lifting the phone's receiver, he heard excited voices echoing on the line. He hung up. Folks on the party line had heard his click in. Minutes later, he tried again and the line was clear.

"Tom, know you're off today, but have you got a minute?" He repeated Bo's request.

"Anyone besides you and me seen the roster?" Tom asked.

"Santo. Why?"

"I'll run it by him. If he's okay with the kid playing, I'll have Bo sign the sheet. Then back into the file, no one wiser."

"You're the man."

"I'll let you know if Santo's on board."

Matt was making his way back down the gym hallway when Mulany approached.

"Where's Bo?" Matt asked.

"In the locker room. Can I talk to you?"

Now what?

"Sure, what is it?"

"Bo passed the word last night. If he's gotta git a crew cut, so does everybody else. He told us 'bout the ironed shirt, polished shoes, and shower too. Can I take time off for a haircut?"

Matt tucked his head, trying to conceal his grin. *I'll be damned.* He was tempted to thank Bo for passing the word about the new dress code, but no.

"So . . . what do ya think?" Bo asked as Matt and Mulany entered the locker room. He squeezed a dripping, soapy rag and pointed to the shower area.

Matt grabbed a white cloth and wiped the top of the shower tiles. He showed Bo the slightly soiled fabric.

"Much better. A decent job," he said as he moved toward another section.

"Decent? That's all?" Bo placed his hands on his hips and stood strong.

Matt spoke evenly, but with determination. "I will inspect every area until I feel each one meets the high standards of this gym. Do you have a problem with that?"

Bo relaxed his stance. "No, sir."

"Good. Now, let's discuss more intriguing aspects of the crew members' job description." He signaled Bo to join him in his office. "Let's talk baseball."

Matt pulled out the baseball roster and read off recognizable names, like Bell, Castor, Williams, and Gonzales.

"Gonzales is a good guy," Bo said. "He's a little short, but he can sure shoot those basketball hoops. I call him 'Shorty Spic.'" The boy chuckled.

Matt's head jerked up. "Watch what you call people. Nicknames can hurt."

Bo tilted his head in question, and a frown wrinkled his face. He appeared to have caught the chill in Matt's voice and shook his head as if he couldn't figure out why Matt was frosted.

"Oh, and there's one other name on this list," Matt said. Bo looked up.

"A late-comer, Beauregard, Harry Beauregard."

"Thanks, Coach," Bo said softly. Matt tipped a "you're welcome" with his cap.

"I mean it," Bo said.

"I know."

Matt turned his head away to give the impression it was no big deal. But it was a big deal, for both of them.

***

In his first life as a successful football player, Matt had little practice or patience with delegating responsibility. The only thing he had ever passed off was a ball. In order to get more time with football, he was determined to teach crew members how to take over some of his tasks.

Under his and Tom's supervision, Bo and Mulany became the new ramrods of the crew, alternating first and second in command. The other two crew members operated the same way on alternating days. Classes would run like cattle drives, both boys keeping all the doggies together, leading them in every activity.

After spending extra time with the boys, Matt announced they were ready to go. Both boys nodded their heads, scribbled notes, and even spoke up to offer suggestions.

At the start of the next gym class, Matt forced himself to step back, nodding to the two to take his place in the front. He moved to a nearby, strategic position and braced himself to jump in if the situation demanded it.

"We help Coach run a tight ship 'round here," Bo spoke with confidence. "This place will be sparklin' clean, and we expect everybody to do everything by the book. When you finish up, put the equipment back right. Everybody know where it goes?"

Bo continued for several minutes, the number of affirmative head bobs increasing one by one. The crowd of smiles indicated his words hit home. Standing less than twenty feet away, Bo spurted off previous quotes Matt had delivered, almost word for word. Matt swallowed a lump of pride. His new recruit never gave him first rights to the inspirations, but then again, that was how it should be.

"Anything else, Mulany?" Bo asked his crew mate.

"Just, listen up," Mulany added as he turned to the boys. "What me and Bo want is 'xactly what the coaches want. Hit the field!"

After the group moved outside, Tom joined Matt on the bottom bench of the bleachers.

"You know, Matt, I'm not a betting man, but I wish I had placed one on seeing what just happened. Is it for real?"

"For now, I think."

Classes over, baseball and football drills began, scheduled at separate times, because several boys wanted to play in both sports.

"Have you decided what baseball position Bo should play?" Matt asked, flipping through his notes.

"Outfielder," Tom said. "He has to cover large distances, so speed, instincts, and reaction time are key. Bo has all three."

"I've seen him chase down a fly ball over his head, even on the run. But how about his arm strength? Can he throw the ball accurately into the infield or home plate?"

"Who's the head baseball coach here?" Tom asked with a grin.

Tom had played baseball in sandlots for most of his younger life, with no one available to teach him the rules of the sport. Only by observing baseball players and imitating their moves had he discovered how to run, throw, bat, field, and catch a ball. His watch-and-learn method had worked. His chest swelled when he spoke of his makeshift diamond of the past being the school's reality today.

"Game in two weeks?" Matt asked.

"Yup."

"Maybe having Bo on the team will have a fringe benefit. The boys are scared shitless every time they look at his wounds. As long as his dangerous escapade is fresh in their minds, they'll not take a chance on running."

Under the lights on the third Thursday in April, the Ospreys played against Anhinga Bay High School. From the dugout, Matt focused on Bo's play.

"He's not the best batter we have, that's for sure," Tom said, "but he's not afraid to crowd the plate." On the second pitch of the third inning, all thoughts of strategy became irrelevant. A high-speed pitch curved the ball downward and cracked into Bo's left knee.

Matt and Tom jumped to their feet, as the crowd rose to theirs. In a flash, Matt's memory of a past hit to his knee after a rapid change in direction caused him to wince in pain. Bo skipped and limped toward first base before collapsing onto his hands and knees to touch base. Rising, he waved that he was okay. Tom and the makeshift medical crew ran onto the field.

"I'm okay. I'm okay," Bo yelled. Matt's hands clenched the railing of the dugout.

"He's fine, Matt," Tom said upon his return. "He'll be just fine."

Matt shook his head. "I know too well that a player can be out for a long time from a wild pitch. I've seen it happen more than once."

Bo's limp to first base forced a score. Bell singled, moving Bo to third base. Minutes later a throw from the catcher picked Bo off for the final out.

Matt kept an eye on Bo's every move for the remainder of the game. Despite the team's early lead, they were unable to outlast the Anhinga Bay nine, winding up on the short end of a 6–5 score.

"Good effort. That's what counts," Matt said and patted each of the players on the back as they boarded the bus. "You okay?" he asked Bo.

Bo nodded.

Matt wasn't sure he believed him. "See Doc when we pull up. Don't wait until tomorrow."

Tom stood in the front aisle, supporting himself by grabbing the metal bar above the back of the first seat. A pep talk followed.

Matt only heard a soft rumble of distant words. The infinite number of scratches on the window before him blurred as he dwelt on possible injuries that could bring down a player, and bring a season's victories to an abrupt end.

CHAPTER 12

Matt checked off the days in April, noting that Bo's physical condition improved every day. The boy's drive to compete appeared to intensify with every practice, every game.

"Coach, when are we gonna compete again on the shuttle run or the forty-yard dash? I'm faster now."

"I'm the old man here. You better be close to beating me by now. Concentrate on the next baseball game. I'll time your laps and then pitch to you. Coach Faber tells me it'll be a tough game on Friday." The teen shrugged his shoulders and picked up the ball.

The prediction of a difficult game came to pass. The Ospreys held the lead against the Cougars by one run going into the fifth inning, when Bo's error allowed two unearned runs to score.

"I fuck up every time I go for the damn ball!" Bo pouted, passing Coach Grazi on his way to the dugout.

"Hold it, young man. Turn around." The boy stopped and faced his coach.

"Have you forgotten who you are and why you're here?"

"Huh?"

"Your foul language indicates to me that the team is not your priority. If this was football and I heard that remark, I'd bench you."

Bo removed his cap. He appeared to weigh a further comment in his mind but remained silent.

"Bo, don't come down so hard on yourself. You played a great centerfield. I was impressed with the great jump you got on that last hit to the outfield. You have good instincts and you cover a lot of ground. Errors happen. Shake it off."

"I'll try."

"Just do it," Matt said, "But we're not done here. We'll talk about it later. For now, sit down and watch your mouth."

The Ospreys lost in the last inning by a run, and the team slumped toward the locker room.

"We should've won that game!" echoed across the room. The language was contagious. Lockers slammed and fists connected with inanimate objects like the wall or lockers.

Matt looked toward Tom. Coach Faber stepped up on a bench and looked down at the group. The frenzy continued until, one by one, the players looked upward and recognized the coach's displeasure. Within minutes, the impetuous outburst subsided.

Tom stepped down off the bench and faced the players.

"Anyone choosing to whine, curse, or swing a fist won't play the next game. Is that clear?"

Bo glanced over at Coach Grazi. The others shifted their positions on the benches. Some looked downward at the floor, others looked away.

"Do I hear a 'Yes, Coach?'" Tom yelled at the group.

"Yes, Coach," sounded from all sides.

"Good, now hit the showers."

"Guess we're okay, huh Coach?" Bo asked.

"Not at all. I'll see you on the bus."

Bo's sigh indicated that was not the response he was looking for.

The bus departed on time, despite the extra seconds it took for Matt to relocate the boy sitting next to Bo and slide into the seat.

"So tell me what you thought of your contribution to tonight's game," Matt said.

"I messed up."

"And you were the only one to make mistakes?"

"No, but I can't . . . I mean I let the team down. It was my fault we lost."

"So you're bad behavior tonight was justified. Your language indicated you were in total control. You were concerned for the team, not about yourself or what your team mates might think of you."

"I . . ."

"Bo, you're number one job is to put the team first. When you need to sort things out remind yourself your team needs you at your best one hundred percent of the time. It's our job to sit you on the bench if you can't do that. And until you realize the team is bigger than you are, you'll remain on the bench." He paused. "Do you want to be on this team?"

"Yes."

"What else?"

"Yes, sir."

"No, I mean just wanting to be on the field is not enough. Accepting a position on a team means you accept the responsibility to make the team stronger. Either you're in all the way, or you're out. There's no gray area. If you're not your best, the team isn't their best."

"Won't happen again, Coach."

"Oh, you'll slip up again," Matt said. "You can bet on it. But you can also bet from now on, if you don't have your priorities straight, I'm calling you on it. No slack."

"I can handle no slack."

"One other thing. Anything you're having a problem with, get your ass into my office and let me know before or after game time. Not on the field. Not in a locker room." Matt sighed. "Stop feeling sorry for yourself and let's figure out why we didn't win. Any ideas?"

"Don't think we were good enough."

"Improving skills," said Matt, "is one problem you, Coach Faber, and I *can* do something about." He stood with intention to move up to the front, placed his hand on the back of Bo's seat, then as an after-thought, leaned downward.

"We'll work on this together."

***

"I cut more hair in the last three weeks than in the past six months," Castor said to Matt as they walked together toward the field. Tell you what though," the boy said, "Teachers grumble about our new look."

"What do you mean?"

"They're jealous, Coach. We let them know that we like being in the gym or on the field a hell of a lot more than being in those dumb classes."

"Whoa, take it easy with talk like that. It doesn't make any points with your teachers, or with me, for that matter."

Castor gave a quizzical tilt of his head.

"Everything has its place, Castor. You understand that?"

"Guess so."

"School is important. The more you learn in class, the easier you learn on the field. The academic and sports worlds will cross over your whole life. You need both."

Castor tipped his hat in agreement and parted from Matt. Bo stood in a seated circle of boys, looked up and waved to his coach. He continued talking with his arms and hands, making his point of view clear. When the bell sounded, signaling the last class of the day was over, he joined Matt.

"How about a walk with your makeshift counselor?" Matt asked.

"Oh yeah, that's what I need, more conversation with my bad-ass shrink."

Bo let out a laugh, startling Matt, the sound of giddy, child-like laughter. Matt couldn't hold back a smile as Bo's nose wrinkled at the brow in another chuckle.

"We need to remind the groups about the importance of academics in the next gym classes."

"What do ya mean?"

Matt discussed the sports versus academics situation. "But don't get me wrong," he said. "I'm more than pleased that the boys are starting to enjoy sports. It's just that they shouldn't go on about it in class."

"It's really gittin' to be fun," Bo said. "But I see what you're talkin' 'bout."

"A place for sports. A place for study."

"I know," Bo said, kicking the dust with his shoe as they walked.

"Okay then, let's talk football."

They discussed possibilities of cutting or adding team members, and Matt asked Bo's opinion of a player.

"Don't go there, Coach."

"Okay, I understand. Let me put it to you another way. I'd appreciate your insight on what makes a boy tick. Knowing more, allows me to make better decisions."

Bo seemed to like that.

The boy smiled whenever a comment received a positive nod from his coach. They finished discussing the talent pool and proceeded toward the gym.

"Bet you had it pretty easy growing up," Bo said. "Not like us."

"What do you mean?"

"From what I know about you, bein' a big college football star and goin' on to the pros and all, you must'a been born with a lucky spoon in your mouth."

"Silver, Bo, a silver spoon," Matt said, slowing the pace. "I'll tell you a secret," he said facing the boy. "Nobody has it easy. Trust me when I tell you, I sure didn't. Unlike you, however, I did have a great advantage, a mother *and* a dad. I was number two of five boys, raised by a hardworking Sicilian father who quit school before the sixth grade to support his family. Both my parents were strict and kicked my ass often, my padre being the more frequent heavy hand."

"Nobody kicks my ass if I can help it," Bo said as he tightened his fingers into a fist.

"Ah, but here's the difference," Matt said. "I respected my father. There were just as many times he rewarded me for trying hard. He was fair."

"Coach?" Bo asked as they continued the walk. "Are you fair?"

"I try to be . . . now."

"And before? You know, when you were a kid like me?"

"For a long time I thought life wasn't fair to me, so I wasn't either."

Matt talked about his teen years, how he had caught shit because of his heritage, how being raised Italian in an Irish-English town wasn't easy. Harassment had escalated during World War II when the enemy spoke Italian.

"We banded with German immigrants to form our ethnic group."

"What's an ethnic group, Coach?"

"A bunch of us who had parents who weren't born in America. We spoke differently and came from a different place than most folks in town."

"Is it like being in a gang? I was in one in Pensacola," he said with pride.

"Not exactly," Matt answered. "We looked out for each other, but tried hard not to go against the cops." Bo shrugged.

Sometimes we didn't succeed at that part. Matt had seen the inside of a police car on more than one occasion.

"Bo, the point is, don't assume because I had successes it was easy. I busted my ass. People disliked me because of my nationality, and it pissed me off. I wanted people to like me. I was determined to be somebody. I fought for recognition and dignity."

"Me too. That's why I chose boxing. Thought I'd get respect by winning in the ring."

"And?"

"And I did, from the kids. But the adults were different. They thought it proved I was a dumb hoodlum."

"Know how you feel, Bo. You chose boxing. I chose football. Both of us are doing something we're good at. Matt sensed a look of admiration in Bo's expression.

"Boxing is important to me. I'm good at it. I have a trophy that means more than anything. My brother helped train me for that fight. You have a favorite prize, Coach?"

Matt told Bo about his football coach at FSU who pushed the team to move to major college status in 1955. He described the pride he felt three years later when the FSU Seminoles stepped onto the Gator field in Gainesville for the first time.

"We didn't win, but it was the first time we were allowed to compete against the best team in Florida. I have the game ball."

"Wow, no kidding?"

"No kidding. Before college, my high school coach was the most important person in my life. He pushed me, and pushed me, and pushed me, demanding I give my all. At times I resented the pressure, but he was the first one to see something in me I didn't know I had."

The temperate Florida wind swirled near the ground and a red-tailed hawk circled the sky. Bo looked upward.

"You see somethin' in me?" he asked.

"We're just getting to know each other. I'm learning to trust your instincts, but I don't know how far you can be pushed, how determined you are. I don't know if you'll bail when it gets tough, or stick it out."

Matt paused to give Bo time to comment, but with no words forthcoming, he finished his thoughts. "Listen, I don't know what burns within you, only you do. But I do know this: You're capable of working your ass off. You can get there, wherever 'there' is for you. The question is will you?"

"Dammit, I do everything wrong," Bo blurted out. "I lose my temper. . . . I ran."

Matt swallowed hard and the memory of Bo's torn and bruised body flashed to the surface. He recognized the frustration in the boy's tightened body and felt the angst in his harsh words.

"Bo, I . . . ,"

"It's hard, Coach. Control I mean. It's hard."

Matt wanted to pull the boy close, to comfort him. He wanted to tell him how he too had lost control in a game, with his teachers, with his coach. But that response was not what the boy needed.

"Damn hard."

After a long moment, Bo peeked out from under his Osprey cap. "Coach, "I done decided a few things in that hospital bed."

"Like what?"

"Two things actually."

"Okay."

"I want to be a better athlete, a good football player."

"That's been my intention. Glad to help with that. And the other thing?"

"Be a coach, like you . . . only better."

Matt stared into Bo's determined eyes. "A coach?"

"I watch you. I could do it. Will you teach me?"

"I have picked up on a potential coaching instinct about you at times. Your peers seem to respond, that's for sure." Matt watched a smile inch its way across Bo's face.

"Lots of work before any payoff. It wasn't easy for me, and I won't make it easy for you. You're asking me to come down on you whenever I think you've made the wrong move."

"Don't you do that now?"

"Good point. But there would be times when you'd hate me."

"I know, but things are different now."

"You'll sweat and even cry."

"Probably not that last one. I'm done crying."

"Glad to see a grin, Bo, but some days it won't be there."

Bo's voice rang clear. "You'll see. When do we start?"

***

"Will you save room for me at the guys' table for supper?" Matt asked Bo, after waving him down on his way to the dining hall. "I need to hit my room to grab the new practice schedule."

"When you get back, Coach, load your plate from our side."

"Oh, and why should I do that?"

"Us inmates are planning a 'get even' meal. You know, for crapping on us for the nothing things. Tonight's menu . . . unwashed toenails."

"What?"

"You'll love this, Coach." Bo chuckled. "It's called 'toenail revenge.' We save our clipped toenails and pass 'em on to the kitchen crew. When we have enough, they dump them into something crunchy on the menu."

Matt's jaw dropped.

"Hey, don't look at me, Coach. Not my idea. I'm guilty of a lot of things, but not this one. The guys' been doin' it for years. The crunch lightens the mood."

"Lightens the mood?"

"Yeah, only we know, and nobody gets hurt," Bo said. "Same with the other stuff."

"There's more?"

Bo went on to tell Matt how boys spit into the pitcher of milk set out for the coffee. Inmates blew snot from their runny noses into the chicken and rice dishes. "Blends right in."

"Stop," Matt ordered, scrunching his disgusted face.

"Really cool are the scrambled eggs. If you see Andrews with a real yellow helping, you'll know somebody's piss never reached the toilet."

Matt's stomach churned with the urge to vomit as he recalled the numerous plates of golden eggs he'd eaten.

"Why did you wait so long to tell me?"

"Cause before, I didn't care what you ate. You're okay, so I'll keep you posted."

"I'm going to have to say something to someone about this."

"Sure the big shots want to hear?" Bo asked. "Besides, we have a code about puking."

"Okay, I'll bite."

"Don't ever do it."

"But you just told me about your supper plans."

"Not puking if nobody gets hurt, and like I said, nobody gets hurt, right?"

Matt felt a slight smile cross his face. He couldn't help admiring the creative audacity, and he found a certain justice in the boys' retribution. He warmed to Bo's show of concern for him, and he enjoyed the trust between them, but he faced a dilemma. How could he protect the staff from food contamination without harm coming to the boys?

After struggling with his plight, Matt made a visit to the kitchen. He spoke with the supervising staff member of the kitchen about the boys' shenanigans.

"Which one of the little creeps is greasing the food in my kitchen?"

"Don't know," Matt said.

"Wait till I get my hands on . . ."

"You're in charge here, right?" The kitchen supervisor nodded.

"I can't imagine you want Dr. Strickland or Santo to hear about this. It's a sure bet they'd assume it's been going on for a while. Punishing the boys might generate an investigation, don't ya think? Wouldn't look good for you."

"Shit."

"Don't worry," Matt said with a finger zipping across his lips. "Mum's the word. We faculty have to stick together. Perhaps you should have a talk with the boys, or make a subtle announcement to let them know you're watching things more carefully. Use your mean voice. That alone should do the trick."

The supervisor lowered his eyebrows and presented his most threatening look.

"Yeah, like that. I know you can figure out how to keep a closer eye on the meal's ingredients without it seeming like these games were happening right under your nose. "

The supervisor appeared to weigh his options. "I'll take care of it."

Matt kept his stoic demeanor until well distanced from the dining area. A smug grin broke out accompanied by his resolution to minimize trips to the staff serving line. Until future efforts by the kitchen supervisor had resolved the antics, Matt would use the pretext of wanting to chat with the boys to receive food in their line before moving back to the faculty area to sit with his cohorts. Dining at The Country Club now had two benefits, seeing Betty and not questioning the food dished onto his plate.

CHAPTER 13

May's track team training became another brick for Matt to carry in his backpack. He attended the majority of the meets, assisting Tom, scouting out boys who were fast and agile, and scribbling in his notebook.

While timing a new inmate during a fast jog around the bumpy, weed-covered trail, the boy's shoe caught causing him to plunge forward.

"You okay? Matt shouted, dashing toward the boy. The teen nodded as he rose from the ground and brushed himself off with scraped and bleeding hands.

"Get to the hospital, and have Doc clean you up." Matt waved to a Pilot, who escorted the shaken boy across the field.

"That dirt trail is downright dangerous," he said to the air. "Damn roots and dips everywhere, jumping pits are crap."

Matt turned to find Bo had overheard his remarks.

"Don't mind me," Matt said in a lowered voice. "I'm on overload today."

"Ya know Mr. O'Hurley in maintenance?" Bo asked. "He's got all kinds of stuff."

"And?"

"Like graders, tractors, and backhoes."

"Really?" Matt asked. "Maybe smooth out that trail a bit?" Bo signaled an affirmative.

"Has lots of sand over there too," Bo added. "Might be able to throw some at the jump pits."

Back in his office, Matt bit down on his lip in concentration and called administration to discuss the track's possible improvement with Santo. His boss had left for a long weekend, so he left a brief message.

Classes over for the day, Matt grabbed his cap and made his way toward the maintenance area.

"Didn't I meet you last month at a faculty meeting?" he asked the maintenance supervisor.

"Eh?"

"I said, didn't we meet at the faculty meeting?"

"Oh, yeah. Coach Grazi?"

"Matt."

Wearing wrinkled skin below thick tufts of white hair, O'Hurley turned his ear toward Matt who described the needed improvements for the track area.

Becoming more and more animated with every detail, Matt finally took a breath. "So, what do you think?" he asked.

O'Hurley rubbed his chin. "Perhaps."

Matt waited.

"Mm-mmm," the old man hummed as he squinted and pressed his lips together. He bit down on his thumbnail. "Young man, I like what you're thinking. Haven't worked on that field path in a coon's age."

Matt continued his wait.

"Might be nice to have a new challenge. I do pretty much the same thing here, day after day, year after year. Not that I don't like my job you understand, been here for twenty-six years."

"So, what do we do?"

"What's that?"

"So, what do we do next?" Matt repeated a little louder.

"Got any good helpers?"

"I can round them up!"

"Tell you what. Let's work out the materials and man-hours needed, or 'boy hours' as the case may be. Then we'll calculate the dimensions and see what we're looking at. I'll bring the stakes and measuring tape, and we'll lay it out. Meet you in the morning. Early."

"Bo and I will be on the field at eight sharp!"

"Bo?"

"My young assistant. Make it seven. We'll do breakfast after."

Matt caught Bo and Tom before they left for the day. He shared the highlights of his conversation, noting Bo's enthusiasm as the boy began to babble about the project they were about to do "together."

When Matt arrived at the field at seven Friday morning, O'Hurley and Bo already had their heads bowed close to each other, a pad and two pencils between them, buzzing like two worker bees.

"Okay you two, fill me in," Matt said.

O'Hurley winked at Bo, and they escorted Matt to the first measured and staked area. After the second set of measurements, Matt and Bo reluctantly left for breakfast, then class. Their mission of the day was to work on 'boy' power.

After classes ended, Matt and Bo sprinted to the field to join O'Hurley. The two men and a boy completed the measuring and staking.

"Let's do it," O'Hurley said.

Matt made another call to Santo, this time leaving a more fired-up message.

***

The weekend project began Saturday morning when Matt arrived at the boys' cottages, where he picked up Bo, Mulany, and over two dozen volunteers. They made their way to the field to find O'Hurley chugging toward them atop a backhoe. Another crew walked alongside the man and his machine, carrying extra shovels and rakes.

Under the direction of O'Hurley, the boys graded and hauled out dirt, moving the soil from one area to another before packing it down. Occasional outbreaks of horseplay included water splashed through the hot air and light sand kicked about in fun. Boys were boys, but no fights broke out. During the clean-up, smiles on sweaty faces confirmed their pride. Everyone agreed to return on Sunday to complete the job.

During a break the next day, O'Hurley wiped the sweat from his brow with the back of his hand. "I've never done track construction, Coach," he said as he turned to admire their progress. "Not bad for a bunch of amateurs."

"It's a new one for me, too," Matt said with pride. "The boys seem to be getting a kick out of this, especially Bo. This was his idea you know."

"Let me tell you, that boy is one smart cookie."

"No kidding?" Matt asked. "I know about his street smarts and athletic skills, but hadn't thought much about his academic abilities."

O'Hurley smiled and handed Matt a glass of water. "With a little help, that kid could figure out just about anything."

The two of them sat down on a flat area of undisturbed ground. They were more than glad to be off their feet for a few minutes. Blinking back drops of sweat, O'Hurley grabbed a cloth from a rear pocket and passed it to Matt.

"You know," the maintenance guru said, "you look at these boys, and see some of them are good, hard-working young men. How many will return to Colby Hill, or end up someplace worse?"

That thought had crossed Matt's mind on more than one occasion. He didn't want to think about it. He was enjoying the positive force that filled the air during the two days it took to grade the track, dig the pits, and spread the sand and sawdust. The boys could truly call the new track and field their own.

How great is this?

***

Santo's call to Matt came only seconds after he had arrived at his office.

"What did you think you were doing this past weekend?" Santo asked.

"Wait till you see it," Matt said with pride.

"My office, please. Now."

Not understanding the stern tone, Matt wondered if he had forgotten something. Crossing campus, he entered Santo's office and plopped into the lower chair in front of the large desk.

"You started your own construction project this past weekend?" Santo asked with a scowl.

"You're going to love it!"

"No, I'm not going to love it. You had no authority to do it."

"I know, but Santo, a better track area was needed, and O'Hurley and the boys did a fantastic job."

Santo caught his breath and raised his hands in exasperation. "Matt, you don't think before you rush into a project. I'm out of town and you start operating on your own rules, getting the staff pissed off because your new track seems to take precedence over everything else. Staff members are calling *you* the 'damn prima donna.'"

"Wait a minute," Matt protested. "I was only making things safer for the kids."

"We're *all* trying to make things better! This was not how to do it. You know damn well if you had gone through the proper channels, I'd have seen to it you got everything you needed."

"Shit, we'd have spent more time on red tape getting . . . "

"Enough! Don't give me any lip! I said I would support you, and I will, but you can't run this institution as your own."

Matt slumped down in the chair. For the first time he considered that, in his enthusiasm, he might have moved too fast. He hadn't meant to antagonize Santo.

But kids were getting hurt!

"Look, Matt, your impulsiveness creates a problem, which in turn, becomes mine. I have a board and state administrators to answer to. Rules are rules."

"The boys took pride in their work and look at . . ."

"And what if a boy had got hurt?"

Matt lowered his head. "Okay. I see your point but . . . "

"Do you?"

"I left you a message," he said in a weak voice.

"That's not good enough. I didn't respond." Matt understood. He now worried their solid working relationship had suffered an irreparable breach.

Bo had a brilliant idea, and I jumped on it.

Not one shovel of dirt should have been dug without requesting permission. Matt admitted to himself that he too would have given hell to anyone under his supervision operating without approval.

"Santo, I'm sorry."

"I'm sorry too, Matt. I have a lot of explaining to do."

"I'm really . . ."

"I need to work this out," Santo interrupted as he rose from his chair. "And you need to go." He turned his back on Matt and moved toward the door. "It's a big deal, not getting approval," Santo said, "a really big deal for a whole lot of reasons. And who pays for the cost of supplies, equipment, and labor for this little brainstorm? You?"

Weariness shrouded Matt as he trudged the short trek to his office. Regret covered him like a heavy, rain-soaked cloak. He imagined yet another consequence of Santo's anger, losing the protection and respect of a boss and friend. Lifting his eyes toward the clock, he gave himself a few more minutes before making the trek down the narrow hallway toward his first class in the gym.

Will Santo fire me?

Matt wished he didn't have to teach class today and instead could go back to his room. He'd place the 45-rpm record on the record player, listen to the sound of Elvis or Patsy Cline, and try to figure out how he might have approached the whole thing differently.

Despite everything, Matt secretly admired the renovated 440-yard track. He had paid a price for the track construction, but the boys' safety was worth it. Santo would realize that after he calmed down. Bo's new pride in doing something important together with the boys would have a lasting positive impact.

But . . . Matt swore to take extra pains to avoid another conflict.

CHAPTER 14

"Technically, Bo's in the third grade?" Matt asked the boy's English teacher. "What happens when he returns to his hometown high school?"

"That's just it," Gary Lissitar said. "We've tried to explain how the lack of progress will make his return to public school difficult. He could have to repeat grades, but he seems unconcerned."

Lissitar explained that after taking an initial placement test, Bo had received a workbook based on his performance. Because Bo chose not to complete assignments, he had made little academic advancement.

"The contract book system says you can work at your own pace, right?" Matt asked.

"And with the class. That's where the boys learn the most."

"Let me talk to him. Maybe I could take him off campus, and make him see the advantages of keeping up with his friends."

"Unless you're family, you can't take a boy anywhere without permission from the director of the school."

Matt was quick to call Dr. Strickland's office. Learning Dr. Strickland would be available in twenty minutes, he zipped across campus. He wiped his damp palms on his pants and slowed his breath before entering the building.

The memory of his first day when Santo had risen and pointed his finger at the portrait of Dr. Strickland flashed in his mind. Then he recalled how adamant Tom had been when he told him, "Whatever Strickland wants, Strickland gets."

"Right on time, Coach," Dr. Strickland said as he pointed to the chair in front of his desk. "Grazi, right?"

"Yes, sir."

"What can I do for you?"

Matt sunk down into the overstuffed chair in front of the director's ornate mahogany desk. Its carved legs supported a five-foot polished top. In all the time Matt had spent at CHB, he had never seen a piece of furniture this elaborate. It didn't fit the general décor of the facility, which up to this point, could have been described as secondhand and heavy-duty.

Matt wanted to stretch out his long legs but knew he would sink down even further into the sponge-like chair. Instead, he sat erect on the edge of the cushioned seat, looked upward toward Dr. Strickland, and took a breath.

"I need a man-to-man chat with Harry Beauregard," he began. "Want to talk to him about his grades, take him off campus for supper."

The director rubbed his chin and raised his eyebrows in question. "And what's wrong with a talk in the gym?"

The tension in Matt's neck remained tight. "Being off campus would give us both a chance to relax. I think I'd have a better chance of convincing him he needs to improve his grades."

"I have questions about this boy, Matt. Appears you've made head-way with him since he ran away, but is he really on your side?"

Without waiting for an answer, Dr. Strickland rose from his seat and raised his arm, shaking his index finger for effect. "The boy is still a handful, and I'm not convinced he wouldn't be scouting out the area more than listening to you."

The drop of Matt's shoulders showed his disappointment.

"I must admit, however," Dr. Strickland said, "I do get a kick out of how Mr. Beauregard responds with a confident no, sir or yes, sir when-ever the staff speaks to him. So, tell me. Is he mocking us?"

"No, sir. I don't think so."

"Has he bought into your plan?"

"My plan?"

"I assume there's a reason you spend so much time with this boy."

"Well, yes, I mean, I'm hoping he becomes the leader of . . ."

"Our football team?" Strickland interrupted. "This boy has what it takes to help the Ospreys win?"

"Yes, sir. So it's a yes?"

"Not yet. Let me investigate how other staff members feel about him. Check back with me later."

"But . . ." Matt stopped himself. Dr. Strickland cocked his head.

"Thank you, sir," Matt offered. "I'll do that."

***

The following evening Matt still had not heard from Dr. Strickland. The faculty members could be saying anything. Bo had made tremendous progress at the gym as a crew member, but Lissitar had said he needed to buckle down in the classroom. What other reasons could the faculty give for not supporting an off-campus jaunt?

It had been days, even weeks since Matt had seen Betty. He stared at the phone. If he were to call her after all this time, would she slam it down once she heard his voice? Better to face her in person.

He settled onto a wooden stool in The Country Club's bar area opposite the dining room, overlooking the pool. He spotted Betty with an armful of dishes, pushing her hip into the swinging doors of the kitchen. Matt lit a Lucky Strike, ordered a beer, and fumbled with his change for the jukebox. He rehearsed his excuses for not calling.

Maybe I should start with a . . .

"Look what the cat dragged in," Betty said, interrupting his thoughts. "Last week it was a half-eaten mouse."

"Hey," Matt countered. He couldn't help but smile.

"So . . . What brings you in?"

"I'm . . . Buy you a beer after work?"

"And why do you want to do that, Coach?"

"Uh, because I like your company?"

"Okay. Any other reason?"

"That little space between your teeth works for me." Betty tried to conceal her amusement.

"And?"

"Okay, it's your hands. I love that you never wear nail polish, and your hands always look beautiful."

"Sold," Betty said. Then she added, "Except I can't tonight. A date."

Matt's ego shrunk to mid-size now that his charm had failed to win the prize.

"On the weekend?" He asked. "Sunday?"

"Possibly."

"Joe's Spaghetti House on Mahan Drive in Tallahassee has good food and the service is slow. Plenty of time to enjoy a meal, and share an overdue conversation."

"We really haven't talked in a while, have we?" Betty's voice softened. "What time?"

***

"So you're back," Dr. Strickland said to Matt two days later in his office.

"Yes, sir."

"I've done a little investigation, Coach. Let me ask you something. Do you realize how long it's been since we've had a runaway?"

Matt didn't recall when the emergency phone last had rung. His focus had been on classes and team preparations.

"Four weeks. In addition, there have been subtle, positive changes on campus, like fewer incidents in the cottages, inmates dressing better. I suspect one person could be responsible for that."

Matt gave a slight nod, his chest swelled.

"It's Bo," Dr. Strickland said.

Matt blinked. His smile faded. Then a new kind of pride washed over him.

"Really?" he asked. "Why do you say that?"

"Staff members tell me Bo has an influence on these boys. They listen to him. They respect him. Some are even afraid of him."

"Yes, sir, I know that."

"His positive change seems to be contagious. The atmosphere has calmed down a notch. The cottage fathers have communicated in their weekly reports that the boys haven't been as aggressive as usual. No major fist fights. Small problems like tardiness or foul language, but fewer issues of a serious nature. They tell me the boys are talking about baseball, track, football, and even gym class."

The corners of Matt's mouth turned upward, exposing his white teeth and indicating his pleasure.

"You know, Matt, I believe when things aren't good, it takes a certain burst of energy to change direction. Bo appears to have delivered that burst."

Dr. Strickland halted for a short moment. "Or, I don't know," he began, "maybe it's the spell of good weather we're having, or the boy might have received a bit of assistance from the staff. What do you think?"

Matt answered his question with a wide grin.

"Yes," Dr. Strickland said with a smile. "Take Bo off campus. It'd be good for him." He scribbled his signature on a notepad, instructing Matt to take it down the hall to the receptionist who would acquaint him with the sign-out procedures.

"And Matt," Dr. Strickland cautioned as Matt headed out the door, "be careful."

"Yes, sir!" Matt turned as he walked, and gave him a friendly salute. Striding with a surge of confidence down the hall, he put Strickland's warning out of his mind.

Almost sprinting back toward his room, Matt freshened up and drove to Bo's cottage. The boy sat on the front stoop and sprang to his feet seconds before Matt's Ford slowed to a stop.

"Glad I caught you. How about a bite to eat?" Matt asked, leaning his head out the car's window. Bo's eyes widened. "Change into clean clothes, and I'll drive us into town!"

Bo bolted into the cottage, returning in a blink of an eye, stuffing his arms upward into a striped polo shirt. Snapping his khaki slacks closed, he hopped into Matt's car.

"Don't you look sharp."

Bo beamed and tied his tennis shoes as he settled into the front seat. "Like your wheels," he said, "especially all the chrome."

"Thanks. Me too. Name your supper choice."

"A big juicy cheeseburger and a shake for me!"

After discussing which place in Colby Hill offered the best burger in town, they settled on Chatters Drive-In. Not exactly the dining experience Matt had envisioned, but Bo appeared to be thoroughly satisfied. Matt watched him chow down the cheeseburger deluxe, French fries, and a large vanilla shake. The boy pinched a crumb off his shirt and, with precision, placed it on the plate in front of him.

"Can I order a side of cheese grits, Coach?"

Matt had forgotten how large an appetite a boy could have. He nibbled at his country fried steak swimming in gravy on the plate in front of him. It was time.

"You're doing great, Bo. I'm proud that you're helping out the boys in gym class. Great ideas."

Bo gave a signal between bites that he appreciated the comments.

"How do you feel about your work assignments in your classes?"

"Easy."

"And the additional evening practice sessions?"

"Lovin' it, Coach. Getting in great shape." A smile peeked around the ketchup-covered beef dripping from the corner of his mouth.

"Glad to hear that, Bo, but you've got a problem."

Bo spooned the remaining cheese grits between pressed lips. "Yah, hut's dat, Coach?" he garbled. He held up his hand in a just-a-minute gesture. His table manners still needed work, but that had to come at another time.

"What grade are you in?"

"The grade I'm really in, or the grade I got into when I faked my test here?"

Matt rolled his widened eyes at the raw honesty. "At CHB."

"Third. Why?"

"How do you expect to play high school football in the third grade?" Bo swallowed his last bite of fries and wiped his mouth with the back of his hand.

It appeared Bo hadn't thought of his grades as being a criterion for playing ball. He had been in the eighth grade in January when he had arrived at CHB, but according to his age, he should be in the tenth.

"What are you talking about?" Bo said in a defensive, agitated voice. "I've gotten this far with no problem. Grades in this place don't matter. I'll be retested after I'm released, and the school will put me in the right grade 'cause of how old I am."

"You've outsmarted yourself, pal."

"What do ya mean?"

"I mean test wise, you'll have to go from the third grade to the tenth in the time you have left, or you might not even be in high school. They could easily put you back into junior high." Matt let the news sink in. "Look, I've spent time talking to you about football and where we're going with it, right?" Bo nodded. "This work means nothing if you can't carry on when you return home."

A moment passed before Bo spoke. "So what should I do?"

"You tell me."

With no response from Bo in the following seconds, Matt prompted further conversation. "Do you try as hard in your academic work as you do in sports?"

"I try to sleep as much as possible in class."

Matt shook his head. "Teachers let you?"

"Some do. Anything to keep the peace I guess."

Matt let out a long, wistful sigh. "No wonder you haven't moved up."

"Never mattered to me."

"It's about time it mattered," Matt said with determination. "You're the one who told me how you couldn't wait to serve your time so you could be on Pensacola High's football team."

"Yeah," Bo said. "I did. I do." He pushed his empty plate away. "Sometimes at night, you know, I picture me runnin' down the field, a ball landing like a helicopter right into my hands." He shook his head as if to shake the vision away. "So I really gotta move up? But even if I'm allowed to take a retest, not sure where I'd test out."

"This time around, you could study."

Bo used his napkin to wipe up the crumbs on the table and then shook it over his plate. He leaned back in the booth. "Even if I did good, I'd never pass high enough to be in the tenth grade. How'd I catch up?"

Matt took a slow bite of his meal. It was his turn to offer silence.

"I could find out from my teachers, I bet," Bo finally offered.

"You're starting to get the hang of this."

Bo began talking about contract books, how quickly he could move up, and how difficult it was going to be. "How about my teachers give me permission to take my contract book back to my cottage? I've seen guys do it."

"Sounds like a good idea."

"Would ya hep me?"

"Might be able to do that."

Bo babbled on with one question after another, ending with "Could ya answer questions or check my work?"

Matt shook his head. "No time during classes."

"I could come to the gym on weekends when . . ."

"Now wait a minute. On weekends I break."

"We sure could git a lot done on Saturdays and Sundays. Know you spend half the weekend working out. Couldn't you break once in a while and correct my assignments?"

"Bo, even when I stay on campus, I do have my own life."

"Got'cha," Bo said "Keepin' company with a lady friend?"

"None of your business!"

"Okay, okay, but Coach, don't ya think we could have just a little time?"

"Enough. I'm paying the check."

Matt tried to talk about other things on the drive back, but Bo kept returning to his new plans. Before the car had come to a complete stop, Bo swung the door open and hopped out. He moved around to the driver window and extended his hand.

"Thanks for supper, Coach." The firm handshake seemed to initiate a journey in a different direction. Bo turned and waved over his head. "Don't forgit to sign me in."

Matt had never imagined that words indicating academics were as important as football would ever spout from his mouth. The clash was almost enough to make him rethink his recommendations.

Bo appeared to accept the challenge to hit the books. But Matt couldn't shake the feeling he might have put too much on Bo's plate. A day had only twenty-four hours, and those hours were already jam-packed.

CHAPTER 15

The Sunday afternoon sun shone into his car's interior, as Matt squinted into the mirror on the back of his visor. Spitting into his hand, he pressed down on his inherited cowlick. The wavy hairs that refused to lie flat had always irritated him. He adjusted his collar.

He escorted Betty to his car and opened her door. The gentlemanly gesture didn't go unnoticed.

They breezed by the Florida Panhandle towns of Sneads, Chattahoochee, Gretna, and Quincy. Matt chuckled at the unique names of the small towns, especially when he had spotted the turnoff to Two Egg. They cruised past the deep Southern woods, the leaning barns, and the unpainted, wooden homes. The open windows allowed the earthy smell of manure to emerge from the sprouting, plowed fields.

"The smell only a farmer could love," Matt said.

"Actually, I think most everyone around here loves that odor. It is the essence of life. It means the crops will come again. When a farmer rubs a handful of rich earth between his fingers, he gives thanks."

"I never thought of it that way. My mom was from a farm in the Midwest."

"Really?"

"Mere spots on the road," she had said when she described similar settlements of her childhood. Matt remembered her lilting voice and again felt a tingle of the warm hug she had given him on his last visit home to an icy New York.

In less than an hour, a friendly waiter at Joe's Restaurant in Tallahassee seated them at a table decorated with a used wine bottle holding a fresh candle. The bulging multicolored drippings down the side indicated countless visits by previous patrons.

"Mind if we move to a side booth?" Matt asked. With a nod, the waiter led them over to the cozier table. In the candlelight, Betty glowed.

Has she been this pretty all along? How foolish to have ignored her for so long. He took her hand in his.

"Betty, I owe you an apology." She appeared puzzled but touched by his gesture. "I'm sorry for not calling you sooner. I'm an idiot, I know."

"Yes."

"Yes, that you accept my apology, or yes that I'm an idiot?"

Betty grinned. "Actually, I called you once."

"You did?"

"Oh right. Didn't get the message, huh?"

"Who'd you talk to?"

"Don't know, but she had a *really sweet* Southern drawl."

"Ah, probably Mary Jo in admin, one of the few women on campus. Not sure why she didn't put you through."

"Maybe . . ." Betty said as she leaned across the table, "she wants you to herself." The sparkle in Betty's eyes seemed to bounce around her body. Matt imagined Alice's Cheshire cat when he felt the white-teethed grin spread across his face. He lifted his glass in a toast.

Over a spumoni dessert, the conversation turned more serious. "I tell you, Betty, the longer I'm here, the more messed up this place seems. The juvenile justice system is nothing like I expected it to be."

"And how did you expect it to be?"

"Different, I guess. I know good people work at Colby Hill, looking after the welfare of the boys, or perhaps I should say, 'trying' to look after the boys. But when I point out crap like sic'ing the dogs on a boy for running, or archaic rules that prevent change, a brick wall goes up. I mean, how do I fight that kind of mentality?"

"The administration doesn't agree with you, and they're the ones who make the rules?"

"Yeah."

"And you're the only one who knows what rules work best?"

"Betty, you know what I mean."

"I know. I know. It's Bo and the boys."

"Yeah."

"You haven't shared much with me, but you've been there for over a couple months, doesn't anyone else see the need for the changes you want?"

Matt frowned. "I haven't really talked with anyone about the boys except Santo, Tom, and you."

"So what are you going to do?" She rested her free hand on top of Matt's, sandwiching his hand between hers.

"I've got to keep focused. Concentrate on doing my job."

"The boys need you to keep *them* focused. Isn't that your job?"

Matt liked this girl, really liked her.

"Talk to me, Matt. Tell me something good that's happening at CHB." Betty raised her eyes. "There is *something* good happening out there, right?"

Matt told Betty about the athletic progress of the boys, the pleasure of spending off time with them. He jabbered on about the last two games of the baseball season when the Ospreys played against the Mississippi Boys' School and Louisiana Technical Institute. His voice rose in tempo and volume when he narrated how CHB went out in front in the opening inning on a walk to Bo. The first game had ended in a 7–3 victory, and the second when they defeated LTI 15–7.

"The boys loved it!"

"Good for them, congrats to you and Tom. So, now baseball is over, how many will stay on for football?"

"You've really got my number, don't you? I'm always recruiting. Each play in baseball relates to a play in football. A throw from deep left field to first base translates into a strong arm, a possible quarterback."

Without even realizing it, within minutes Matt returned to Bo, explaining how the boy had asked to be retested, had been assigned a new test date, and had received extra study materials from the teachers.

"Despite the kid's former penchant for avoiding school work, he appears to be putting a high degree of effort into the new venture."

"Worried about how long it will be before Bo's commitment to his studies fades?"

"I'm more worried studying will interfere with the upcoming football schedule, that the team might suffer for it."

"We all battle with commitments, Matt. Never enough time. Bo needs to choose what's important to him, and you need to choose too. It's how it works."

Sipping wine, they lingered for another hour. The conversation turned toward Betty, and Matt found himself enjoying her battles at the college, her conversations with her dad, and her plans for the future. He wished an evening like this for the boys, to someday share a conversation similar to the one he was having now.

He listened and he talked, but in the back of his mind, he worried how much weight Bo would be able to carry.

***

Once as remote as snow falling on campus, Matt and Bo sat near the bleachers discussing news events, a topic covered in Bo's studies. Neither of them could have predicted sharing outlooks on Navy Commander Alan B. Shepard, Jr.'s blast into space for a fifteen-minute, sub-orbital ride. Everyone on campus had gathered around the black-and-white TV screens, cheering when the "out of this world" Freedom 7 space capsule shot into the sky.

"It's so cool, Coach," Bo said. "Can you believe it?"

"A cosmic achievement. Ever feel like that?"

"When I win a boxing match."

"You do like throwing a good punch, don't you?" Matt asked with a grin.

"In fact, got in a little fist practice last week with a jerk from the chorus."

Noting the hint of anger on Bo's tongue, a knot tightened in Matt's stomach and his smile disappeared. "That's *more* than disappointing."

Bo thrust his open palm in front of Matt's face. "No, no, don't worry. I didn't hurt him."

"Still . . . You have something against this kid?" Matt asked.

"Not really."

"Not into music?"

"Not into that kind of fun and games." Matt tilted his head in question. "In case you haven't noticed, Coach, there're no girls around here, and fellas in the chorus class have their own way of getting it on . . . if you know what I mean."

Having no experience talking about this topic to anyone younger than himself, much less a boy he coached, Matt searched for a way to end the conversation. Bo seemed oblivious to his discomfort.

"Mostly, the choir boys and I leave each other alone," Bo said. "I don't report their stuff, and they don't snitch on me when I'm sneaking a cigarette, or whatever, but this kid pushed."

Matt watched Bo shift gears.

"Most times I'm okay with what's going on here. We use'ta go to the Ritz on Fridays to see a flick, and some used the place as a hook-up spot. Until they banned us from the theater that is, for throwing ice, soda, and popcorn off the balcony. Oh, and spitting down into the audience."

"Nice guys, but *where* is this going?"

"Well, boys gettin' it on is one thing, but this is different." Bo hesitated. "It's . . . it's not right. It's the music teacher."

"I still don't understand."

"He's into it," Bo said matter-of-factly. "The teacher's into it." Matt's mouth opened. He stared at Bo, not sure of how to respond.

"The choir teacher is into the boys?" Matt asked. "Wait a minute, Bo. You can't go around making an accusation like that unless you're pretty damned sure."

"Aw, Coach, there's no way that kind of stuff can go on in class without the teacher knowin' 'bout it." Bo shrugged his shoulders along with a gesture saying "not my business, just thought somebody should know."

"You're sure about this?"

"I don't lie."

"I know that," Matt said, looking directly at the boy.

"You didn't hear it from me."

"Yeah."

Returning to his room, Matt debated what to do. He had encouraged Bo to share his feelings, but this had gone an entirely different direction. Was it really his business? He was only one person, what could he do? Could it be true that a member of the faculty was involved in this type of activity? If a staff member abused a boy, he should be arrested, dismissed at the least. If Matt believed Bo, he had to do something. Bo had put his confidence in him, and he needed to return that trust. He couldn't accuse anyone without proof, and yet, he rotated the phone's dial to his boss's extension.

I'll just make an inquiry into the rumor.

Minutes into the conversation, Matt's head moved back from the phone and a look of surprise covered his face. Santo revealed that an investigation into the extracurricular activities in the chorus classroom was already in progress.

***

Any boy interested in being part of the future football team was to show up to meet with Matt and Tom on Sunday afternoon.

"Where's Gonzales?" Matt asked, reviewing the prospective football roster. He had earmarked Mike Gonzales as a boy who could be a definite asset. "Anybody?" Bo shrugged his shoulders.

"Jeff would know," one player offered. "He's over there," he said pointing his finger across the field.

Looking up from the group, Matt spotted Jeff Argot, the older Pilot who had proved to be quite the detective.

"Hey, Argot!" Matt shouted.

Argot turned toward the voice, and recognizing Matt, smiled, waved, and continued away from the field. Before Matt could flag him down, the bugle blasted its musical signal for lunch. *"Come and get your chow, boys"* rang clear, and the boys immediately moved toward the dining hall.

"Damn it," Matt cursed. "How many times have I told you I dismiss the class?"

"Yes, sir!" they yelled in unison, and froze in their footsteps.

"Dismissed."

The boys broke en masse for their afternoon meal.

Matt followed the boys' lead and searched the tables for Argot as he edged his way toward the food line. He had given up trying to find the boy, when Gary Lissitar fell in line behind him.

"Got a minute?" Matt asked the English teacher. "I got a kid missing from practice."

"Aw, sometimes kids don't show," Lissitar said, pushing his black-rimmed glasses upward on his nose.

"Wouldn't I be informed about a boy who had signed up for a team and then dropped out?"

"You never got a memo saying he would miss practice?" Matt shook his head. "You mark him absent?" Matt indicated an affirmative.

"Then it's no big deal. We often receive notices after the fact. Reasons vary. Could be for health, discipline, transfers. Things like that.

You'll be notified, eventually. Check with the counselor's office."

Returning to his office, Matt placed a call to the guidance center to hear the weekend crew confirm a follow-up. Absorbed in scanning a stack of mail and new messages, he jumped when the phone vibrated with its loud ring. Expecting a call back from guidance, he relaxed when the voice of Larry, his past college buddy, boomed a rush of fresh air across the line.

"About time," Matt said. "Thought you forgot about me."

"No way. These sportswriting gigs have me going full time."

"Sure, and lots of elbow bending at the bar too, I bet."

His friend laughed. "Actually, I could down a few later tonight. We need to catch up."

"Got that right, but boys are scheduled for a track workout in an hour, and I have paperwork due tomorrow morning."

"Got you running ragged, eh, buddy boy?"

"Yeah, but that's not the thing. I'm finding the job more personal than I thought."

"Okay, spit it out. You can talk to me. Remember, I coached there too."

Matt was questioning himself about a possible overreaction to a kid who didn't show up for class when Larry pressed him.

"Come on, Matt. What's bugging you?" Matt grinned. Larry knew when to probe.

"One of the boys. Gonzales. Another toughie, but real likable."

"So what's the problem?"

"A no-show at football practice today."

Silence hung in the air. "Anybody told you why that might happen?"

"Yeah, lots of reasons. Haven't checked them out," Matt said. "I'll stop by his cottage. They'll know if he's in the hospital or something." Larry's uneasy breathing was the only response. "Larry, what aren't you telling me?"

"Could be the discipline."

"Oh, I know all about the goon squad and their crazy dogs, if that's what you mean. I would've heard if Gonzales had run."

"No, I mean about the 'bed.'"

"What bed? What . . ."

His friend cut him off. "Sorry, my interview walked in. Have to catch you later."

Matt hung up the phone in slow motion.

A bed? A hospital bed?

Two minutes later Matt recognized Bo's whistling as he moved down the hallway. He entered Matt's office still tapping his foot to the whistled tune.

"Bo, you ever heard of a bed used for discipline?" Bo's twisted his head toward the door.

"Why ya askin' me?"

"Because you're sitting in front of me."

"Oh."

"Well?" Matt snapped.

Bo hesitated. "I'm not the one to be talkin' 'bout that."

"Bo!"

"Okay, okay."

Matt watched Bo glance both ways down the corridor before shutting the door.

Is Bo afraid, even in my office, that someone might be listening?

The teen appeared to struggle with his words, so Matt encouraged him to relax and take a seat. When Bo spoke, it was in a whispered tone.

"You know 'bout all the rules, Coach, the things we ain't supposed to do. And you know how the guards and dogs get their licks in when they catch anybody on a run."

"Go on."

"'Member when I told you how lucky I was when nobody whipped me for running?"

"I'm familiar with the whipping concept. Nuns in my private schools wacked my hands with a ruler, or smacked my butt with a yardstick on more than one occasion."

"Yeah, well . . . we call the whippings here 'swats.' They're different than that."

"How?"

"They use a thick, nasty wooden paddle."

"What?"

"And they make us lie on a bed to do it. After a few swats, we can't walk too good."

"Show it to me. I want to see this bed."

Bo lowered his head. "Can't do it. Ask Coach Faber."

"Why?"

Too risky for the boy?

"Just ask him," Bo said. "And Coach," he added with a wave on his way out the door, "We ain't ever talked 'bout this."

CHAPTER 16

"Corporal punishment is part of the program, Matt," Tom said in a defensive tone. "You know that."

"Come on, Tom. Help me out here."

Tom signaled Matt to take a seat and moved to the other side of his desk.

"What does that mean?" Matt continued. "Where is this 'bed'? Describe these 'swats'."

"Don't know. Never watched."

"Never watched where?"

"In the small, gray building, downwind of the dining hall. Used to be the sweet shop."

"Thought that was a maintenance building."

"Might be that too."

"You've been in it?"

"No."

"Can we take a look?"

"It's not our business."

"It should be our business."

Tom looked square into Matt's face. "Don't include me on this one."

"You're already included." Matt paused and then softened. "Look,

Tom, I want to see the place."

"As I said, it's not our business. Go to Santo."

"I'm not about to run to Santo until I find out whether there's anything to be concerned about. Does everyone but me know this secret?"

Tom rose, turned away from Matt, and peered through the narrow, dusty window pane of his office. The only sound was the constant clicking of the wall clock's hand. Without turning around, he spoke. "You want to look inside the gray building."

"I want to see the bed."

Tom turned to face him. "What will it accomplish?"

"We won't know till we see it."

"I don't like the 'we' part."

"I want *us* to check it out, Tom."

"Safety in numbers?"

"Yeah, but more than that. You want to see too, don't you?"

Tom waited for several seconds. "Maybe."

"When? When can we take a look?"

"Have commitments after work today. Maybe tomorrow night, after the boys are in bed. No need to be seen. Want to avoid questions from home, so we go after my wife goes to sleep."

"Agreed."

"And you realize if anyone sees us sneaking around in the dark, we'll have lots of explaining to do. "

"Blame everything on me."

"I intend to, but not sure that would help me much." Tom took another full minute to speak. "I'll call you at your gym office, after eleven, and let you know when I'm ready to leave the house."

"It should only take a few minutes. We either see it or we don't."

"It better. You owe me big for this one, Grazi."

***

Matt flicked on the light of his dark office and sat behind his desk. Minutes later he paced about the cramped space, waiting for the call. He knew something wasn't right as soon as Tom's greeting hit his ears.

"My wife's coughing, running a fever. We have to investigate another time."

"Shit," Matt said into the phone. He sighed. "It's okay, Tom."

"Sorry. We'll talk tomorrow."

"Sure."

Matt stared at the phone for several minutes before locking the gym.

Damn. I was so ready.

He crossed the field toward the direction of his cottage, when his eyes fell on the gray cement-block building, barely lit from the distant high beams. The campus was eerily quiet, even the owl mute. He stopped.

Just take a quick peek.

As he initiated a short detour, the shadowed terrain below the misty moon returned him to a time in his life when stealth was required. He approached the lone structure with caution, in the same way he and his delinquent buddies had once maneuvered along the moonlit, beachside streets of Staten Island.

He moved to the left front window and pressed his forehead close to the pane. Wooden slats covered the glass from the inside. The same was true of the window on the other side of the front door. His fingers pressed and rotated the knob. Locked.

About to return to his room, he reconsidered. He glanced over each shoulder to confirm no one was in sight before starting a circular reconnaissance of the building. He stepped around to the side wall, inspecting each of six tall, rectangular side windows and finding them also sealed or locked. Advancing past the solid wall in back, he proceeded to the far side. A rear side door became visible, and he tensed, hearing what sounded like a muffled engine from within.

Matt stared at the door, feeling the moisture dripping from his forehead. A nervous twitch ran down his leg. He cupped his hand to his ear and pressed against the door. A bumping sound filtered through the whirring background, indicating activity within.

He wiped the sweat from his upper lip with the back of his hand and inhaled one, two breaths before gripping the door handle. He braced himself against the door and gently pushed. As the door shifted, a shaft of dim light appeared through the crack, illuminating the tightened knuckles of his right hand. He leaned into the creaking wooden door and sidestepped into the space to prevent the door from opening any further than necessary.

Matt's pupils widened to adjust to the poor light, and he squinted to protect his eyes from the three-foot industrial drum fan churning out near-gale winds from the far corner. The fan spun so high that the air velocity almost caused him to lose his balance. He slid one foot forward and looked down to discover three trembling figures huddled together on the edge of a single, bare mattress.

Despite the faint light, the whites of the boys' eyes glistened in shock at the sudden entrance of an equally shocked Matt. He recognized Luke, a timid boy from his gym class. He recalled seeing the other two, but couldn't remember their names. He raised his finger to his mouth, indicating silence. One of the wide-eyed boys whimpered, and his petrified face sent a jolt through Matt's chest.

"Go back to your cottages," Matt whispered and then waved them to the exit. The boys remained frozen in place. Their heads turned toward the closed door opposite them, further back into the room. Matt turned to the inner door and back again to the boys.

"It's okay," Matt said low. The boys pressed closer together. Matt reached toward Luke and took his hands, tugging the boy to his feet with repeated words of encouragement. He pointed again to the open door, and this time the three boys struggled to their feet. Matt leaned close to the crying nine-year-old, touching the boy on the shoulder, letting him know it was all right.

With the boys gone, Matt slid his way to the inside door. A snapping noise sounded from the other side, another snap, and then . . . a moan. He reached out his hand toward the knob. The door opened an inch, bringing the scene into view.

A young boy laid face down on a bed, gripping two bars of the metal headboard. Naked except for underwear, the skinny boy sobbed into a flat pillow. His back revealed red, swollen welts, blood tinged lines visible on his briefs. A raised arm held a stiff, discolored, twelve-inch strap tied to a leather-covered, wooden handle.

Paralyzed for only a second, Matt lifted his leg, and with all his might, gave a forceful kick to the door. With a loud crack, the wooden door flew open splintering against the room's wall. The hot stench of sweat and urine filled his nostrils, and he gagged as he covered his nose with his hand. Something almost metallic, organic, hung in the moldy air. His stomach pulled into a knot so tight, a wave of nausea flowed over him. He tried to swallow, his throat constricted beyond his control.

Andrews whirled around to see who dared to interfere.

Something snapped inside Matt, and he lunged for the barber-style razor strap in Andrews' hand. His unexpected forward movement took Andrews off guard, and the marine stumbled to his knees. Tight-fisted, the coach clenched one arm around Andrew's neck while his other hand grabbed the strap and pressed it to the man's angry face. The sour smoker's breath laced with beer and barbecue belched into Matt's face, and he instinctively squinted his eyes and pulled away.

It was the opening Andrews needed. With the release of Matt's hold around his bruised neck, Andrews elbowed the coach in the stomach.

Matt groaned as he curled over and hit the floor. "You mother fucker!"

Andrews made his move. His heavy combat boot stomped down on Matt's exposed hand. Matt screamed. The small figure on the bed cried out at the same time, covering his head to shut out the sounds.

Matt rolled to the side, pulling his hand away. His eyes targeted downward from Andrews' face, and he became even more enraged. The son of a bitch had an erection. The stiff protrusion and the stained crotch of his pants left little to the imagination. A faint fishy smell whiffed past his nostrils.

"This is how you get your kicks?" Matt yelled as he dodged another swing of the paddle and rose to his feet. "Big man on campus!"

The marine's hand flew upward over his head.

The whoosh of the leather strap sailed passed Matt's face, missing its target by a fraction of an inch. The miscalculation resulted in a loud crack as the paddle smashed into the bed rail.

Matt thrust his knee as hard as he could toward the soiled crotch, but Andrews pulled away. Shifting his weight, Matt's other foot found its dampened target. Andrews' hands sprang from his side to his groin, and he fell to the floor with an agonizing moan. Matt glared at the crouching figure below him.

"From now on, I'm your guardian angel! Touch one boy, and I'll make you regret it! Matt dragged Andrews to his feet. "You're done!" Using all his strength, he grabbed Andrew's shirt collar with his uninjured hand and shoved him out the door into the waiting area.

"Your wife and boss will hear everything about tonight. You haven't heard the end of this, creep!" Matt yelled to the bent figure on the ground.

Rubbing his throat, Andrews faced Matt head on. "No," he said, his hoarse voice almost indistinguishable. The marine swallowed hard and spit to the side. "It's you who haven't heard the end of this." He staggered to his feet and stumbled once before hobbling out through the side door.

Matt turned to see the tear-stained cheeks of the boy leaning on the wall. He extended his arms toward the boy, and the boy collapsed into his arms. Matt caught him and they both slid to the floor. He held the boy tight and rocked him until the sobbing subsided.

Grabbing the boy's arm, Matt pushed his shoulder underneath to support him. They passed through the doorway of the gray building and headed for the campus hospital.

Pushing the doors open with his free shoulder, Matt deposited the boy into the nearest chair. A gray-haired man wearing wire-framed glasses entered through swinging doors. Matt recognized Dr. Graves.

"What's this?" the doctor asked as he rubbed his beard. "There," he said, pointing to a bed inside a cubicle with tools and medications. He set to work tending to the boy's wounds, removing the boy's torn underwear and swabbing his back and buttocks with a hydrogen peroxide solution.

Matt, his body shaking, focused on the doctor's movements. He clenched his arms around his chest and moved to the boy's bedside.

"You're going to be okay, son." The boy nodded, and Matt dragged himself toward the door.

"Where are you going?" Dr. Graves asked.

"To wash up, and go to my room."

Matt's body was heavy with exhaustion, his hand throbbing. He wanted a hot shower to rinse away the putrid smells. The doctor had other ideas.

"Not before you accompany this boy back to his cottage. He can walk. I'll apply an anesthetic to numb his wounds before you both leave."

"He can't stay overnight?"

"No. The cottage fathers are perfectly capable of follow-up care. The Mercurochrome in their first-aid kits prevents infection."

"Glad to hear the cottage fathers are good guys," Matt said.

"From my experience," the doctor offered, "Many cottage fathers have sympathy for this kind of thing, but others feel the boys' punishments are well deserved."

"Great," mumbled Matt. "Let me hit the john. Stomach doesn't feel so good."

"Your hand doesn't look too good either. Let me take a look."

After the first-aid session ended, Matt stumbled. His foot caught the corner wheel of the bed, and he held onto the door jam.

"You okay?" the doc asked.

With a nod, Matt headed for the terra-cotta tiled washroom, splashing cold water on his face to ease his nausea.

"God," Matt whispered, as he looked at his ragged image in the mirror. He stared at the dripping water on his face, and his trembling hands tore at the paper towel. After inhaling a calming breath, he returned to the triage area.

"Okay, son, back to your cottage," Matt said to the boy. Then turning to Dr. Graves, he added, "That bastard."

The physician cocked his head and peeked over his glasses. He returned the antiseptics to the cupboard and didn't say a word.

CHAPTER 17

Matt rose early the following morning, his mind tagging from one question to another in anticipation of a pending meeting with Santo. He stressed over how to present the most accurate account of his actions, how to describe Andrews' disgusting behavior in a professional way. Andrews had overstepped every boundary. It was time for justice.

Matt burst into the hallway of the administration building and stood in front of Mary Jo's empty desk. He turned and took four quick steps before he spotted Santo sprinting down the hallway toward him.

"What the hell is going on?" Santo demanded.

"What?" Matt asked, his adrenaline pumping.

"I just finished talking to Andrews. You attacked him?"

Damn it! Andrews got the first punch.

Matt's outrage resurfaced. "You bet your ass I attacked him! He . . ."

"My office," Santo interrupted. His quick long stride was matched by Matt's, trailing close behind.

"He's lucky I didn't beat him useless!" Matt yelled as Santo's door closed behind him. He took a breath, but not a seat. "Stop him, Santo. It's not right."

"What in the world are you talking about?"

"That monster was beating the boy, and getting his rocks off at the same time!"

"What?" Santo asked, his eyes widening. He didn't wait for a response. "That's *not* Andrews' version, He claims you must have been drinking last night. He asked me to find out what prompted your ballistic behavior toward him, and he's concerned you injured the boys in your stupor."

"That jerk! He's . . ."

"He's writing up details on your bizarre behavior, and he claims he will press charges. He wants you arrested or dismissed."

"That's not how it went down."

"Really? Because he told me he was doing his job when you decided to play Superman."

"And his job is whipping those boys to a pulp?"

"No, Matt," Santo said with a frown, "but legal and appropriate punishment is necessary around here."

"Well, last night Andrews was beating the shit out of that young boy, and that's neither legal nor appropriate!"

"As I said, that's not what he's saying."

"He's lying."

"Sit down."

Matt collapsed into a chair. Santo took a seat behind his desk.

"So let me get this straight. You dismissed the boys without authority?"

"I thought they should return to their cottages, a judgment call."

"I see. And you crashed into the door between the waiting area and the punishment area, which was already open?"

"Well yes, but . . ."

"And injured Andrews in efforts to stop a procedure that you claim was inappropriate. Do I have this right?"

"Damned straight."

"I don't understand," Santo said. "If the boys were in danger as you claim, why didn't you call me immediately?"

"There wasn't time! I had to do something!" Matt yelled, rising from his chair.

"Okay, okay, sit down."

Matt clenched his fists in a boxing stance and paced about the room before returning to his seat.

"I sent Andrews to the hospital after our meeting, Matt. He could hardly speak."

Matt rolled his eyes upward. "Look, I jumped Andrews to keep him from hurting that boy any further. It was the right thing to do."

Santo bit down hard on his lip. Tension lined his face. "One more question," he said. "Why were you roaming the campus in the middle of the night?"

Shit.

Matt slumped back in his chair and ran his fingers through his hair. He tasted the acid rising from his stomach. He looked at Santo and started from the beginning.

"Do you believe me?" Matt asked. He paused. "He nearly broke my hand," he added, holding his bandaged hand up for inspection. "Do you believe that?"

"I'm not sure what to believe."

"Then talk to the boys. You'll believe them, won't you?"

Santo made a call to the cottage where Matt had escorted the boy, and they headed across campus.

Just minutes with the injured boy revealed Andrews had made a previous visit. The young boy hung his head low and diverted his eyes away from Matt. He told Santo his injuries were, "Nothin' much." He whispered praise for Dr. Graves' treatment.

Yes, he was much better, thank you. The ice packs had worked their magic, and he was fine. When Matt started to speak, the whites of the boy's eyes flashed a look of warning. Interrupting Matt, the boy confessed that he had deserved the punishment.

"The boy is scared," Matt said, on their way to the building where the incident occurred. "My God, you can surely see that."

"Scared of what? Of who? You or Andrews?"

The only sign of damage in the old gray structure was the splintered remains of the door smashed during Matt's fury. No blood or stains on the walls or bed. No lingering odor to prove Andrews' lascivious activity, just the musty smell of mold and moisture. A logbook sat on a neat desk confirming the name, date, offense, and description of disciplinary procedures. The number 1, 2, or 3 indicated the number of swats delivered.

"So, if it's written in the log book, it must be true?" Matt asked. "Andrews could write down anything he wanted if you're not there."

Santo turned away. "Enough. I'll speak with Andrews about the absence of another employee, and question him regarding your charges. Document the incident. I'll read it as soon as you drop it off. You'll hear from me after that."

Heavy with frustration, Matt slumped his way back to the gym.

"Jesus, Matt. You sure shook up a hornet's nest," Tom said.

"Maybe you were right, Tom, about everything. What did I accomplish?"

"From what you told me, you rescued one boy and saved three others from a severe beating. And I bet the word is out."

***

"Did you hear?" Tom said to Matt at the end of the day. "An inmate in the administration office passed the word that Santo read the riot act to Andrews."

Santo had not commented when Matt had shown him the welts on the boy's back and buttocks, but perhaps they had made an impression after all.

"I'd sure like to think Santo won't back down," Matt said. "At the least, he will be forced to keep an eye on the bastard."

"Maybe."

"That brute was standing guard in the dining room at lunch, and waved to me! He threw me a shit-eating grin! I figure he thinks he got the best of me."

"It's a risky situation, Matt. If Santo reprimanded Andrews, it would be a first. And if Andrews gets written up, well, that would create one fuming marine."

Both administration and the state board had always backed Andrews. The plaques in his office thanked him for his service maintaining order at CHB. He had the reputation of running the day-to-day show with an iron hand, with results.

"You don't think Santo could get flack if he believes me over Andrews, do you?"

"I've seen it work that way, Matt."

"And if he believes Andrews, I could be gone, couldn't I? That can't happen!"

Tom took a few steps toward a wooden bookcase, where he fanned the pages of a Resident Rulebook.

"Maybe you need a lawyer to interpret the rules on discipline." Tom said as he flipped the pages, *"Quiet and serious talks with the individual boy resulting in a perfect understanding are quite effective and, in most cases sufficient."*

"That should be written on the damn paddle," Matt said in a lowered voice.

"Whippings, (not severe), loss of privileges, extra hard tasks and, in extreme cases, confinement, constitute the chief forms of punishment."

"Not severe?" Matt questioned. "Anything short of death is apparently 'not severe'."

What makes a person be cruel to a young boy? Matt recognized men in the news who wanted power. The current Cuban dictator threatened the safety of Americans, and Hitler's past rise in World War II had terrified countries all over the planet. But he had never met anyone face to face that he considered villainous or obscene.

While at college he had read published theories projecting brutal people were often themselves victims of abuse, but he didn't buy any acceptable reason for last night's activities.

"It doesn't matter why Andrews did what he did, Tom. It matters that he stops."

"At least we don't shackle boys in the fields or drag them into sweatboxes without food or water like they did in the past."

"Not that you know of."

"Matt . . ."

The word had barely left Tom's mouth when a knock shook the office door. Upon opening it, Matt stood back in disbelief. Mike Gonzales, the Spanish boy who had missed football practice, stood in front of him.

"You're kidding me!" Matt exclaimed. "Where the hell have you been?"

"You look for me, right?"

"Yeah, I was looking for you."

"Sorry 'bout that. Papa came to visit," the boy offered with a proud smile. "I go town with Papa, and then to family's house for long party, forget to sign out," he added. "I in trouble?"

Turning toward Tom, Matt rolled his eyes and mumbled an expletive under his breath.

"We go with lunch and see movie, *The Absent-Minded Professor.* Man, so cool!" Gonzales hesitated when he realized neither Matt nor Tom had responded.

Matt lifted his brows and said, "Cool, huh?" Gonzales missed the sarcasm, and his white teeth gleamed beneath his wide smile.

"Never mind," Matt said. "You ready to play?"

"*Si, si.* Sure am."

"Practice in twenty minutes."

Gonzales bolted for the door, and Matt stared at the open doorway. He turned to Tom.

"Did that just happen?"

***

"Can we talk?" Matt asked, leading Bo away from a group of friends congregating near Monroe Cottage. "Suppose you heard about last night."

"Of course."

"I was thinking. If the boy came forward . . ."

"Hold it right there, Coach," Bo interrupted. "You've taught me a lot and all, but this I know. When you take 'em on. You can't go in full front."

"Wait, you didn't let me finish. I . . ."

"It don't matter what you have to say. Told ya. We have a code. We don't puke. We don't puke on each other and we *never* puke on someone in charge."

Matt read the conviction on Bo's face.

"Look, Coach, we have to survive here. We serve our time until our sentence is over. Puking means somebody will be hurt, usually real bad. Those of us who are smart enough to stay out of the way and keep our mouths shut don't catch flack. But sometimes even that doesn't work. Our word doesn't hold much water against theirs. Odds are, we don't come out on top."

"Bo, I . . ."

"It's over. Only a dummy accuses the head honchos of doing bad. Feel good 'bout helpin' that boy, Coach. Maybe things will ease up for a while. But that's it."

The boys were scared. Matt shifted his position and took a deep breath. Bo threw him a dirty look. "We'll pay if . . ."

"If?"

"If you decide not letting this go is the right thing for you to do."

"Whatever I do, I won't involve you or the others."

"Don't know how you can do that, Coach. I been at CHB before and seen folks open their mouths 'bout things. They're gone, we're still here, and somebody pays."

CHAPTER 18

May ended with a reprimand for both Andrews and Matt, as if the disturbing events equated with being late for work, or not completing an assignment. Administration required Andrews to present the disciplinary logbook for daily review. Matt received a written warning of dismissal upon any future physical contact with a staff member. Both men signed off to report, but not react to, any improper behavior.

"A logbook review? That's it? Nothing about the 'spankings'?" Matt imitated quote marks with his fingers.

"Raising a hand works when nothing else does," Tom said with a sigh, "They're not going to give that up."

Matt's teeth ground together. He shook his head in silence.

"Matt, Andrews accused you of assault! As much as you disagree with corporal punishment and his light sentence, be glad you weren't fired or arrested."

Matt's frown deepened. He was so weighed down with anger he slammed the drawer in his office file cabinet with such fury that the entire office seemed to shake. He looked around for something to punch or destroy.

"Here's a notebook you could throw," Tom said.

"I'm angry, Tom! I'm so angry with Andrews, I could kill him! I'm angry with Santo, too, and the entire state system!" He paused. "And I'm angry with you, Tom, for acting like all this is okay."

Tom returned Matt's tirade with a raised voice. "It's not okay! But don't you see? There's nothing more you can do! And the boys need you, now more than ever. You take this any further, and you won't be coaching any football team this year or ever!"

Where was the world going when folks hired to protect children were the same people who hurt them? Matt's realization that he had to push Andrews aside didn't sit well, but the fight was over because the system had decided it was.

"Passing the baton to you, Matt," Tom said.

"What?"

"Spring football. You ready to take over, or you want to pack your bag?"

***

Like ants from a kicked mound, inmates swarmed out of their residences into a westward flow toward the gym. Locking the door to his room late Saturday morning, Matt joined them.

Bo's voice boomed down the dirt road.

"Outta those sweaty cottages! Butts in gear!"

Matt followed the crowd, meeting Tom and dozens of boys outside the metal gym door. When the key turned, it was Bo and Mulany who directed the boys to the workout areas.

"Hey, you two," Matt shouted, "Assign spotters for guys on the equipment. Here's a notebook to record each boy's reps . . . neatly."

"Will do," Mulany said, as he grabbed the spiral pad.

"'Cept for that 'neatly' part," Bo chimed in. "That's askin' *too* much."

Matt was still smiling as he tapped a pre-selected group of boys on the shoulder.

"You, you, and you," Matt ordered to prospective defensive players, "To the field."

Within minutes, the boys huddled around their coach. "Let's talk 'aggressive'," Matt said with a clenched fist. "Does everybody know what that means?"

"Kick butt!" yelled one boy.

"Right," Matt said in agreement. "But in football, kick only one way, the right way."

"How's that, Coach?"

"Start with this. When a brute from the other team heads for you at full speed," Matt said, punching his right fist into his left palm, "picture a kid who bullied you or your pal when you were in school. You may not have stopped him back then, but guess what? You'll learn how to be tough and stop him now."

"All right, Coach," echoed from the group. "We're with you,"

"Imagine your biggest past nightmare is the one charging you, Matt continued. "You want to stop him, you have to stop him, but . . . ," he hesitated.

"But don't break the rules," Mulany interrupted.

"That's right! Move over here, help me with a demo."

Quizzical looks appeared as if the task at hand seemed impossible. The boys watched Matt and Mulany go through a short series of new football maneuvers, and then dissembled into smaller units as ordered.

Attempts to replicate the technical movements resulted in a clash of bodies. After every encounter, Matt explained how to correct a move to make it more effective. Each one took time and demanded discipline, necessary steps in building a solid foundation.

"You'll learn to recognize and avoid the not-so-legal maneuvers too," Matt said, "Later."

At the end of practice, Bo followed Matt into his office.

"Got a minute?" the boy asked. Without waiting for a response, Bo took a seat across from Coach Grazi's desk.

"Something on your mind?"

"Sort of."

"And you come here to . . .?"

"Yeah."

"Do I guess?"

"Hey, man, the boys are really talking 'bout you."

"Yeah?"

"You're a hero." Bo's statement took Matt by surprise.

"No, I'm not."

"You are . . . whether you like it or not."

"Didn't do anything. Tried, but nothing's changed."

"Don't matter. You stuck up for us, and you took a shot at Andrews."

"Bo, I lost my temper, and I probably didn't handle it the best way."

"That don't matter either."

"I don't want to talk about it."

"Okay, then wanna talk about this?" Bo asked as he slid papers toward him. "Got the results of my new placement test."

Matt scanned the state forms. "You're in the eighth?"

Bo nodded. "Mid-eighth."

"So who's the hero now?" Matt said, rising from his desk with an outstretched hand. "Congratulations."

"Thanks." He shook Matt's hand with what appeared to be reluctant pride. "Got another year to cover before home," he added. "Good thing school is twelve months a year."

"Can you move that fast?"

"Try my damnedest."

"Your damnedest is what you should *always* expect from yourself," Matt said. "And I'm here to hold you to that."

***

Matt slapped the necessary bills on the counter at the general store in Colby Hill. He helped the clerk load a secondhand coffee urn, coffee, and cups into his car. Back on campus, he headed for the kitchen and finagled sugar and cream from the dining-room crew.

Time to dangle a new carrot before this bunch of football wannabees.

The table was set. Surprise covered the prospective team members as the crew led them into the newly designed refreshment area the following Saturday morning.

"Pretty cool, Coach," Mulany said.

"Well, ain't we all grown up?" Bo asked, holding a cup between his thumb and forefinger.

Out of ear range to the boys, Matt leaned toward Tom. "How about we open the pool early after workouts on the weekends?"

Matt's mind drifted back to FSU days when he had used swimming to unwind. Cool water would wake these boys up. It provided a liquid freedom unlike anything else.

"I'd need another pair of eyes, Tom."

"Might be able to arrange an escape from the home lawn mower, but I'd have to negotiate with my sweetie, the warden." Matt smiled and motioned a thumbs up.

"Oh, better check with . . ." Tom began.

Matt thrust out his hand, palm up, fingers splayed wide, toward his coaching partner. "I know. I know. Learned my lesson on that one. My good intentions with the track area backfired. We'll conference with Santo *before* we order kids into the pool."

In the gym after supper, both offensive and defensive prospects gathered before their coach. Matt chalked out plays on the blackboard, watching them struggle to understand. Each boy fought to answer the coach's questions.

Bo raised his hand. "'Stead of just tellin' us how to do it or drawing stuff on the board, could we see how it works for real?"

"Already done. I ordered football game films from FSU. You'll see Coach Nugent's basic, but tricky system in action. Mulany, turn down the lights and let 'er roll."

The boys sat glued to the screen as reels started to spin.

"Watch and learn, boys. Ask questions if you don't understand. Know what you are doing and why. And when we've got that down pat, we'll take the next step, executing a plan."

The boys' chatter told Matt he was making progress. An esprit de corps was developing, and he wished he could package the feeling. He'd need to tap on it when things didn't go smoothly.

"So what makes a good quarterback, Coach?" Bo asked after the evening films had ended.

"You want to be a quarterback?"

"Nah, I'm a better runner than a passer. Jest want to know who could be tossin' the ball to me."

"I'm looking for someone with more than an arm that can throw. A quarterback has to have the vision of what needs to happen before it happens. He must be smart, know when to take command, and when to hand it over. He needs the stamina to withstand pressure, to be a team player."

"Big list, Coach."

"It is."

"Did you hit the mark when you were a quarterback?"

"Have to ask my teammates."

Matt turned toward Bo and opened his notebook. "Take a look at my list of prospects."

"Ah, David Bell," Bo said. "Figures. He may be tall with a strong arm, but I *definitely* git annoyed when he tries to tell me what to do. Bragging 'bout one thing or another, trying to be top dog."

"He tries to be in charge?" Matt asked.

"Not around me."

"Can't imagine."

Matt liked Bell's physical attributes and had only one reservation. He was a manipulator. Employing methods to shape behavior was only acceptable if they pushed the team to fight together, to win.

"You think this loudmouth would really be the best one to be quarterback?" Bo asked.

"If he gives us our best chance to win."

"So if he can throw, it doesn't matter 'bout him being a hot shot?"

Matt tilted his head and lifted his eyebrows in question, encouraging Bo to answer the question himself.

"Okay, I git it. He's a good bet."

"Might be our only bet. But let me know if you spot anyone who has a more accurate arm or can make quicker decisions on his feet."

A loud knock interrupted the conversation, and Tom pushed the cracked office door open. The three reviewed the list of prospective players.

"Might be small, but Ron Stalworth is one tough kid," Bo said after Tom had thrown the boy's name into the discussion. "The boys respect him."

"Good to know," Tom said, "but there's one thing left to consider. He turned to face Matt and Bo. "He's slotted to leave CHB the end of September."

"Shit!" Matt exclaimed. "If Stalworth's leaving soon after the season starts, what good is he going to be? We'd have to replace him and train somebody else."

"Anybody better, Matt?" asked Tom. "We have to play boys when we've got 'em, for as long as we've got 'em."

"Okay. Make a list of all the boys tentatively scheduled for release during the season," Matt said as their meeting ended. "Better to know up front the number of players who might be gone before the season ends."

Matt took the defense to the field later during the day, where he had rigged dummies so the boys could fire off and hit. They charged, keeping their backs straight, their butts low, and their heads up. Right shoulder, left shoulder. Matt was determined to teach the boys the discipline to tackle an opposing player without malice or resentment.

"This is great," exclaimed one of the boys. "I get to slam spoiled rich kids into the ground."

"Whoa!" Matt exclaimed. "They'll be no slamming anyone! This isn't a free for all."

"Okay, okay, you call it tackling, I call it slamming. Same thing."

"Not the same thing!"

"Fall to the ground, you bastard!" cried a boy downfield.

"Teaching these street kids to play fair isn't going to be easy," Matt lamented to Tom. "I want to win games by playing legal, not by bending the rules."

"Remember who you're teaching about unacceptable behavior."

Matt reacted with a scrunched face like that of a young boy forced to swallow a spoonful of castor oil.

"Don't worry so much. You saw how the baseball season went. We won and we lost, but these boys stuck to the rules most of the time. They'll do the same for football."

"Baseball isn't the contact sport that football is, Tom. I've seen temperaments change in a heartbeat when someone hits too hard. I've watched respect disintegrate at the first sight of a fist. I don't want this team seen as a group of thugs."

"Too late for that, Matt. Folks already think of our boys that way"

CHAPTER 19

June's evening heat settled in and the small fan in Matt's room blew full force. He moved to the edge of his bed and focused on the small black and white television propped on the rickety wooden table. *Gunsmoke* featured Marshal Matt Dillon sauntering into the Dodge City, Kansas, saloon. Just as Miss Kitty raised her voice and her finger at an irate cowboy, a loud rap sounded twice on his door.

When Matt opened it, Bo stood with his head down, his foot furiously tapping the cement underneath. Tony Castor and Danny Williams pushed in close. Two faces Matt didn't recognize peered from behind.

"What? Bo, have you lost your damn mind? It's after hours. You're supposed to be in bed."

"Coach, can I come in . . . ?" Bo said in a whispered voice. "Please?"

Matt backed away from the door and motioned for the gang of five to squeeze into the room. He scanned the area outside before closing it.

"What the hell is going on?" he asked.

"Coach," Bo said pointing to the boys, "They were gonna run. We can't let 'em do that. Don't want 'em to break our record of no runaways."

"*Your* record of no runaways?"

"Yeah. We know if nobody runs, you don't have problems. If you don't have problems, we don't have problems. You're out front, Coach.

143

So tonight we jumped 'em and now you tell 'em."

"Christ, you're holding down boys to keep them from running?" He glanced at the two new inmates before turning back to Bo. "Why not report them?"

"You know the answer to that, Coach. We take care of our own. That's our code."

Realizing he was wearing nothing but his B.V.D. underwear, Matt felt awkward trying to investigate while half-naked. He grabbed a shirt and pulled on his pants.

"Maybe so, Bo, but you can't bring every kid who decides to run to my room."

"No, no, you're the end back up. We been doin' this for a while, and this is the first time our plan hasn't worked."

"And how exactly does your plan work?"

"It's like this. The house parents make hourly bed checks, so us football players formed teams to do our own bed check in between. If we hear a new guy is even thinkin' 'bout leaving, one of us stays next to him, or even sleeps beside him. It's been workin' great. Till now. These two are the first to give us a hard time, so we had to gang up on 'em and bring 'em to you. We couldn't convince 'em, but we knew you could."

Matt sat down on the single bed. He wiped his face with both his hands and tented his fingers together in thought before facing the wide-eyed Rookies.

"You're damn lucky these three musketeers," Matt said as he pointed to Bo, Castor, and Williams, "kept you from running. Don't you understand the price you would have paid?"

"I'm going home," the young teen stated, blinking back watery eyes.

"Won't happen. Just more time added to your sentence."

"I shouldn't be here," the other Rookie said with a scowl.

"You're lucky you're standing here, and not being marched off for a paddling," Matt said. "Sliced up by saw palmetto plants, or swollen up after a beating, are bad alternatives."

"But tell me something, Bo," Matt said as he turned and faced the boy. "How are you getting yourself and these boys back, before you're reported missing as runaways?"

Shock swept over their faces. The boys exchanged glances, first with each other, then with Bo.

"Oh," Bo replied.

"Oh, isn't an answer, and we're running short on time."

No brilliant plan jumped into Matt's mind, except that these boys needed to be out of his room, fast.

"All right, all right. Let's find neutral ground . . . The gym."

Matt grabbed his keys and ushered the boys out the door, across the semi-dark campus. Without warning, a winged shadow lunged through the air above them.

"What the . . . ?" came from one of the boys, as he ducked his head.

"Quiet," Matt whispered. "Just a friend."

He unlocked the gym door and the gang of five slithered down the hallway into his office. Biting his lips together, he gingerly picked up the receiver and listened as Santo's phone rang five long times.

"Shit," Matt said as he hung up. *Now what?*

"What are we gonna do, Coach?"

It would be only minutes before phones rang to the on-call emergency staff. Matt calculated the number of minutes needed to cross the field to their cottages. Even if he completed the escort in time, there was the possibility the cottage father could not cover for the boys. Not reporting runaways carried a stiff penalty.

"Let's go, boys, I'm getting you back," Matt declared. After two boys had stepped into the hallway, Matt changed his mind.

"Hold up," he ordered, as he lifted the phone from its cradle. "One last time." After redialing the familiar number, a gruff, strong voice broke the quiet of Matt's office.

"Santo here."

"It's Matt. Know it's late, but could you come to the gym?"

"You okay?"

"Yeah."

"Can't wait till morning?"

"No. Please. It's important."

"It better be. Okay, okay. Your office?"

Matt looked around the small room. "No, the gym." Matt hadn't felt this nervous since he and a friend had smuggled beer into the dorm back at college.

Because Santo lived on campus, it took only moments for the panting supervisor to arrive in his baggy sweatpants and an oversized tee shirt. Attempting to breathe as he fired off a barrage of questions, he stopped when he saw the circle of boys behind Matt.

"So?" Santo asked with his hands' palms up.

Matt explained the situation as his boss stood, not saying a word.

Santo made eye contact with each of the boys before turning to face Matt.

"This situation gets under control," Santo said, "now. Back to their cottages, immediately. We'll address the rest tomorrow."

As they turned to leave, Matt touched Santo's shoulder. He needed to say one more thing within earshot of the boys.

"Santo, no bed. Grub status or whatever for the boys who were going to run, but no bed." Matt felt the fire inside flare with every word.

"Don't talk to me about any of that tonight, Matt," Santo replied, and he turned away from Matt's gaze.

The group arrived at Monroe Cottage where Santo offered a brief explanation to Bart Rourk. He ended with, "Forget about this night, Bart."

"I'll *never* forget this night," the cottage father whispered. "But I swear no one will hear a word about it from me."

Santo had signaled Matt to leave when they overheard Bo's low voice as he pulled the new inmates toward him.

"Like I told ya, this place stinks, but running won't help. You'll end up with bug bites, snake bites, dog bites, or worse. I know. Git the thought of running out of your heads, and keep yourselves busy. You ain't runnin', cause we ain't gonna let ya."

Matt exchanged eye contact with Santo. Matt could feel a lecture coming on, but not tonight it seemed.

"I'll see *you*," Santo said, pointing a finger at Matt, "tomorrow. Come early for your budget meeting."

Back in his room, Matt closed his eyelids as the barred owl echoed from across campus. The sounds increased in volume until the swoosh of heavy, methodical wings neared his window.

You checking on me?

Weeks ago, he would have closed the window or covered his head, but tonight he remained still. He breathed in the moving air.

The evening's drama replayed in his mind until a new thought surfaced. For the first time, he considered Bo's reliance on him a possible liability, for both of them.

***

The next morning Matt had just pushed his breakfast plate toward the end of the boys' food line when Bart Rourk threw open the dining room doors and moved toward him. Matt raised his eyebrows in question regarding last night's escapade, and Bart nodded an "okay for now" response.

At a nearby table, Gary Lissitar put down his folders of creative writing and waved Matt and Bart over to his table. Not five minutes later, Tom stepped through the same oversized doors and joined the three men.

The party of four shared their latest fiascos and small triumphs, and Matt enjoyed the laughter. The comradery lifted each of them a notch. Licking his fingers, Bart was the first to push back his chair.

"Nice talking to you folks this morning," Bart said as he tipped an imaginary cap. "Matt, maybe we should chat later?" Matt nodded an affirmative.

Bart's distinctive jagged walk, his left foot slower to respond than his right, prompted Gary to shrug his shoulders.

"Old injury according to Bart," Gary said to the group. "He doesn't offer details."

"Everybody has secrets," said Tom.

If they only knew, thought Matt.

Minutes later Gary headed off to his classroom. Matt and Tom hadn't taken another bite before Santo bypassed the food line and plopped down on the vacated seat.

"Ready for the big shindig next month?" Santo asked. He eyed Matt with raised eyebrows and a tilt of the head indicating he had not forgotten last night. Matt's fork topped with French toast and syrup had just disappeared into his mouth, and it took every bit of control to keep from choking.

"Our Independence Day committee is making plans for the July picnic," Santo continued. "We're planning an old-fashioned barbecue, a watermelon cutting, a band concert, and an awards ceremony." Santo turned and faced Matt. "This is the one event of the year where parents, family, and friends of the inmates attend. Opening up the campus is a huge undertaking."

"Is O'Hurley clearing and harrowing the outer field again this year?" Tom asked.

"What happens in the field and what is harrowing?" asked Matt.

"A pronged attachment is pulled behind a tractor. Smooths out the ground and turns the bumpy east field into a giant parking lot" Tom said.

"So, which one of you will be joining the committee?" Santo asked.

Matt's jaw dropped low on his tanned Italian face.

"I'll do it," Tom volunteered. "I've been this route before. You can count on Matt and me to keep the boys busy."

"Thanks for heading up the track and field events again, Tom. Explain to Matt about his swimming competition." Matt looked toward Tom and stopped chewing.

Speed contests were always popular at the school, whether on land or sea. In this case, "land" was the athletic field where Tom would preside in the morning, and the "sea" was the pool where Matt would be in charge in the afternoon.

"I'm here to help out in any way I can," Santo said, rising from his seat. "And Matt, if you have any questions after you've chatted with Tom, we'll add that to our list of things to discuss this afternoon. Your budget appointment is at one, right?"

"I'll be there," Matt said. "Early."

"I'm sure you will."

After Santo had moved away Matt leaned toward Tom. "Another assignment? A swim team? "

"Yeah. About that. It's actually Dr. Strickland, not Santo who calls the shots on this one. And since he wants a swim team, there's a summer swim team."

Tom explained that he had coached the track team for the past few years, so Matt needed to take on the swim team. As in baseball and football, they would assist each other as needed.

"Thanks for being on the damned committee, Tom,"

"Don't thank me yet. You'll be involved every step of the way so you can take over and be point man next year."

"Only fair. I'm more concerned about coaching swimming. Never done it. Not even a great swimmer myself. When I do something, I want to do it right. How am I supposed to teach something I don't know?"

"It's not like swimming is a major sport."

"That doesn't matter. Santo hired me to put a winning football team together. I'm good at football."

"What other coach should be assigned to the task?"

"Wipe off that ridiculous smile!" Matt said as he stood and moved behind Tom. He tugged at the back of Tom's chair as if he would pull it over.

"Take it easy. I give," Tom said as laughter poured from his throat. "You need me to finish up this damn budget before you meet with Santo." They took turns pushing at each other through the dining hall, out the door, and toward the gym.

The inventory of football equipment and supplies had revealed deficits beyond Matt's expectations. Equipment needed repair. Gear was missing or in poor shape. The team clothing offered little to no protection. The dilemma had caused Matt and Tom to push the spreadsheets back and forth between them for the past few days.

"We don't have enough uniforms, and oh yeah, there's not enough sizes either," Tom lamented. "Look at this. Size extra-large, extra-large, and oh, extra-large."

"Refresh that cup of coffee, Tom. We need a budget for Santo that will remedy this situation, and not give him a heart attack."

"Roger that. And let me remind you, our state budget doesn't measure up to a school budget in the outside world, so you can't go overboard on this one."

Matt grabbed the scratched-up list they had completed earlier and checked off what the football team needed: exercise and workout equipment, gear including shoulder pads, hip pads, thigh pads, knee pads, practice jerseys, football shoes, and balls. The list kept growing. Being as conservative as he could, the total of equipment and gear came to nearly $2,500. Tom finalized the budgets for the baseball, basketball, swim and track teams, keeping requested funds to a minimum.

"Wow," Matt exclaimed. "And that figure doesn't include uniforms. When *was* the last time the team wore new uniforms?"

Tom shrugged. "Over six, seven years ago."

"They sure fit the description of 'tattered and torn.'"

Matt recalled his college days when the Georgia Tech Yellow Jackets had the most impressive team uniform he had ever seen. The brilliant white and steel gray jerseys trimmed in black and gold complimented the brilliant gold pants. The team walked onto the field with self-esteem and confidence. That's what he wanted for these boys.

"Uniforms would double the already steep budget," Tom lamented.

Like all administrators, Santo was interested in the bottom line.

He may have been familiar with what it took to minimally equip each sport, but Matt wanted much more than the minimum.

Matt would have to justify every item at the budget meeting and anticipate every possible question or rebuttal. One part of him wished he could pass the paperwork to Santo's secretary, return to the gym, and wait for a response, but there was another part that looked forward to the verbal debate, the vigorous offense.

The budget meeting and a discussion about last night's activities weighed heavy on his mind, but he was ready for both . . . he hoped.

***

Entering Santo's office, brief greetings gave way to a serious conversation about the scene from the previous night. Santo agreed that Bo and the other boys' intentions were well-meaning, however poorly thought out. Matt pushed for reassurance the boys wouldn't have to pay too dearly for such a mistake.

"I've given this situation a lot of thought, Matt. The boys who planned on running will be demoted to Grub, along with a restricted curfew and bathroom duty. I haven't decided about physical punishment."

"But Santo, it was my fault that . . ."

"The boys almost ran away! They left their cottages without permission. Do you get that?" Matt lowered his head.

"Are you going to guarantee these boys will not try to run again?" Santo asked. "Can you do that?"

"I'll talk to them. I'll give them extra . . ."

"Enough. Corporal punishment has its place," Santo said, looking directly at Matt.

Matt closed and opened his eyes, took a breath, and fell silent. Words were of no use any longer, the decision made.

Santo moved from behind his desk and faced Matt. "However, this one time, this one time only, I don't feel it's warranted."

Matt pressed his lips together and his head dropped. "Thank you, sir. Thank you. It won't happen again."

Santo threw his hand in front of Matt. "But I'm not going to ease up a second time. Understood?"

"Understood, understood," Matt said with repetitive nodding. He inhaled a breath of relief. He would share this information with Bo, and explain why he could not prevent a whipping for such an offense in the future.

"Thanks, Santo," Matt said again, relaxing his muscles. "May I ask you something?"

"What?" Santo asked, impatience lacing his response.

"Why can't CHB eliminate corporal punishment and use increased work assignments as a punishment for bad behavior?"

"Bad idea, Matt," Santo said, as he moved back behind his desk. "I know other institutions use a work detail as punishment, but we don't do that because we try to teach 'dignity in labor' here."

"What exactly does that mean?"

"Look, these boys will leave CHB, and we hope, settle down and find jobs. But regardless, we want them to feel positive, not negative when they work hard."

Matt paused, cocking his head to the side. "Never thought about that."

"Lots of things to think about when it comes to these boys."

"But there must be another disciplinary procedure that could replace corporal punishment."

"What do you suggest?"

"I don't know." Matt hung his head.

"When you figure it out, let me know. For now, let's move on to your budget proposal."

Matt extended his paper-filled hand toward Santo. Drawing another deep breath, he argued for the increased football budget. He fought for every position, explained every safety issue, and projected every possible positive outcome. He exuded confidence, despite the previous tongue lashing.

"Take a gander at what we've put together, and give me a buzz when you've agreed to it," he said, ending with a wide grin.

"Thank you, Coach," Santo said without returning Matt's smile. On that final word, Santo rose and ushered Matt to the office door and gently closed it behind him. Matt stood outside Santo's door for a few moments, feeling like a dismissed defendant who waited as a jury deliberated.

CHAPTER 20

"Hey, Matt, heard the rumor about the missing chorus director?" Tom asked, his hands cupping a hot mug of coffee on his desk.
"Undercover police agents arrested our preacher in a Panama City
bathhouse."

"No shit!"

"Bet Santo's having a cow trying to keep publicity down on this
one. Chatter in the dining room says Santo suspended the guy."

"Do you think he let him go before or after the arrest, Tom?"

"Does that make a difference?"

"Yeah, it does," Matt said. "It would prove Santo had a spine, or it
would support the idea he let the cops do the work."

"Where's this coming from?"

"I'd just like to see Santo stand up to whatever he thought was
wrong, that's all."

"You sure you're not just stressed out about our budget?"

"Yeah, maybe that too, but I've never seen Santo really buck the
system."

"You talking about the shed scene, Bo's run, or the dogs?"

"Yes, and a few other things."

"For gosh sakes, let it go. Go forward, man."

Tom explained he had received word that the school found a substitute. A chorus class became a study hall. Teachers would have to rotate their hour of prep time to fill the gap until a full-time substitute was hired.

"We cover study hall?"

"That's what I heard, Matt."

Before sunset, the word passed through campus that the officially dismissed choir director was gone forever, and CHB had initiated a scramble to replace him.

Substitutes came and went for a week until a full-time sub was hired. A few weeks later, Alan Jules, a young, friendly guy with short, auburn curls and a wide smile, arrived.

The new permanent replacement hadn't passed his Florida State teaching certification as a college student, so he needed to live in Florida for a year to be eligible for residency and retake the exam. The job at CHB enabled him to earn a living while he studied. Not a preacher like previous chorus directors, CHB chose him to fill the position because he had majored in music.

Close to Matt's age of twenty-five, Alan spoke at a fast pace, indicating either nervous energy or genuine excitement about his job. He and Matt hit it off the first minute they met.

"Be happy to show you around, Alan. CHB can be pretty overwhelming. Should we start with your classroom or walk to the church? Both places are where you'll be spending most of your time."

"I'll take the walk."

"Right. We'll loop past the boys' cottages and pass the clothing store, barbershop, upholstery shop, and canteen on the way to the chapel."

"Canteen?"

"Yeah, a small store where the boys can buy extra things, like candy."

"Inmates have money?"

"Sometimes families send spending money," Matt responded. "But I've seen more than one cottage father give change to boys who didn't receive money from home. In exchange for the cash, the boys do extra chores around their cottage."

"Got a sweet tooth myself. Am I allowed to purchase a Sugar Daddy or a Chunky Bar?"

"No problem." They strolled through the lush, manicured campus.

"It's beautiful here, Matt."

"Yeah," Matt said in a lowered voice. *I thought so too.*

He pointed across the main road, near Colby Hill's side entrance. "That's the North Side, the colored side." A steeple of a white gabled chapel edged upward into the cloudless blue sky.

"With a wreath on the front door and a little snow, that church makes a perfect Christmas card," Alan said, moving both hands to his waist and clicking on an imaginary camera. "The only things missing are the welcoming signs showing the times of the services and the biblical sayings. If there was a black iron fence around an attached cemetery, I'd feel like I was in front of my church back home."

"Cemetery on the hill round the back."

"Really? Why?" Alan asked.

"Some boys didn't have folks to transport them home if they died. Doesn't happen anymore. Tom told me boys died from influenza and other fatal diseases years ago and that boys and a faculty member died in a fire in the early 1900s."

"Shit," Alan said. "That's bloody awful." Matt nodded.

"See that land past the cemetery?" Matt asked. "The coloreds work hard at farming over there. Cows, chickens, turkeys, and pigs, and just about any vegetable you can think of. Even have a few fruit and pecan trees. I understand the boys harvest something every month of the year."

"I had no idea."

"Oh, yeah. They butcher, cut, cook and serve the meat for tables on both sides of campus. Makes them employable when they go back home."

"And the boys over there have their own chorus, right?

"And their own football team."

They moved further down the dirt road until Matt turned to face Alan. "Before we move on, let me tell you something about the music class."

"Shoot."

"I could never figure out its popularity," Matt mused. "Chorus was never big when I went to school."

"It's great so many participate."

"Not exactly." Matt filled him in on the class's current reputation.

"Shit, you're kidding!"

"No, unfortunately not. Thought you should know."

"Thanks, I think."

Entering the education building, they bumped into Gary Lissitar coming out of his classroom.

"Got a minute, Gary?" Matt asked. "Any chance you could finish up the new guy's tour? I'm needed at the gym."

"Thanks for the walkabout," Alan said, "and the heads-up."

***

Two long days passed. One by one, the faculty received a request for a follow-up budget meeting. On the fourth day, a Pilot handed Matt the instruction to call Santo's office. Nervous as a schoolboy awaiting a report card, he dropped his notebook and pencil and made the call.

Seconds later, he waved his crossed fingers at Tom and yelled for him to "hold down the fort." He bolted from the gym.

"Pretty hefty budget you've given me," Santo said, as he smoothed the proposal on his desk. "Over $2,000 for equipment and gear? That same amount again for uniforms? A lot of money."

"Yes, sir."

"That's more than we've spent on the football team in five years. Do you really need all of this?"

"Yes, sir."

"If you could cut one thing, what would it be?"

"If I had my druthers?"

"Yeah."

Matt swallowed hard. "Nothing."

Santo looked up. He wasn't amused.

"Santo, listen to what I'm saying," Matt pleaded. "These kids have been working their asses off. They're enthused, hyped up, and ready to go. If you put them back out there in garbage, that's how they're going to feel and how they're going to play. The team needs an extra boost to give them some self-respect."

Santo eyed him as he continued.

"We need this. For all the right reasons, we need this."

Santo rubbed his chin between his thumb and forefinger. "Okay, tell you what. Make do with the current exercise equipment and I'll go along with your uniform request. I'll make cuts somewhere else. The way things are going with your pre-season activities, well, I'd sure hate to see the momentum stop. This is important for the boys, and it's important for the school. I'll sign off. Go ahead, order it."

Matt jumped to his feet and shoved his hand across the desk to shake Santo's.

"Thank you."

With great relief, Matt bowed his head to leave and then stopped to ask, "When will the new uniforms come in?"

"Late summer."

"That works. We can start practice in the old uniforms, and when the new uniforms arrive at the end of the summer . . . Perfect."

"Anything else to discuss? Your swim team?"

"Naah, I'm good." He shook Santo's hand one more time.

Perhaps Matt had been too hard on Santo. The guy had sure pulled through for him today. He winked at the secretary as he floated by. When the sunshine hit his face, he let out a loud yell.

"Yee-haw!" he shouted with all his might. He was sure the whole campus could hear.

Matt ran the entire way to his office where Tom was waiting. When Matt told him the results of the budget meeting, they slapped each other on the arms, letting out victorious "hurrahs." Uncharacteristic to their nature, they spontaneously linked arms by their elbows and circled each other in one direction. Then linking opposite elbows, danced the opposite way.

Except for new exercise equipment, the football team would have everything they needed. Matt had no excuse for creating anything less than the winning team he had envisioned on the first day he had arrived.

***

Since Matt's first few days of gym class had included spitballs and back-talk, he worried Alan might run into the same issues. Tom covered the beginning of gym class while Matt slipped into the back of the chorus room.

Alan stepped onto the pedestal the previous minister had once occupied. He stood erect as he introduced himself. Starting with a cheerful hello, he told the inmates a little about himself and then burst into a nontraditional dialog.

"Boys," he began, "this is a chorus. We will sing here. I've been told other activities have taken place during this class. Starting now, that's going to end. There will be no hand jobs and no blow jobs in this classroom. Your only job will be to sing.

"If you need such entertainment, find it elsewhere. If any of you have trouble with this new policy, tough shit. I intend to teach you how to sing, and when we're done, we'll have the best damn chorus in the state!"

Standing in the back of the room, Matt stifled his laughter with his hand. This guy was going to handle these boys just fine. He hoped that Alan's choice of words wouldn't get back to Santo. CHB could be a place where you could do bad things, but you needed to say nice words.

CHAPTER 21

Mulany came to football practice as part of his crew responsibilities but didn't think of himself as a football player. He had never played the game and, despite Coach Grazi's encouragement, protested when Bo suggested he'd be a good tight end.

"I'd make an ass out of myself," Mulany said. Bo patted him on the shoulder and appeared ready to make an argument when Matt's voice interrupted from behind.

"With this crazy bunch, you're worried about that?"

"Coach is right, man," Bo interjected. "We need a tight end. All ya gotta do is run down the field and catch the damn ball."

"With your height and speed already up to par," Matt added, "you'd only have to concentrate on being in the right place at the right time."

"Maybe I should just work crew."

Bo threw his hands into the air. "You can catch a ball, I've seen you."

"Hold off, Bo," Matt said. "Mulany knows we need him. Leave it at that."

"Okay," Bo said, "for now."

That afternoon the boys' practice played like an ancient and chaotic *Keystone Kops* film with sound. Players couldn't replicate assigned tasks and crashed into each other.

"Watch where you're going!" Coach Faber yelled.

"Your shoulder, use your shoulder!" Matt bellowed.

Although a sense of unity was developing on and off the field, frustration erupted after an unsuccessful play.

"Okay, everyone, gather round," Matt commanded. "I've preached how winning depends on how hard you've practiced, and on your precision in execution, but that's not what I care about right now. Today I want to see you handle yourself when you *don't* hit the mark. Mistakes are good, sometimes more important than completing a play. Each time you make one, build on it. That's how you learn. Each mistake makes you better, smarter."

Matt's deep inhale and exhale preceded his next decree. "Mistakes are *not* failures. Say it."

"Mistakes are not failures!" echoed from the group.

"Believe me, there will *always* be another play. Take pride in the things you accomplish, but just as important, have the courage to hang in there after you've screwed up. And you will screw up."

"So . . ." Matt began. The boys waited for his next words.

"So, try not to screw up," Bell chimed in, "but when you do, make sure to learn something so the next time you do it right."

Matt's eyebrows lifted in surprise. "Listen to the guy who might be your quarterback."

All heads turned. Bell beamed as if he had just thrown a winning touchdown.

The boys thrived on Matt's suggestions and criticisms and pushed each other to improve. They worked until they dropped and wanted more. Despite additional practice on Saturday mornings, the boys clamored for time on the field on Sunday after church.

"Keep drills short and sweet, Tom," said Matt. "I don't want to test these guys' attention span."

"How long?" Tom asked.

"No longer than an hour and twenty minutes, including stretching and loosening up."

The boys talked to each other, encouraged and assisted. Humor became part of the activities, and waxing and waning sounds of laughter emerged from the field and locker room.

In between practices, brainstorming sessions took place outside Matt's office, and the little percolator in the back corner never worked so hard. The team was coming together. Fifty-nine boys signed up to play on the football team, one of the largest numbers to report for any sport at CHB. Mulany was one of them.

***

"It's a lot, isn't it?" Matt asked Bo, pulling him aside after a practice session.

"Football's great, but school's tough."

"Grades okay?"

"Made it."

"What did you make?"

"Honor roll."

Honor roll required grades of "B" or better in academic classes for a month. Having that distinction meant Bo's name would appear in the *Flying Osprey* and be listed on Monroe Cottage's bulletin board.

"Good job!" Matt exclaimed.

Bo looked downward and scuffed his shoe against the wooden floor.

"You don't want it? Honor roll is something to be proud of."

"Yeah, but . . ." Bo moved his focus from Matt to the schedule on the office wall. "But that's not really the thing."

"Spit it out."

"There's never enough time, Coach. Love sports, but I can't do studyin' with lights out at nine." He paused. "And it's . . . don't have time for the little kids anymore. Miss it, and they miss it."

"Okay, I can relate." The conversation with Betty about "not enough time" flashed into his mind.

"Extra credit assignments and teachers puttin' in a good word for me will speed me up to Pilot, but . . . Coach, I don't know what to do."

"Slow down, Bo. Let's think about this. How about you cut back a few after-class hours in the gym?"

"Okay. That'd work. Then I could help the kids during homework time. Yeah, that would work great, Coach."

"And how about I write up something positive about your efforts in class? Be happy to hand in something to admin. Might make your next promotion go a little faster."

"I like cuttin' down gym time," Bo said. "But better skip the writin'. You're good with the boys, but you're not popular with the teachers who sign off on my stuff."

CHAPTER 22

The positive, clear air clouded over when Matt's favorite prospective quarterback, David Bell, entered his office with a limp.

"You look awful. What happened?" Matt asked.

"Andrews dragged me and a bunch of other guys out of bed last night, and whipped the hell out of me."

"What? Explain!"

"I didn't do nuthin'!"

"Are you all right? Did you see a doctor?"

"Shit, no. They made me limp back to my cottage."

Matt felt the hairs on the back of his neck rise up. "Let me get this straight. Andrews whipped you for no reason at all?"

Bell remained quiet for a few seconds before answering. "I had one stupid cigarette."

"Oh, one little cigarette." Matt moved his hand back from his forehead, along the top of his head, pressing down on his neck.

Shit.

He could see that the boy was hurting, but he also knew the rules when it came to smoking.

"I can't walk right! I was awake all night with the pain," Bell lamented. "I don't see how come we can't smoke, anyway. It's not right. They shouldn't be able to beat the shit outta you for one fucking cigarette!"

"So you knew if you smoked, a whipping would be the consequence?"

"I guess."

"And orientation included information about the bad fire a few years back caused by a burning cigarette?"

"Rubbed it out with my foot." Bell's chin dropped toward his chest.

"So how did you come by cigarettes?"

"One of the inmates selling 'em."

"Who?"

"You know I ain't gonna -"

"Never mind, you ain't gonna 'puke' on nobody."

"Yeah."

"Sounds like you screwed up."

"You mean you won't go to bat for me?"

"I don't believe any of you should be whipped, but I don't run the place. The solution is to follow the rules."

"Stupid rules."

"So, can you follow them?"

"I guess."

"And I guess you'll be off the team if you don't."

Without a word, Bell threw one last searching look at Matt before dragging himself out the door.

Matt stared at the empty doorway. He had to do something. The health of the team was at stake. If he intervened in any way, would Andrews take his frustration out on his players?

Did Andrews whip this boy to get even with me?

That thought clarified Matt's next step. Bullies depended on their prey to be weak. He picked up the phone.

"Santo, you've got a problem, and if you don't fix it we won't have a quarterback or a winning season!"

CHAPTER 23

"Bell okay?" Tom asked Matt the following day on the field.

"Doc says he's pretty swollen. Nothing broken."

"Anything from Santo?"

"He was livid that Andrews dare touch one of the players, especially the quarterback. They're off-limits to the man for now."

"So you got one snorting mad marine even madder than before," Tom said. "Great."

"He can't touch the boys without hurting himself, so he should behave."

"Yeah, right."

"At least Santo came through. I think he was scared I was going to attack the man and get fired."

"I was afraid of that too, Matt."

"Ha."

"So what's on the agenda?"

Matt had determined it was time to press the boys on defense before the real heat set in. They had learned how to launch themselves from a three-point stance, avoid blocks, and rush the quarterback, but one major obstacle remained.

"It's one thing to tell and show these boys how to hit dummies,"

Matt said, "but it's becoming obvious that it's a whole new ballgame when they are required to hit real bodies."

"They'll come around," said Tom. "I've seen them on the field. There's more than one player who strikes a pretty good blow. Give them time."

Matt stayed on the field after Tom and the boys had left. He flipped through the pages of his notebook, brushing off bits of erasure, like cookie crumbs from a plate.

"What are these boys really made of?" he whispered to a nearby headless dummy. "You watch these boys every day. Are they ready for combat?"

Matt waited only a moment for the response that would never come. "Tell me. *Will* they hit?" He leaned in toward the dummy. "Speak up. Will they hit?"

Matt punched the dummy's stump where a head should have been. "I guess we won't know until the time comes."

Finishing his one-sided discourse and returning to the gym, Matt caught Tom wiping down the equipment.

"Richard Bern," Matt said.

"Yeah?" Tom asked. "What about him?"

"We've both known from day one that he'd be an impressive hitter, and he's shown talent lately."

"Time to encourage him to show his stuff?"

Bern's six foot one, massive frame had a place on the team. He was the biggest guy around, weighing in over two hundred fifty pounds, and despite his weight, his muscle tone was excellent.

"Talk about a vicious kid," Tom said. "He could teach the boys how to hit a moving target."

"Too dangerous. His behavior could easily trigger a return to 'street' mode." Matt had seen Bern slip back into his neighborhood tactics on more than one occasion.

"Okay, so what do you have in mind?" asked Tom.

"More one-on-one with the guy," Matt answered. "I've got to re-wire his natural impulse to stop anyone in his way. He can never intentionally hurt an opposing player. Any question about this, and I won't play him, no matter how good he may be."

Matt needed players like Bern who had no qualms about hard tackles. He would schedule extra time with the boy and other defensive prospects, explaining the right and wrong ways to hit.

"Another thing, Tom, Bern has to be more careful. I don't want him getting hurt. He's got to master how to turn his head the right way when he tackles someone."

A few days into the next set of drills, a runner came to Matt with a note directing Bern to report to the guidance office. After Bern missed the next three practices, Matt called Wayne, his friend at the guidance center.

"Know Richard Bern?"

"Can't miss that guy, Matt."

"Know where he is?"

"Why? You want to meet and go over his file?"

"No, just tell me the scoop on why he isn't at practice. I need this guy on the team."

"No football for this boy, Matt. He's undergoing treatment with Dr. Hemlick."

Matt remembered meeting Dr. Hemlick once before when he had requested permission to meet with Bo back in March.

"Details, Wayne. I need details."

"Nothing you don't already know. Bern has an aggressive side to him and the doctor is helping him with that."

"What?" Matt asked. "Damn it, Wayne."

Matt had learned enough about medical guidelines and treatment plans to know he would have to wait until Bern completed his program before the boy could return.

"Damn, damn, damn," Matt muttered under his breath.

***

"What's the story on this Dr. Hemlick?" Matt asked Tom in the gym.

Tom seemed to note Matt's agitation and took his time removing his tattered Osprey baseball cap. He rubbed his sweating head. "And what do you mean by that?"

"I mean, what kind of medical regimens does he prescribe?"

"I don't know."

"And let me guess, nobody objects to it."

Tom shook his head. "Climb off your high horse, Matt. Sometimes medications improve life for a boy; sometimes they don't."

"I'm just saying . . ."

"Let me spell a few things out for you," Tom interrupted, "real clear."

Tom argued that despite Matt's juvenile criminal justice courses at FSU, Matt was not an expert when it came to the best way to handle delinquents.

"Textbook procedures sound good, but often don't benefit these boys. If the gurus were able to figure it out, these kids would be in and out of here. All cured. Doesn't work that way."

"Tom, I . . ."

"You encourage these boys, you treat them fairly. I respect you for that. But sometimes you live in a fantasy. You expect the miracle of rehabilitation to occur with everyone. Always be fair, be kind, blah, blah, blah. At Colby Hill, it's not that simple. Sometimes they need more help than that."

"So medications are justified?"

"I didn't say that. I'm not a doctor."

"I hear what you're saying, but I don't agree with you. My God, Tom, Bern has come a long way. Why pull him out without even consulting with his teachers?"

"Maybe he has."

"He hasn't asked for my opinion."

"Imagine that," Tom said as he turned to go. "You do what you have to do, Matt. We've been through this before. Stick with something you're an expert at, football."

Matt knew Tom had a point, but something inside him couldn't let it go. He made an additional query at the guidance office but gained no further information. He pulled Bo aside after his afternoon class.

"Yeah, I've known a few who drank the 'soup,'" Bo said. "Hell, Hemlick tried to give it to me when I met with him once a week. But I wasn't gonna drink that crap. He tried convincin' me it was for my own good, but you know me, I don't listen all the time."

"You turned down this 'soup'?" Matt asked. "The soup was optional?"

"Guess so," Bo admitted. "Since I said 'no way,' I guess anybody could. Tell you what though, his soup gives you a damned good high."

"If you never had the soup, how can you say what kind of a high it causes?"

"Repeatin' what I've heard."

"And you never thought to tell me this when Bern disappeared?"

Bo shrugged. "Not my business."

Matt sighed. "Have you seen him?"

"A couple times."

"When I dropped by his cottage to talk with him," Matt said, "his cottage father told me he was sleeping. I asked him to have Bern drop by the gym, but he either didn't get my message or doesn't want to talk to me. Think he'd talk to you guys?"

"Maybe. You gonna talk to Hemlick?"

"Just do me this favor, Bo . . . and let me know what he says."

***

Betty had managed a weekend night off so Matt invited her and Santo to join him at The Country Club.

"Hey, did you see Alan King's skit last night? The one on the *Ed Sullivan Show*?" Santo asked.

"The one about the shortcomings of airline travel?" Betty laughed as she tossed her hair to one side. "Too funny."

Laughter came easily for the trio, but tonight Matt had more than a good time on his mind. Announcing a needed trip to the ladies' room, Betty said she would drop a few coins into the jukebox on songs by Patsy Cline and Eddy Arnold. Matt took advantage of her absence and brought Santo up to date on his defensive player.

"So, Santo, do you know anything about Dr. Hemlick's so-called soups?"

Santo eyed Matt, his lips pursed, his smile gone.

"Matt, are you at it again? Hemlick is a qualified Doctor of Medicine and Psychology with the degrees and the experience to back him up. As far as his 'soup' treatment, yes, and I've seen it work."

"Is it a sedative?"

"Don't know."

"A narcotic?"

"Matt, I'm not the doctor."

"Is it possible these concoctions are doing harm to the kids?"

"Why would you think that? I haven't seen anything to that effect."

"I saw Richard Bern this past week. He's lost a lot of weight."

"Losing weight may be a good thing for that boy."

"It isn't just the weight loss, his whole appearance is different. His complexion is pale, and his eyes seem vacant, sunken-in. Call him into your office. He's different."

Santo shook his head. "If he's not feeling right, have him make a trip to see Dr. Graves. But I can't imagine Dr. Hemlick not treating a boy properly. Are you reporting things that aren't real so your player returns to the team?"

Matt looked at his boss in disbelief but then questioned himself as to whether this could be a possibility. No, no way.

Spotting Betty striding across the room, Santo finished the conversation. "Do we need to talk more about this later? I can always call the review board together regarding any impropriety, but . . ." Santo slowed his voice. "If you call that play, you better have damn good evidence that something bad is going down."

"Hey, have you two been keeping up with the news?" Betty asked. Matt rose from his chair and pulled hers away from the table so she could be seated.

"Some," Santo said. "Why do you ask?"

"I keep reading about Berlin, Germany, and I don't understand what's going on. What's all this about a wall?"

"I talked to my dad last night," Matt said. "He told me that since World War II ended, East Germans have been crossing over their border by the thousands. Seems like communism isn't as attractive as folks thought."

"Where are they going?"

"To West Berlin, and to West Germany or Europe," Santo offered. "A wall keeps them from leaving."

"That's unreal. A wall to keep folks in? I thought walls kept people out." Betty took a breath. "You think it's really going to happen?"

"Seems that way. Reports say they're building trenches along the streets and shutting down the railroad lines as we speak."

Betty turned toward Matt. "I hope you don't have family over there."

"Most of our family's in Italy, although I do have a friend whose aunt lives in Germany."

"Problems in Cuba, too," Santo added. "Got numerous friends who have either enlisted or gotten called up."

"Guess we can't solve the world's problems tonight," Betty said, "Ready to eat?"

Santo glanced at Matt over the menu, lifting his eyebrows in question.

Matt returned his gaze and nodded. He had raised his concern about Dr. Hemlick and Santo had, after a reprimand of sorts, tried to put his mind at ease. Instead, Santo had unknowingly succeeded in making Matt more determined than ever to keep his eyes and ears open.

CHAPTER 24

"Hey," Matt called when Bo appeared at his office door. "I'm reading letters from friends and family in the 'mail call' section of the *Flying Osprey*. Made me think. You hear from home?"

"Mama 'n them got their own lives I guess," Bo said, "and Pensacola is down the road a piece."

Bo rarely spoke of his family. When he did make an occasional quick comment, bitterness laced his words. Matt hadn't probed for further information and Bo never elaborated.

"No calls or letters?"

"Mama's not much of a letter writer, but she might visit soon. Maybe next weekend, or for the big July Fourth thing."

"Really? Can I meet her?"

"I guess, if she shows."

"I'll be on campus both weekends."

"Okay, I'll tell her, but don't git your hopes up. Oh, and she works all week, usually sleeps in on weekends. If she comes, I reckon she won't git here till after lunch."

Matt made it clear to Bo that any weekend, any time, would work for him, but he still jumped to attention when the gym doors swung wide the following Saturday and a thin woman approached.

An unexpected sight on campus, she wore her light brown hair tightly pinched back with silver clips and wore a large dose of makeup on her narrow face.

He recognized the determined wide eyes above the visible dark rings and noted the familiar tightened square jaw. She extended a rough, reddened hand, one that had seen more than its share of hard work. He knew her identity before she spoke.

"Hi there," she said with a twang. "Harry's mama. Coach Grazi?"

Matt toweled the sweat from his face and arms and returned her vise-like handshake.

This is one tough lady.

"Nice meeting you. Let's move to my office," he suggested, as he motioned down the corridor.

"I saw Harry," she stated. "He tells me you're fair, even though you push him real hard. He likes you."

"Bo, I mean Harry, has made incredible progress," Matt said after they had settled into the two office chairs. "He seems to be able to do anything he puts his mind to, and he wants to graduate from high school. He wants you to be proud of him."

"You heard him say that?"

"Not in so many words, but . . ."

"Thought not." She turned her head and took in the sparse surroundings.

"I'm glad you visited today. I'm sure it means a lot to Harry, too."

She lowered her head, "Not quite."

"What's not quite?"

"Let's just say, I've not been there for Harry as much as I should. But it ain't really none of your business, Coach."

Taken aback by her bluntness, Matt didn't know what to say. "I want to learn more about your boy, Mrs. Beauregard."

"He can tell you whatever you need to know."

Matt didn't have time to respond before she continued. "Well, lookie here, time is slipping away. I came by to thank you for being a decent coach and a friend to Harry. So thank you." She stood.

"Wait, I . . ."

"Good-bye now," she said as she pushed her hand toward him a second time. She turned to leave. "You have a nice day."

This was a critical meeting for Matt and he wanted more than a handshake. He needed time with this woman. Much more time.

"Stay, please, Harry is . . ."

"Sorry, next time."

"Are you coming back for the Fourth of July activities?" Then in a lowered voice, he added. "It's important for parents to be there . . . if they can."

"Don't know," she replied as she waved her hand over her head and headed down the hallway.

"Try to make it," Matt yelled after her. "For Bo."

She waved again without looking back. Matt wanted to tackle her before she disappeared. How could he stop her? He couldn't.

Her actions puzzled Matt, but at the same time, they explained why he had a hard time reading Bo. In some ways, he and his mama were alike.

Absorbed in his thoughts about the curtailed visit, Matt locked the office and made his way toward the dining hall.

"Grazi!" Santo called out to him, sprinting to catch up. He spoke first, not allowing Matt a word about the meeting with Bo's mom.

"Guess what? The Country Club has offered to sponsor the upcoming swim team. You select the swimmers yet?"

After spending sessions at the campus pool, Matt had confirmed what he already knew. His aquatic sports knowledge was much less than average. "I'm working on it, but you should have someone who knows more about a swim team than I do."

"You can swim, right?"

"Sure but . . ."

"That's good enough. You're the only one we got."

"I can do the strokes, but I have no clue how to teach them, or their associated turns, for that matter. And God forbid, you put me on a diving board."

"You have to do this, Matt. I've been bragging about you and our boys."

Matt heaved a deep sigh. Santo responded with a wave of the hand as he turned to walk away. "Knew I could count on you."

One step forward, two steps back.

***

Days later Matt sat across the table from a lightly tanned Betty. He couldn't take his eyes off her royal blue dress and low scooped neckline. Their reservation allowed them to sit in one of the smallest private dining rooms at *The Silver Slipper* restaurant in Tallahassee. The establishment had a license to sell beer and wine, allowing patrons who desired stronger drinks to bring in their own bottles hidden in a brown paper bag. Smoke-tinged air, dark pine paneling, and wallpapered borders contributed to the ambiance.

He pulled out the bottle of Southern bourbon and ordered a mixer for two highballs. The waitress laid the ice bucket, ceramic plates, and menus on the checkered tablecloth. She slid the louvered doors closed behind her.

"This place is sultry," said Betty, as she lowered a shoulder toward Matt, giving him a quick wink. "Like we're back in the days of prohibition."

"Governors and legislators dine here whenever they're in session," said Matt, as he inflated his chest like a member of the privileged elite. "U.S. presidents and movie stars have been known to wander in, too. The best Tallahassee has to offer."

In a toast, he lifted his crystal tumbler and clinked it with Betty's. Her smile widened and she reached across the table to squeeze his hand. After consuming a perfectly grilled steak from the finest local farm, they ordered cheesecake and coffee.

Matt lapsed into silence. He didn't want to think about the school, but couldn't help himself. He was unaware of how long he had disappeared until Betty broke the spell.

"What's bothering you?"

"Nothing."

"Can I help with nothing?"

"Nah."

"You're sure?"

"I met Bo's mom."

"And?"

"And that's the nothing. It was over before it started."

Matt described his frustration with the brief encounter. "No end to the questions I wanted to ask her. She wasn't interested."

"Sounds like a mama and teenage son problem."

"Yeah."

"But she came to visit," Betty reminded him.

"That's something, I guess."

"It really is, Matt. How many other parents have you met?"

Betty was right. He had conversed with only two other parents at the home baseball games.

"I live down this road," Betty said when they returned to Colby Hill. "Left at the next stop sign."

Seated next to him, she triggered a familiar physical sensation. Matt downshifted and then stopped in front of a Victorian-style home. Betty pointed out her living area on the top floor. The intensity of the stars' brightness complemented the half-moon peeking between the pillars of high reaching pines.

He leaned over and cupped Betty's chin in his hand. Then his lips brushed hers.

"Time to come up and see the place?" she asked. The whispered question he longed to hear prompted his heart rate to shift into second gear.

"You know I want to," he said softly. "But Betty, sometimes I don't know how I feel about things anymore. I want to be honest about that. I don't know if we should start a real relationship or if . . ."

Betty didn't let him finish. She smiled as she leaned over to touch his lips with her gentle fingers. Matt never enjoyed being told to shut up as he did now.

He quivered when her hot fingertips slid across his mouth, and he closed his eyes as her arms wrapped around him. Warmness moved throughout his body, setting in motion a craving he had not experienced in too long a time.

"How often is it clear what step to take next?" she whispered. "There's no time line with us. Let's take it as it comes."

She led him, step by step, upward. Their lips met, and ecstasy followed. They made love until satisfied and then leaned back, wrapped in each other's bodies. Betty butted her head against his chest, letting her hair rub his skin. Matt enjoyed the aroma of honeysuckle shampoo as he returned the push by squeezing her tighter.

"Betty?"

"Yeah?"

"You said something last time we met."

"Which was?"

"Me concentrating on the boys, both in class and on the teams. I've been reminded of that quite a bit lately."

"That's a good thing, right?"

"Yeah, but sometimes things happen on campus where . . . As you said, there aren't enough hours in the day."

"Go with your gut." Betty pushed a pillow behind her and pulled his face close to hers. "That cliché doesn't help much, does it?"

"Yeah, actually coming from you, it does."

She smiled. "And Matt, if you figure out how to do it with the boys, you might just figure it out with me, too."

CHAPTER 25

Later that week, the skies turned dark and heavy raindrops pelted the ground during a full-pad practice. The boys raised their heads and arms toward the sky, welcoming the cool, stinging wetness. Matt and Tom took advantage of the traditional Florida downpour to coach the boys on how to play under such conditions. Rarely did officials cancel a game because of inclement weather.

The boys slipped and slid on the wet grass and muddy field. "Pack everything in tight!" Matt yelled. The tight formation run game was what an opponent expected.

"Now that you know how to pack it tight, open up! If you learn how to go forward with an open attacking offense during slop like this, we could surprise any team we come across.

"The key to this play is comfort in handing the ball off in the rain, and running on a sloppy field." Matt gave Bell a quick cadence and watched him snap the ball without slipping.

"Again," Matt shouted. "Again."

Practice over, Bo and the wearied boys returned to the gym and pulled off their soaked, grimy uniforms. A thin swathe of water spread across the floor as they hung their gear on the hooks and locker doors.

"Drape your uniforms on the benches to dry," Matt ordered. "Take your leather shoes back to your cottage, and dry them with any towel you can find. Your cottage father has the polish you'll need to keep them from dry rotting."

The boys hopped to the commands. Exhausted, they completed their tasks, slinging their soaked shoes, tied together by their shoe-strings, over their shoulders. Sliding wherever they touched the wet tile, they inched their way out the door.

***

The following morning, administration called Matt, requesting his presence at a last-minute meeting.

"Any idea what's going on," Matt asked Tom as he peeked into his cohort's office.

"Nope, nothing happening that I know of."

"Did you get a call?"

"Nope."

"Budget problems?"

"Maybe."

Mary Jo directed Matt toward Dr. Strickland's office. Taking a moment to tuck in his shirt a little tighter, he knocked.

"Come in!" boomed a voice from the other side.

Matt glanced at the guidance department head and a counselor sitting to one side of the director's desk. Each held a legal pad or folder on his lap. Matt recognized the counselor as the one who had challenged him months ago when he had requested the file on Bo.

Dr. Hemlick sat on the opposite side of the room.

What kind of meeting is this? Where's Santo?

"Have a seat, Matt," Dr. Strickland said, pointing to the empty seat that faced his desk in the middle of the room.

Four pairs of eyes followed Matt as he stepped halfway into the room and sat down.

"All right, let's get started," Dr. Strickland said, addressing the group. "I received your request to discuss concerns with Coach Grazi."

This meeting is about me?

"You mind answering a couple questions for us, Coach?"

Matt's body tightened. "What kind of questions, Dr. Strickland?"

The director deferred the question to the guidance team by pointing his finger toward the department head, who then stood.

"Thank you. We want to discuss what we consider 'inappropriate behavior.'"

"What?" Matt's gaping jaw revealed his disbelief.

The department head raised a notepad and shook it at Matt. "It is reported our new coach assumes the authority to run this place like a country club. His idea of coaching is enjoying movies together with the inmates and serving coffee and cake after it's over."

"Oh, come on!"

Without acknowledging Matt's lament, the guidance department head continued in a matter-of-fact manner. "For those of us who enforce CHB rules, this is a problem. Our jobs are difficult enough without the inmates pressing us to serve doughnuts and beverages. When we report an inmate for bad behavior or other infraction, they lament that Coach Grazi doesn't operate that way. We come off as the bad guys because we follow procedures while he comes off the hero because he chooses to ignore the rules."

"Matt?" Strickland asked.

"Okay, okay. I plead guilty to bending the rules a bit to reward good behavior. I thought it would give the boys an incentive to participate, and it seems to be doing that."

"For you, maybe," the counselor said under his breath. A hard glint became visible in his eyes.

"This can be further resolved after hours. Next item?"

Dr. Hemlick took a deep breath and rose to speak. "I have more serious concerns," he said as he enunciated each word.

"Go ahead, Doctor."

"What I want to know," he said, facing Matt head on, "is why you're better qualified than I to determine the course of medical treatment."

"I have never . . ."

Dr. Hemlick shook his head at Matt and held up his palm to silence him.

Matt looked down at the floor for only a second before straightening his posture and returning Hemlick's stare.

"Your unprofessional opinions have interfered with the boys' treatment plans," Hemlick said, "not to mention distracting them from their educational objectives. Is it your long experience as a football hero or your desire to make a name for yourself that contributes to your superiority?"

"Just a damn minute," Matt yelled, now standing.

"Calm down!" Dr. Strickland warned. "You'll have your turn."

"Damn it. It is my turn!"

Dr. Strickland glared at Matt before asking the good doctor if he had anything else to add. Doctor Hemlick cleared his throat and used the opportunity to cite research procedures and medical protocols.

Matt struggled to hold his tongue.

"I think you've enlightened us, Dr. Hemlick. Coach?"

"All that sounds real good," Matt said. "But here's the thing. I made multiple inquiries about our 'soup doctor' here, and asked questions regarding his procedures, his concoctions, and what they were doing to my players." A glance toward Hemlick showed the doctor's face turning red. "I have never received satisfactory answers."

"You son of a . . ."

"Should I apologize for . . ."

"You have no right . . ."

"Stop it!" Strickland yelled as he stood behind his desk. The room went quiet.

"Dr. Hemlick, can you clarify why Coach Grazi's concerns have not been addressed?"

"You are informed," Dr. Hemlick said, turning to Matt, "when a student becomes part of our medical program. You received recommended behavior modifications in writing, including procedures for you and the inmate. You have no need to know any details about treatment protocols. They are private."

"Private to who? The boys don't seem to know what the hell is going on. Do the parents know 'the details'?" Matt took a breath. "Dr. Strickland? Doesn't the faculty need to know what medications are given and why?"

Dr. Strickland took a moment, appearing to consider both positions.

"Matt, your intentions seem honorable, but Doctor Hemlick is correct. You are not privileged to access inmate medical records during treatment." Matt's shoulders fell.

Dr. Hemlick's look of satisfaction spread across his canary filled, cat-like face.

"Doctor," Dr. Strickland said, "perhaps you could provide the staff with more information about your work and the type of treatments in progress at the next faculty meeting. A presentation would help us all understand your important work."

The glimmer of satisfaction had almost disappeared on Dr.

Hemlick's face when a voice shouted from across the room.

"This coach puts our boys in danger!" All heads turned toward the counselor.

"He makes inmates practice in a lightning storm, and he runs a sloppy operation down at the gym. No one seems responsible for the dirty locker area, the germ-infested showers or the . . ."

"Stop!" Matt raised his hand and waited to be recognized. "I want to assure all of you," he stated in a slow determined manner, "that no lightning occurred when the boys practiced yesterday. Before practice, yes, but not during. And as far as the locker area, the gym, lockers, and showers are spic and span. The crew down there takes extra pride in keeping it that way."

"Oh, right," the staffer responded. With a flick of the wrist, he produced Polaroid pictures of the locker room after practice in yesterday's rainstorm. "These boys have no regard for state property."

Everyone stared at the photos of muddied evidence.

"Matt, are you refuting these pictures?" Strickland asked.

"Not at all. Can we continue this meeting in the gym?"

"Is that necessary?"

"It would help."

"Okay, by all of you?" Strickland questioned.

"I don't have time to . . ." Dr. Hemlick began.

"Let's make time for this, shall we?"

"Gentlemen, come with me." Matt turned, his long legs taking brisk strides, the grumbling faculty scrambling to keep up.

The gym doors slammed behind the group and they filed into the locker room. Pointing to the draped uniforms and still damp equipment, Matt accounted for yesterday's activities.

"Do I need to further explain the proper way to dry equipment and uniforms, how to protect shoes?" Sheepish faces filled the room.

"We have seen enough," said Dr. Strickland. "Matt, anything else?"

Matt weighed the comfort of ending this confrontation, or saying what he needed to say, but might regret, later.

"Yeah, there's something else." The guidance counselor looked at his watch. The others focused on Matt.

"I've experienced resistance to everything I've tried to do here, and I can't figure out why. I work with these boys the best way I know, to put together the most successful football team possible. I'm not perfect, neither are these boys, neither are you."

Matt took a breath and slowed down.

"I'm making progress. I may rub people the wrong way, and I may be bending rules, but I haven't snapped any. Things are going in the right direction."

Matt turned toward Dr. Strickland. "Haven't you seen a decrease in the number of Grubs in the inmate population? The team decided to do what it took to move up from Grub status. They encourage the other boys to do the same. I didn't decide that. They did.

"Practice is seven days a week because they ask for more time in the field. These facts mean more than petty procedures." Matt looked at the faces around him, hoping for a sign they understood. Dr. Hemlick's look of disdain said it all.

"And the number of runaways? Dr. Strickland?"

"None in the last six weeks," the director confirmed. Matt silently thanked Bo and his team for their initiative. He fought to keep control. *Slow down.*

"A boy has a reason to run. A boy needs a reason to stay. So do I dig for anything I can find to reward these boys when they make the right decisions? Do I question any procedure that appears to hurt the boys? You bet I do."

"Look, I don't claim to understand the politics of this place, and maybe I've stepped on a few toes, but the boys are behaving better and are eagerly participating. That's worth a lot. So decide what you're going to do about these so-called 'issues.' Determine if you want me to go or stay. But know that *if* I stay, I need to coach this football team and run gym classes my way. It's the only way that works."

Matt turned to Dr. Strickland. "May I be excused?" The director nodded.

The inquisition over, Matt moved down the hallway toward his office. He listened to the mumbling behind him as the tribunal exited the gym. He sensed a satisfaction in saying things that had long been on his mind, but he grappled with despair in learning he had more enemies than he had realized.

Matt pondered the kangaroo court until his phone's ring broke into his thoughts.

"Sorry I wasn't at this morning's inquest," Santo said. "Dr. Strickland chose to hold the meeting despite my scheduled appointment off campus."

"Wondered why you weren't there."

"Heard you gave quite a performance."

"If I had told them exactly what I thought, bet we wouldn't be having this conversation. Probably fired on the spot. I tried hard to keep myself from exploding, held my tongue when I thought about the boys."

"*You* held your tongue?"

Tension released a notch from Matt's shoulders and a partial grin appeared.

"Sorry. Hope I didn't embarrass you or put you in any compromising position."

"I'm fine. Sorry I wasn't there. The guidance team may not like your playbook, but Dr. Strickland and I like what we see. You may be a pain in the ass sometimes, but you're getting results."

"So I'm not fired?"

"Actually, I understand you threatened to quit."

"Yeah, I guess I did."

"Your mouth gets you into trouble, Matt, but I believe you have the boy's best interests at heart."

After a moment, Matt spoke. "If you're on my side, kemosabe, it'll take more than an ambush for me to leave."

CHAPTER 26

The football prospects held their heads high whenever they strutted in their ironed shirts and polished brogans. They wouldn't practice again until the end of July, so Matt gathered the group together.

"Each of you has his own reasons to be here," Matt said to the crowd-packed gym, "but for the most part, I suspect you had trouble following rules, either in your family or your hometown. Now you're stuck with the even stricter rules of CHB."

A soft murmur of groans and the shuffle of feet filled the air, tapering off until quietness gave Matt his cue to continue.

"When you signed up for football, you signed up to follow its rules. And yet, I still see anger and frustration when I penalize a player for breaking one. Why is that?"

Matt tossed the football into the air above his head and caught it. The ball crossed from his left hand to his right and back again. Every eye focused, every ear cocked to listen.

"This coming football season gives you the chance to prove that you're capable of toeing the line. Continue improving your physical fitness every day. But with that being said, remember your physical condition is just one ingredient for success. Lifting weights and running laps are necessary but real strength comes from within."

"I think I got it, Coach." Matt looked toward Bo.

"It's not only what's here," Bo said slapping his arms and legs, "It's here," he said, pounding his chest, "inside. And it's what's up here too," he added pointing with his index finger toward his head. "Isn't that right, Coach?"

"You've got it. Use your head, for decision control, patience. Listen to your heart for dependability, concern.

"Don't let your teammate down. Your fellow players deserve better. Play for the team, not for yourself. That's what wins a game.

"Chances are good the boy beside you won't be there at the end of the season. Some will quit when they don't hit the mark because that's what's been easier in the past. Don't let that happen. Don't be a quitter. Don't be one of them."

Matt turned his head toward one player after another. "Don't be a quitter," he repeated until he had scanned the eyes of every boy.

An invisible force rose like steam.

"Not me, Coach," a boy said. Like a bull, he snorted air through his nose and mouth, as if he was about to fight his toughest battle ever.

"I'm gonna be here," another boy grunted.

"I ain't leaving," voiced a boy from the back. Simultaneous bursts of commitment rushed from the boys' mouths, accompanied by clenched fists and forceful arm movements.

"Together!" Matt yelled. The boys rushed forward. Hands and arms reached to the center of a newly formed circle, like spokes in a wheel.

"Together!" the boys returned the call.

The teens filed past Matt, each receiving a shake of a hand and giving back a smile.

"That was great, Coach," Bo said to Matt on their way down the gym hallway.

Matt nodded to him, coming around the desk and leaning against it, facing him. "I'm feeling it too."

"We're hyped!" Bo yelled. He jumped up and then bounced around the room as he would in the boxing ring, throwing one punch after another.

"You've gotten into great shape, Bo. Can you come back down to earth for a minute? I'm curious about something."

"Like what?"

"Like you helping the younger boys with Sunday school."

Bo stopped his one-sided boxing match and met Matt's gaze.

"Mr. Rourk asked me."

"You didn't have to say yes."

"I wanted to say yes."

"I see."

"Shit. I better not find out who puked on me."

"It's not a secret, Bo. And it's a good thing, but . . ."

"But?"

"But it won't interfere with your football when practice starts back up, will it? Sure you'll be able to play, crew, keep fit, and study? It sounds like too much."

"Doesn't git in the way of anything, Coach. It's fun. Those kids pump me up, kinda like you do, only *I'm* the coach."

"Okay, *Coach*, as long as you think you can manage it. And Bo, one more thing."

"What's that?"

"As long as you've taken this on, could you start putting in a good word for us on Sunday, especially when we hit that first game with Bakerton?"

Bo gave him a smile and a thumbs up on his way out the door.

***

Matt and Tom spent time with the swim team hopefuls, continuing to scout out new recruits. One new inmate caught Matt's attention when locker room chatter included a rumor that he was a top-ranked, all-around, Junior Olympic diving champion in Florida. The Rookie had a real liking for driving Thunderbirds. Problem was, they weren't his, and he wasn't old enough to drive them.

Matt had more than socialization on his mind when he talked to the high school athlete. "I understand you're a decent diver, Dodd."

"That's what they claim. What I do, I tend to do well."

Bo leaned against the doorway and appeared to be listening. He let out a muffled, "You didn't steal cars very well." Both Matt and the young diver turned at the sound of his voice.

"Yeah, at least I didn't have a gun with me, like somebody else around here," the new boy responded.

A gun?

"Bo," Matt interrupted, "don't you have something else to do?"

"Yeah, yeah, I'm going, but you better watch this guy, Coach. He thinks he knows it all."

Matt remembered early spring when Tom had made a similar comment about Bo. He held his tongue until Bo pushed off the side of the doorway, then turned his attention back to the new boy.

"Want to compete for the swim team?"

"Why not? Since I have to be here, might as well do somethin' I like."

"Good. The July Fourth swimming events determine who we select."

"Works for me."

"And son, one more question," Matt said. "Ever play football?"

CHAPTER 27

On the morning of July Fourth, the bugle's sound of *Reveille* bounced across the campus air and mingled with the aroma of slow-cooking pork and beef. Matt inhaled the tangy odor as he passed the covered, steaming ground pits.

He waved to O'Hurley's masonry and carpentry crews, as they added the final touches to the newly constructed outdoor tables and barbecue pits. Routine school and crew activities canceled, the boys buzzed over their holiday assignments, preparing for their families and friends.

Matt sauntered into the dining hall and pushed his tray through the student line. He continued the practice of receiving food from the student side, despite the kitchen supervisor's assurance that he had long ago eliminated toenail revenge.

Carrying his food tray to the staff dining section, he sat behind a divider next to the student area and dug into his smoked sausage and grits. The clink of silverware, amid the sound of boys conversing between slurps and bites of breakfast, came through the partition.

He sopped up the last of a runny egg when he heard the hard shuffle of approaching footsteps on the other side. The metal crash of a tray slamming against a table broke the hum of the room.

Coffee splashed from Matt's cup as he jerked in response.

"What da hell is your problem, asshole?"

He stood, considering whether to move toward the sound, but stayed put. Matt recognized the irritation in Bo's familiar garbled voice.

"Jest got word I'm to direct visitors into the fuckin' parking lot!" Mulany bellowed.

"So what?" Bo asked.

"Me, run traffic? I should be workin' with Coach Faber! What about you? Why aren't you helpin'?"

Matt pictured the back of Bo's wrist wiping his lips.

"'Cause I haven't been told to," Bo said in a now controlled voice. "Got any other questions? Ask Coach."

"Oh, you're not a parkin' boy," Mulany declared. "Cause I reckon you're Coach Grazi's favorite!"

The squeal of a chair against the floor came in a blink. "Enough!" Bo demanded.

A hush settled over the dining room. Still, no staff member moved to settle the argument. Matt stared at his half-empty cup of coffee.

Thank God, Andrews isn't on duty.

A full minute passed before conversations resumed. He had witnessed Bo and Mulany sparring in the past, but not with this animosity. Resentment was an ugly animal. Matt pursed his lips and shook his head, realizing the effect of his favoritism.

He scrapped his tray, placed it in the return alcove, and maneuvered around the partition to the boys' side.

"Morning," he said.

Jolted by his sudden appearance, Bo covered his mouth, initiating a bogus cough which appeared to give him time to gather his thoughts. Mulany looked first at Matt, then at Bo for possible guidance.

"Great food," Matt said. "Things okay here?"

"Oh, sure. We was just talking about ya," Bo stammered. "I mean, you bein' a great coach and all."

"Is that right Mulany?" Matt asked with a straight face.

"Yes, sir."

"Assignments start in twelve minutes," Matt said, looking at his watch. He focused from one boy to the other. "Expect you on time."

"Yes, Coach!" Mulany replied. "Sure, Coach," Bo said at the same time. They scrambled to the tray return line.

Matt dropped Mulany off at the parking lot and told Bo he would meet him at the pool. The sight of boys reuniting with moms and dads, relatives, and friends caused Matt to squint back memories of home. The campus swelled with hugs, kisses, and tears. A few youngsters ran barefoot, normally an antic resulting in disciplinary action.

"Glad you're early," Tom said, greeting Matt. "Have everything? The individual and cottage trophies ready to take to admin?"

"Ready?"

"Then let's load 'em up. My car's out back. I'll grab the final lists of boys competing in each event." Separate pages existed for the pony, junior, intermediate, and senior divisions.

Matt described the showdown at breakfast. He asked Tom if he thought it best to confront the boys or let it go.

"What have you done about it?"

"Stepped back to see if they can work things out."

"Check. Sounds like a plan to me. I'm relieving Mulany after the trophy drop-off. Bringing him over to the race area. I'll fill you in if any more comes of it."

***

During the morning series of track and field events, Matt gave an extra pat on the back to any boy not getting a personal greeting from home. His chest filled with pride when Tom announced that Bo had won the senior hundred-yard dash.

"What a morning, Tom," Matt exclaimed. "Can't believe the races went off without a hitch."

"Been doing this a few years. Swimming relays should go the same."

"I'm nervous. Never overseen a swimming event before."

"Follow the procedures we put together, and you'll do fine. The gym crew is on crowd control, and I'll be working the opposite side."

Lunch refreshed everyone, and the crowd moved to the pool. Similar to the morning's activities, the audience clapped rigorously after every medley and relay event.

As Matt threw a towel to one of the young swimmers, Andrews pushed toward the sidelines. The overbearing man was whispering to a staff member beside him, all the time looking at Matt.

Matt rubbed his fingers against his palms. His discomfort heightened until the crowd's cheering and whistling returned him to the moment.

He awarded points to the first three boys finishing in each division.

The points counted toward a boy's own certificate and added to the total score of his cottage.

"It's amazing how proud the boys are in the winning cottages," Tom said. "They can't wait to display their trophies."

"Ah, that sense of pride."

"Yeah, works most of the time, but nothing's ever a home run with all of them."

"Except the barbecue. I hear from the boys it's a hit one hundred percent of the time."

The final diving exhibition, led by the car-stealing rookie, was an unexpected display of talent, popular with inmates and guests alike.

"That was really neat," Bo said, as he leaned toward Matt. "Maybe I'll learn to work with this new guy after all."

"Working together is a definite asset Bo, but a leader has to strive for something even higher."

"Like what?"

"Like finding something about a person that sets him apart, his talents or interests. Then using that information to build up confidence."

Bo thought for a moment. "Boxing. You found out about my boxing." Matt nodded.

"There's a harder part, playing down a player's shortcomings."

"Like I should forget about this South Florida big shot thinkin' he's better than the rest of us, and give him a hand for being a neat diver?"

"Yeah, like that. Admire anyone who excels," Matt said, "in any sport."

"Even boxing?"

"Especially boxing."

The evening ceremonies included a motivational speech by one of the local judges and the presentation of the American Legion awards to the outstanding student. Matt and Tom presented the athletic certificates and trophies. After picking the last of the barbecue from his teeth, Matt bade his farewells and headed for his room.

As he rounded the bleachers, Andrews appeared in front of him. The massive man shifted his oncoming gait to move directly into Matt's path. Matt slowed, but Andrews picked up his pace, crossed his arms in front of his chest, and attempted a hard body bump. Matt sidestepped in time to catch only a slight push, but the massive man continued to lean toward him.

"Sorry, Coach. Didn't see ya."

Matt stepped back from the man. "What the hell do you want?"

Andrews ignored the question. "Amazing how the boys who were put in their place did just fine today," he said.

"Put in their place?"

"See? A little whipping goes a long way in getting them back on the right track," the marine's voice hissed, drooling with satisfaction. "Part of the job, thank you."

Matt tightened his arms and clenched his fingers, glaring at Andrews. He tried to pass the man again. Andrews grabbed his shoulder to pull him back. Matt, in response, raised his fist.

"Eh, eh, eh," Andrews said as he stepped back. "Calm down, buddy boy. Don't get yourself in trouble again."

Matt's face flushed red, and with fists tight, he watched Andrews turn his back, chuckling as he shrugged off.

***

Following the picnic, interest in joining the swim team increased. Matt recruited the talented new diver to assist him and heard from inmates with acrobatic and gymnastic skills.

Bo seemed to take a renewed interest as he approached the appointed swimming assistant during an afternoon session. Matt kept on task with the breaststroke relays, at the same time repositioning himself to hear the boys' conversation.

"You're somethin' else," Bo said to Dodd. "I never was much good at diving."

"Wanna get better?" Dodd asked. "Might be able to help with that."

Bo nodded and the two of them headed toward the end of the pool. Matt pressed his lips together, wishing he could follow close enough to hear what came next.

Matt regrouped after the tiring afternoon swim session by taking a quick nap. He greeted Betty that evening at The Country Club for an Osprey swim team fund-raiser. Surprise showed on his face when dozens of club members walked through the door.

"Gosh, Betty, the people of this town are sure supportive of the boys."

"Lots of folks care about these kids," Betty said. "A few ladies from the Women's Garden Club have approached me about raisin' money from the community for things like shirts, books, belts, and pen and pencil sets. They're already in the process of collectin' things for their Christmas project."

"Santo told me about that."

"And see those two men over there?" Betty asked. She pointed to the far table. "They're from the Kiwanis Club. They collected new board games for each of the boys' cottages. They have a network of good ol' boys set up throughout the state to employ boys after they're released."

"Is that right? Do the boys take advantage of that?"

Betty related that she didn't know the actual statistics, but the program had been in effect for years. "The club posts communication from boys who succeed in the program. Comes in fairly regularly."

"I hear most boys talk about returning to their old group of friends as soon as they return, not about job opportunities."

"At this age, friends are a priority. That's the reality."

"Peer pressure can be good or bad," Matt said, "but at CHB and on the street, it's bad."

"I imagine pressure from a coach can be good or bad too," Betty said as she cocked her head and raised her eyebrows in question.

"Oh, yeah, it can be tricky. When I don't pressure on a player, he's tempted to hang on to the old ways of his buddies or not give his all to the team. On the other hand, when I crack the whip . . . ," he caught the connotation and jerked his head toward Betty in time to see her frown.

"I mean, when I demand more than a boy can give, he can become frustrated and start giving me problems, or even worse, quit."

"A real balancing act, huh?"

"Like most things, I'm finding out."

"Who follows up these boys when they leave CHB, Matt?"

"A social worker I imagine, but I really don't know."

"I wonder if any of the boys return to CHB," Betty continued to probe.

"Now that's a question I can answer. Boys definitely return. In fact, Bo's a repeat offender."

"Bo's been to CHB before? You mean . . . ?" Betty began, her mood appearing to dampen. "All the effort that . . . Never mind."

"What is it?"

"Nothin'," she said, turning away from him, toward the table. Without raising her eyes, she collected the completed index cards for both donations and volunteer positions.

"Here's the donation list. I need a break." She disappeared into the crowd.

CHAPTER 28

After closing the gym door on the bright swath of July sunlight, Matt strolled into his office where Tom greeted him. "Nice to have a day back in the eighties," he said.

Together they walked down the hallway to the gym where the class assembled.

"Listen up, guys," Matt instructed. Today we start with laps and move onto practice shots. You know the routine. Ready?"

"Ready!" voices rose from the group.

"Go, Ospreys!" cried another.

Matt wished he could bottle enthusiasm like this. He always warmed to outbursts that confirmed he wasn't wasting his, or their, time. After laps and hoop shots were fully underway, he moved to the side of the gym to crack another window.

Before completing his task he heard a thud behind, and then a collective moan of "Oh, my God."

The intensified padded smacks of boys' running feet on the wooden floor filled the air, and Matt's head snapped toward the sound. He saw the boys' scrambling toward a common point in the gym, and he hastened to join them. An eerie silence followed. Something was wrong. Very wrong.

"Back away! Give him room to breathe!" Tom yelled.

"It's Danny Williams! He's hurt!" shouted another.

Breaking through the throng of boys, Matt saw the still body on the gym floor.

"Get the doctor! Somebody, find the doctor!" Matt managed to shout as he dropped to his knees. A Pilot took off running.

"He's not breathing!" came from somewhere in the crowd.

Matt held motionless as he focused downward on the young boy's face, the teen's wide, glazed eyes staring into nothingness. Scanning the boy's body and seeing no blood or wounds, Matt dropped to his knees.

"Wake up, son!" he yelled. Leaning closer to the boy's head, he gently slapped his cheeks. "Danny! Danny!" His restrained fists lightly pounded on the boy's chest. "Wake up, wake up."

Where is the doctor? Why is he taking so long?

Sweat dripped down Matt's face, drenched his armpits, and rolled down his chest. The sounds of whispering boys filtered into the surrounding air.

The gym doors crashed open, and Dr. Graves sprinted across the floor. "Step back!" he ordered. The hospital crew pushed the crowd apart and slid a stretcher closer.

Matt stumbled away from the boy. Dr. Graves moved in, listening with his stethoscope. The doctor's fingers moved the probe from the boy's chest to his neck, and back down to his chest again.

"Is he . . . ," someone whispered.

Matt flashed a look at Tom. *How can this be happening?*

Tom closed his eyes and swung his head left to right and then left to right again. A tear found its way down his cheek.

Dr. Graves rose from the floor and motioned for help to move the boy onto the stretcher. The medical crew lifted Williams' limp body like they would have lifted a newborn. The doctor sent an I'm-so-sorry look toward Matt.

He signaled boys to hold the gym doors open, and Matt started to follow. Dr. Graves' open hand flashed as a stoplight. The doctor shook his head.

"Nothing you can do," he mouthed. The medical team rushed toward the CHB hospital.

Matt stared at the closed doors. His frantic wave caught Tom's attention, followed by his shaking finger, pointing to the exit. He had to leave, now. Tom nodded his understanding.

The crystal sound of silence shattered as the gym doors slammed open. Matt broke into a sprint before the doors had closed behind him. He peered through a wall of liquid that pooled up close to overflow but refused to run down his cheeks.

He ran hard and fast toward his cottage where he snatched his keys and jumped into his car. Speeding down the road, he held the wheel tight with his white-knuckled fingers. He didn't know where he was going, nor did he care. He swerved onto a small dirt lane, threw the door open, and staggered out. Vomit rushed upward through his nose and mouth, splattering onto the dusty ground. He couldn't stop until the heaves became dry.

Williams is one of the good ones, he silently repeated to himself. *One of the good ones.*

Matt's tight chest and clenched stomach were sore. With bent knees nearly bringing his body to the ground, he wrapped his far-reaching arms around his chest and rocked. He had recently promoted Danny to a higher athletic crew position, and the boy consistently made good grades. He was to be discharged in a few short months. He had never been sick other than a few allergies.

He'll be okay. He's got to be okay.

He ran his long fingers through his dark hair and wiped the sour wetness from his face. He sat on the side of the lane for another twenty minutes, and then wobbled his way toward his car.

What happened?

He drove back to campus, returned to his office and confirmed what he already knew. The scribbled announcement of the boy's death sat on his desk.

Matt was sitting in a trance when Tom and Bo walked in and plopped down in front of him. Matt stared at the note on his desk while Tom and Bo exchanged glances. No one spoke. After moments, Tom broke the silence.

"Where did you go? Were you at the hospital?"

Matt sat there.

Bo tried. "Coach, it wasn't your fault."

Matt stared toward the boy, glazed eyes looking through him as if he weren't in the room. The *tick tock* of the wall clock was the only sound, becoming more deafening each second.

When he finally spoke, Matt's voice was raspy. "Tom, find out about the funeral arrangements so we can make sure flowers are sent from the team. I've talked with Santo. I've asked if we can hold a short memorial service tomorrow. Williams' family wants his body laid to rest in his hometown." Matt rose. "I'll read the announcement in the last class and call for a quiet study hall."

Matt passed on the evening meal and jogged the campus. Back in his cottage, distorted visions of the day's events played havoc with his body's need to rest. Hours after nightfall had laid down its heavy cloak, he fell into a restless sleep.

Hoo, hoo, too-HOO; hoo, hoo, too-HOO, ooo sounded through his dreams, and within minutes, the blurred image of an owl perched high above him appeared. The raptor clenched a squirming rodent in its beak until the talons braced the struggling, furred creature against the branch, and the meal began.

Matt woke with a start and pushed his legs over the side of the bed. His drenched T-shirt clung to his shivering chest. The surrounding room inched into full focus, and he remembered where he was.

He was angry, mad that such a thing could have happened to such a young boy. His body had failed him when he had needed it most. Both his knees and his stomach had collapsed. He stared into the shadowed space around him and asked himself, over and over again, if there was more he could have done.

How could he rise in a few hours and return to his classes? Lifting his hand to his forehead took every ounce of strength he could muster.

Everything looks the same, but nothing will be the same again.

He was awake, sitting in bed when the morning alarm went off before the bugle blew. He moved from the bed to the shower. Brushing his teeth wouldn't remove the bitterness in his mouth.

Matt and Tom gathered the boys together before each class and took turns saying a few words. Moments of silence followed.

CHB sent a red rose blanket to the boy's hometown for the funeral. "Passing of Boy at CHB Shock to School," reported the *Flying Osprey*. "A local sixteen-year-old student collapsed and died from an apparent heart attack Monday while attending a physical fitness class. The student had established an exceptional record since coming to the school and held the rank of Pilot. During spring football practice, he had made his position as defensive right end secure, and was popular with coaches and other players."

It went on to describe the scene in the gym, the attempts to save his life, and the deep sorrow and loss felt by every staff member and student alike.

What the paper failed to describe was the unspeakable ache, the throbbing in the heads of the coaches and every team member. It couldn't answer the inaudible questions asked over and over again nor could it lighten the grief that would weigh forever. The scene burned into their memories. They had lost one of their own.

***

A loneliness seized Matt's body and wouldn't let go. It was as if he existed apart from everyone and everything.

"It hit all of us hard," Tom said to him on their way back from the field.

"Should we somehow be making things safer for the boys?" Matt asked. "I still don't understand. Was he sick? He never looked sick to me."

After months of pushing the boys together, Williams' death began pulling them apart. Anger surfaced and boys pointed fingers at the staff and teachers for not saving their friend. As Matt made his way toward the gym for a class, he overheard words that cut him to the bone.

"It's the coaches' fault," said one boy. "One of 'em should 'a saved him."

"The doctor's the one who let him die," argued another.

Matt stopped his approach to the class and fell backward against the hallway wall. He squinted hard, bringing a tear to the surface, and brushed it away with his towel. He swallowed, swearing he would never speak of the incident again.

Time became the enemy, not moving fast enough to ease the pain, moving so fast everyone seemed to feel guilty if they put their grief aside to partake in school activities. Matt kept his mind and body busy. Sleep didn't come until total exhaustion took over.

Days turned into a week as Matt and the swim team tried in vain to be ready for their next meet. "The CHB Ospreys' swimming team added their scalp to the town's own Colby Hill Academy's list of victims," reported the Flying Osprey's newsletter. The boys hadn't been able to find what they needed to prevent their first loss, and it didn't seem to matter.

"I'm postponing the football practices and workouts that were to start next Monday," Matt announced to Tom.

"Why?"

"Can't do it. Doesn't seem right to think football without Danny."

"And what is right for the boys who are left behind, trying to find some kind of meaning in all this?"

"You think facing the hole in the team will help, Tom?"

"Will it help you?"

"I don't know. I just don't know."

***

"Listen up," Matt announced to his classes after the weekend. "Anybody who wants to resume preparation for the football season is welcome. We start tomorrow afternoon."

He tried to be enthusiastic when every boy appeared at the designated time. Boys fell in line to do exercises and go through assigned drills.

The cottages were close to empty on Saturdays and Sundays as July ended and August began. The boys worked out on the field and in the gym, dousing their sweaty bodies under the showers before cannon balling into the pool.

Keeping active helped on two fronts. Less opportunity for the boys to mourn eased the pain, and increased physical activity led to a better night's rest.

"Look at them, Tom," said Matt, pointing at the boys splashing about on their free time.

"I like them being kids," Tom replied.

Bo pulled himself up the ladder on the side of the pool and walked around the deck toward Matt.

"Is it okay if I bring my math over to the gym?"

"Yeah, sure," Matt said.

Bo's mouth widened into a smile. "I'm glad you're back, Coach."

Matt cocked his head toward Bo and then nodded. He wasn't back, and he knew it.

Later that day, he resurrected his notebook and scribbled a few notes. He met with Tom, Bo, Mulany, and the new diver to proceed with the selection of the football players.

"You're really good at football, Bo," said Dodd.

"You ever play?" Bo asked.

"Yeah, a little."

"Wanna get better? Might be able to help with that."

Matt looked at both boys and managed the first small crack of a real smile.

CHAPTER 29

August days became shorter, reminding everyone summer was in full force. Matt had one week to decide which boys made the team. He had selected most players, but five spots remained open, three on defense, two on offense. With such a large number of boys trying out, the task was difficult.

By the end of the week, forty-two boys earned the privilege of being members of the 1961 Colby Hill football team.

"In the past, I dreaded summer ending," Tom confessed to Matt. "I enjoyed the rest. It was a relief over too soon. But this year my wife says I'm driving her crazy with my constant talk about the upcoming season."

"Know what you mean, Tom. These boys are ready. We're ready."

"We'll soon find out if hard work pays off, won't we?"

"It's been a ride," Matt said, "for sure. Bo has come a long way. He's an integral part of the offense and . . . get this, he's moved up from eighth grade to ninth."

"Doesn't surprise me. Must admit, that boy has shown real leadership skills, on and off the field. A candidate for team captain?"

"Don't think so, Tom."

Bo made it clear to staff and inmates alike that he didn't want to be captain. His role as a leading crew member and an assistant coach was rewarding and earned him the admiration of the entire team. He preferred the responsibilities of working with players off the field, not during a game.

Within days the team elected two co-captains, Tony Castor, defensive captain, and David Bell, on the offense. Castor had the most football experience, while Bell had become more congenial and was widely accepted for his quarterback skills.

"The boys couldn't have picked a better captain, Castor," said Matt, "but I suspect you won't have much time to cut hair anymore."

"Got that right, Coach. The barber said he'd hire a new kid to help fill in, although I've been noticing you've sure eased up a bit on them short crew cuts."

Matt laughed.

The long-anticipated uniforms and gear arrived at the gym in mid-August as promised. The team watched with wide eyes as helmets, shoulder pads, spikes, footballs, and mouthpieces tumbled from their boxes.

Prior to the baseball season, Matt and Tom had fought for, but never received, jockstraps or protective cups. But for football, both coaches repeatedly insisted on the safeguard they offered. It became obvious which boys were seeing cups for the first time when a boy pulled one over his head, thinking it was a nose guard.

Gonzales pulled a set of bulky shoulder pads from a box.

"Hey, Gonzales," yelled a teammate, "flex those biceps in those pads, and you'll look like a Spanish Mighty Mouse!"

"Oh, I know that cartoon!" the boy said and started to sing the first line of the mouse's theme song with a Spanish accent. 'Here I come, to save ze day!'" He flexed his arm and curved his fisted hand toward his shoulder in the cartoon figure's bodybuilding pose. After a period of unrestrained laughter, the boys confirmed their assigned sizes and pulled their issued uniforms to their chests in admiration.

For the first time in years, the team practiced under real game conditions in brilliant white and dark green jerseys, trimmed in black and gold. From the sideline, Matt watched the boys perform together as a team, switching from offensive to defensive positions and back again.

The players followed his signals, grins crossing their faces whenever he motioned a thumbs up. They sought approval whenever they improved.

The boys showed determination to win by practicing long and hitting hard. Their bodies ached, sweat, and even bled together. Bo maneuvered his way into the middle of things, stopping the bickering and strengthening the sense of camaraderie.

Matt beamed each time a boy indicated he understood his directions. The boys' timing and strength had improved over the past month, and Matt logged comments and numbers about their speed, endurance, and body condition into his sweaty notebook.

The pressure was on. With each passing moment, Matt became more determined not to let the boys, or the school, down.

Matt pulled Tom aside as they finished up practice at the end of the day.

"These guys will run out of Bakerton's locker room looking damn good on the field, but the first impression really comes when they step off the bus."

"I'm aware of that."

"I don't want the boys to feel like a bunch of crooks and thieves when they arrive at an outside school."

"Matt, they are crooks and thieves."

"Oh, right. But still, how can we increase their sense of pride before they fight their first battle? If they step off the bus dressed in what now is their best clothes, I can imagine the taunts."

"There's no budget to address style. Be happy with what we got."

The comment from Tom triggered a brainstorm. Matt returned to his room and picked up the phone. Betty couldn't see him, but she sensed his pride when he described the final team member selection, the election of captains, and the comic uniform scene in the gym.

"Only one thing though, the boys' state clothing when they arrive at a competing school makes them stand out like the plague."

"Are they allowed to wear other clothes?"

"If they have them. But not many do. I could try to get permission to talk to the parents of the players, but for the most part, that goes against the rules. Money is scarce. New travel clothes like slacks, shirts, ties, and sports jackets are the answer, but just shirts and ties would help. Any ideas?"

"Hmm. Maybe. Let me run it by a few folks. Reckon we've raised funds for things like this before."

"Appreciate anything you could do."

"You could persuade folks better than I could," she whispered into the phone.

"Never. Wouldn't even ask. The people of Colby Hill have been more than kind to us already, and they support their own local high school too."

"Let me tap on their soft spot, and see if anything's left."

***

Local high schools were apprehensive about coming to Colby Hill. In fact, school officials had again voiced the opinion CHB shouldn't be taking part in the Panhandle League at all. The opposition to the football team's participation reinforced the need for the boys to dress appropriately and behave when on the road.

Within the week, a call came through to the gym. Between the boys' parents and Betty, they raised and spent the needed funds for travel clothes. In addition, the local general store rose to the challenge and donated a carry-on bag to each boy.

Blank stares replaced the routine gibber and horseplay as crisp white shirts, dark green sports jackets, and pressed khaki pants lifted up from underneath plastic bags. With open mouths, the boys watched satchels of belts and ties open before them.

"A special class today, guys," Matt announced. "The late Emily Post is going to be proud."

"Emily who?" asked Bell.

"The good manners lady, fool!" yelled a voice in the back.

"You gonna teach us manners, Coach?"

"Today you learn the intricacies of putting on a tie."

"Huh?"

"Drape that tie around your neck with the wide side on your right," Matt demonstrated the motion.

"No, your other right, Bo."

"Watch me. Extend the wide end about ten or twelve inches below the skinny end," Matt said as his fingers slid the tie in place. "Not even close, Bell. It will be down to your knees if you keep that up."

"Guys, pay attention! Cross the wide end of the tie over the narrow end and then continue underneath. The wide end *over* the tie, over the tie." He adjusted a tie for two more players.

"OK, everybody with me? Cross the wide end over the narrow part one more time, and . . . Did I say reverse direction? Did anybody hear me say, reverse direction? No."

"Coach, can we start over?" one of the boys asked.

"Of course we can," Matt sighed.

Thirty minutes later most of the boys were close. The ones who mastered the technique assisted the other boys.

"You're almost there, guys. Now center that dimple."

Bo jumped into the center of the room. "Come on, team, you heard him! Oh, and Coach, 'xactly where's our dimple again?"

That did it. The boys burst into laughter.

"Anything else, Coach?"

"Yeah. Tighten those knots." Even Matt laughed.

"Yes, sir!" they all repeated, one after the other.

Only a few more sessions and the boys would be looking sharp and feeling good on game day. Matt visualized the group all cleaned up, getting off the bus in coat and tie, carrying their gear low and their heads high. Classy.

***

As practice ended the following day, Matt saw a familiar figure making his way across the field.

"Bern?" Matt asked. The memory of Dr. Hemlick's rage flashed before him.

"Hi, Coach. Wanted to wish ya good luck at the first game with Bakerton."

Matt hardly recognized the boy. Once active, perhaps even hyper, he appeared sluggish, his face swollen. His massive, muscular shape was gone. A drooping gut protruded over his belt.

"Are you okay, son?" Matt inquired.

"Oh, I'm okay," he slurred. "Sometimes even *better* than okay." His quirky grin caused an acidic pool to form in the bottom of Matt's stomach.

"Are you staying out of trouble?"

"Oh, yeah, that I'm doing. I don't have any desire to slam any of my cronies anymore. Actually, I don't really care about anything. Cool, huh?"

He reminded Matt of a walking zombie.

"Dr. Hemlick still giving you the joy juice?" The lull in the conversation elicited no response. "Bern, did you hear me? Why don't you cut back on that crap and come back to the gym?"

"Too much trouble. I'll hang in there with the Doc until my release."

Matt's mind spun. "If you change your mind, we could always use you."

"Yeah, well, maybe. Anywhoo . . ." Bern's voice dropped off. "Good luck."

"I'll tell the boys you stopped by."

"Do that," Bern said, turning to leave. He shuffled back across the field.

A single burst of hoots sounded from far away and disappeared. The thrill of the team coming together faded, and sadness covered Matt like a shroud.

CHAPTER 30

September snuck its head in the door without asking permission from anyone. The first three games would take place on the road and at full strength, the team would travel with thirty members. October would roll around before the Osprey's faced an opponent on their home turf.

Inmates on the print crew ran to distribute extra copies of the Osprey newsletter. It boasted that since Coach Grazi had arrived, he initiated a new physical fitness program, organized a varsity swimming team, and created a football team that will make everyone proud.

The biweekly edition did its best to incite school spirit by reviewing Matt's history at FSU, making it clear he was no ordinary guy.

Ospreys Have Outstanding Young Coach

While in college, The Associated Press named Matt Grazi the 'back of the week' of the entire nation. Fraternities of the Nation named him to the second All-America team in his last year at FSU. If the honors he received are any reflection of his coaching talents, the 1961 CHB football team will be a real force. So, Go Ospreys!

Matt's brow knitted together in anger as he glared at the article.

Tom knocked and opened the door to Matt's office. "Wow, did you see the spread in the newsletter?"

"Not discussing it," Matt said.

"Okay, I . . ."

"Why the heck didn't they print something about the team? Not a word about how hard the team worked on this. They're the ones who deserve the credit, no matter what happens next."

"I understand."

"This is the time the boys need positive press, Tom! I sure as hell don't."

"May I speak, 'Cowboy Grazi'?"

"Sorry. I'm pissed."

"Geesh, you're really wound up tight about this, aren't you?"

"I'm tired of hearing about what a great guy I used to be. I want to be a great guy today, and that only happens after the team gets credit for being the great players they are."

"That will come, if they win."

"*When* they win," Matt corrected him. "When they win."

"Enough already. Can we move on to the strategy of the first game?"

Matt sighed and gave Tom a nod. The two coaches reviewed plans for the opening game against Bakerton, a small-town high school located northwest of Colby Hill in a place local folks called, "Alabamaland."

"Alabamaland?" Matt asked, looking at the map in front of them. "Can't find it."

"It's not a town, a region of Florida near the Alabama border. Here," Tom said sticking a map pin into the parchment.

"Looks like we have to travel several hours to find out how good, or bad the team plays."

A *tap-tap* on the office door caused both coaches to look up as Santo pushed his way in.

"Want to wish you guys luck Friday night."

"Thanks," Matt said. "Your timing's perfect."

Matt and Tom had brainstormed on how to keep the team occupied the day of the game, but needed Santo to buy in.

"About Friday, we have a couple hours before boarding the bus for Bakerton."

"So?"

"Tom and I don't want the boys doing anything to use the energy they'll need, but at the same time, it's inviting trouble to sit around the cottages or lay around the gym after classes end. We want to take the team off campus for a ride."

Santo's eyes widened.

"You know, dress them up and show them off around the country-side. We'd like to borrow the truck down at the laundry department, along with one or two of those flatbeds."

It seemed a simple request, but Santo didn't appear to share Matt's point of view.

"You're kidding, right? I can't let you take these inmates for a joy-ride! If just one thing happens, the state has my head."

"Wait, hear me out. I know the state is responsible for these boys, and as a state employee, *I'll* assume that responsibility. You're the one who told me we're capable of taking care of them on the road. What's the difference? They've gone the extra mile for football, for CHB. Don't they deserve a little reward?"

"Matt, you've brainstormed wild schemes before, and you've con-vinced me to change my mind on occasion, but you can't, in all honesty, believe this is a rational, well-thought-out plan. What are you going to do if one of them decides to run?"

"Why would they run? Once a kid has worked to become a team member, he has a connection. If a player was going to run, he would have bolted long before he put in the effort to stay."

"But this is handing these inmates an opportunity they've never had before. And there are other things to consider."

"Like?"

Santo threw his hands into the air. "There could be repercussions if any boy misbehaved or was hurt."

"The same as if they ran before, during, or after an away game?"

Matt played his role with patience, as Santo verbalized the reasons why the ride shouldn't happen. After his boss paused to take a breath, Matt straightened his stance and stepped closer.

"I'm supposed to be the worry wart," he said. "I know these boys now. It'll be okay." He spoke about their recent learning curve and ma-turity. He argued that this was the perfect time to loosen the leash.

With a deep sigh, Santo's shoulders dropped a notch. Victory was Matt's.

"Two conditions," Santo said, having the last word. "O'Hurley has to drive the truck, and you take extra staff with you . . . in case."

"Agreed, I'll recruit Bart, Alan Jules, Wayne, and maybe Gary

Lissitar. Tom is already in, right, Tom?"

Santo looked at a smiling Tom, shook his head, and rolled his eyes upward. "I'll have the paperwork ready."

***

Nobody would guess the boys from CHB were delinquents on this second Friday of September. The newly showered team arrived at the gym and changed into their travel clothes. Their clothes squeaked with newness, yet not one grumble about a stiff collar or a tight fit came from their mouths. They admired themselves, adjusting each other's ties and brushing off their teammate's shoulders.

O'Hurley drove the rust-spattered truck and flatbeds into place.

"Even hosed it all down for ya." O'Hurley bragged.

After the players and recruited staff members climbed aboard, the caravan sputtered its way past the entrance sign, onto the paved country road.

When a local farmer waved to the group, Tom leaned over and whispered to Matt, "If that guy knew who these kids were, he sure as hell wouldn't be waving."

"Maybe running, or locking his door," Matt agreed.

The ride was what everyone needed and went without incident. After an early supper, coaches and players climbed onto the bus.

Despite the successful romp around the countryside, Matt couldn't calm the nerves playing havoc with his stomach. A lot could still happen.

The yellow CHB bus drove westward for nearly two hours and pulled into Bakerton's designated high school parking area. A typical high school, it boasted newly constructed wooden bleachers visible from the lot.

Nervous, but excited, the players held their heads high as they exited the bus. A young man in a Bakerton High School T-shirt greeted them and escorted the team down to the locker area. Matt's intuition had paid off. Appearances meant a lot.

The players changed into their stylish green and white uniforms, the added line of gold contributing to the positive aura surrounding them. They emerged from the corner of the field, warmed-up, loosened-up, and wearing the sweat of anticipation.

After getting their timing down, they sprinted back to the locker room for the pre-game talk. Matt rarely prepared his pep talk. He relied on his gut. The boys gathered around him, and a feeling of family hung in the room.

"Tonight is the culmination of your hard work. The results of your patience and pain will unfold on Bakerton's field. Go out there and show who you are. Represent yourselves, me, and above all, everyone back at CHB. Show these people you can play this game by the rules. Show them you're a class act."

Matt placed his foot up on a bench and continued. "Go out there and knock people down. Then help them back up. After that, get back on the field and knock 'em down again." Every eye focused on Matt.

"If you're tempted to argue with a referee who comes down hard on you, don't. That's not your job, it's mine. Your job is to regroup and stay in the fight. If you lose your cool, swing at another player, or run away, you'll let yourself and your teammates down."

"Coach?" whispered a soft voice from the back of the locker room.
"Yes?"
"Let's play this one for Danny Williams."
"For Williams!" another shouted, and soon the room filled with the name of the boy who had died so suddenly.

The sound of Williams' name reverberated through Matt's body. As the volume of the cheers decreased, Matt attempted to speak. The words choked in his throat and he coughed to clear them away.

"Let's do it!" he said in a solid voice.
"Let's do it!" the team repeated in unison.
"For you, Williams," Matt added in a whisper. He sighed before following the charging Ospreys back onto the field.

The opposing team, much bigger in stature than the Ospreys, marched onto the slightly muddy field, ready to play. CHB won the toss and elected to receive the kickoff. For the first two quarters, the two teams held each other at a virtual standoff, and the game remained scoreless at halftime.

"You're doing great," Matt said to the team, gathered at the half in the locker room. "No matter how you feel about the score, dig deeper. Don't let fatigue take control in the second half."

"Coach, it's blowin' up a storm!"
'Fixin' to rain like a cow pissin' on a flat rock," Bo added.

"All of you know how to handle that. You practiced it. Go out there and do what you know how to do, the best you can do it. Continue, no matter how wet or nasty it gets. Play with as much ferocity on your last play as you do on your first, and we'll win this game. Remember, your true strength is inner."

A typical Florida downpour erupted in the beginning of the third quarter, and the Ospreys took it in stride. The brawny and more experienced Bakerton High School Panthers methodically executed their plays against the younger squad from CHB. The Ospreys fired back with vicious hitting, and as the game wound down, still no points appeared on the board. Both defensive units were determined to hold the line, both teams fighting for that important first victory on the rain-soaked field.

Late in the third quarter, Bakerton scored a touchdown but missed the extra point. Castor told Bo and the offensive line, "We've got you covered. Make somethin' happen. Put us on the board!"

The rain tapered off, but the field was a muddy mess. Questions dodged through Matt's mind like a tight end through a defensive line. Did I spend enough time with the offense? Will I call the right play?

As if Bo had read his mind, he caught the next throw, tucked his head, and plowed through the mist. He crashed through Bakerton's line for the first touchdown, and Bell ran the ball in for the extra point.

The Panthers couldn't regroup before the game ended 7–6. The Ospreys had won! Smacks on the butt, hard pats on the back, and wide grins followed the group back into the locker room for the final time. The reality began to sink in.

They had done it! The boys were proud, ecstatic at how they had played. Matt looked at Bo, whose head bobbed back and forth. Laughter carried above the celebration. Matt savored the moment.

On the return trip outside of DeFuniak Springs, the bus sputtered and lurched forward. The driver pulled the vehicle off the road as it took one last gasp. Several attempts to restart the engine were futile.

The murmur of voices became less and less audible as the night wore on. Fatigue laid its hand on each boy's shoulder and dragged him into sleep.

"Matt," Tom whispered, "here we are in the middle of the night, on board a bus loaded with kids who could have made a break for it. Instead, they're sleeping like babies."

"Yeah, watching over them makes me realize they're just a team of boys like every other high school team. They did a great job didn't they?"

"Think we'll make it back to CHB before breakfast?" Tom asked.

A yawn escaped Matt's mouth. "After a night like tonight, it doesn't matter, does it?"

It took hours for CHB to locate a mechanic to drive out and make the repairs. The bus returned to the school after three in the morning.

The next day, word spread fast about the Osprey's first win of the season. Everywhere on campus, someone patted somebody on the back. A seldom felt euphoria rushed from one cottage to the next. "All right!" and "Great job!" echoed throughout the day.

The celebration continued at The Country Club. Glasses lifted to the air as toasts sounded throughout the room. Waitresses balanced rounds of beer and delivered cocktails nonstop. Santo's chest swelled with pride.

"What's your secret?" one of the club members asked Matt.

Matt smiled as he winked at Tom. It was impossible to explain what had gone into this effort for the last seven months.

"All we have to do is figure out how to do it again with East Chattahoochee, right?" Tom asked the crowd. Everyone laughed and folks relaxed, moving into smaller, familiar groups.

Betty weaved through the crowd toward Matt as the get-together was ending.

"Mr. Hero, how about you and I mosey on over to the jukebox and listen to a little Ray Charles or Brenda Lee?"

Matt maneuvered Betty in the direction of the music. After two dances they moved from the dance floor to a table. He stepped behind Betty's chair and pulled it out, allowing her to take a seat. As he pushed the chair in, his lips brushed her ear.

"You look particularly enchanting tonight, pretty lady," he whispered She was still blushing after Matt had taken his seat.

"So, want to talk to me, Coach Grazi?"

"About the details of our first victory?"

"Ah, no."

"Okay, how about something other than conversation?"

He squeezed Betty's hand, and they moved back to the nearly empty wooden floor for one last dance.

***

By the following Monday the jubilation on campus had wound down to an almost normal hum, but the boys were still psyched. Matt and Tom scheduled practice right away, knowing the team couldn't rest. Their next game would be even more of a challenge than Bakerton had been.

"You guys were phenomenal," Matt said to the group on the turf. "I couldn't have been any prouder."

"I never won anythin' like this in my whole life!" sounded from the group.

"Me neither," echoed back and forth.

"That's great, but it's time to let it go. East Chattahoochee, known as 'Hoochie,' by the locals, is our next opponent, reportedly the best team in the division. They have an advantage Bakerton didn't have. They know more about us because they've seen our plays."

"Yeah, and they know we keek ass, right, Coach?" Gonzales asked.

"We're unstoppable!" Bell cheered as he spun around, punching the air.

Hoots and hollers of agreement carried into the blue Florida air.

"Snap back to reality," Matt's voice boomed. "The time to celebrate is over!" Shouts of celebration lessened into murmurs until seconds later, silence ensued.

"Listen up, one win is only the first step. After each game we play, we must become sharper, or we'll go down in flames."

Matt initiated the revised practice regimen and the team jumped into action. Only after the players were exhausted did Matt, Tom, Bo, and Mulany gather the equipment and head for the gym.

"Coach?" Bo called out as they started walking.

"Yeah?"

"Thanks," he said. "It was a great game."

"You made it happen," Matt said to the boy's back. "That touchdown saved us."

Bo stopped and turned.

"No, Coach, *we* made it happen." And with a grin he turned again, waving over his shoulder.

Relaxed in his office, Matt took a sip of freshly perked coffee and brushed the clutter from his chair and desk. Shuffling through the delivered mail, he noted a letter from his mom, a magazine, and flyers from sporting-goods suppliers.

Yep, the usual.

As he threw the mail back onto the desk, one letter fell to the cement floor. He leaned over to pick it up. Turning the envelope over, he stared at the formal correspondence. Examining the letter closer, a thumping in his chest palpated in a wild, irregular rhythm. Before his knees had a chance to give out, he collapsed into the chair.

"Oh my God!" he whispered aloud. *It can't be.*

CHAPTER 31

The stamped return address stared up at Matt as if it were alive, Department of Defense, U.S. Army. Reluctant to tear the envelope open, minutes passed before Matt slipped his finger under the tight seal. He removed the folded one-page letter and read President Kennedy's "invitation" to serve. Although his eligibility had been determined before he arrived at the boys' school, the unexpected draft notice burned in his hand.

Prior to this coaching job, his selection for military service had fostered an excitement, a pride in country. But not today. Everything had changed since February.

Except the news on the radio and his monthly communication with his folks, Matt had lost connection with the outside world. His priorities focused on Bo and the boys.

Matt read the official words more slowly. It was his turn. He had to report the last week of October.

I can't leave. Not now.

The thought of a job left undone, of deserting a boy and team in the midst of their mission, caused an overwhelming ache in every part of his body.

"Uh-oh, what's wrong?" Tom asked as he took in Matt's blanched face through the open door. Matt turned his head away and stretched out his arm to hand him the letter that ended his coaching job.

"Oh shit!" Tom said. He wrung his hands together, looking down at the floor.

"Don't say a word. I have to think about this." His voice slipped from gravelly to dry and raspy. "When the time is right," he coughed, "I'll tell the boys. For now, it's between you and me." Matt cleared his throat again. "And Santo, I suppose."

Matt slammed his fist down on the desk. It was as if the first half of a game had evaporated, and the time clock had magically spun ahead. His fourth quarter at CHB started this minute, and the team had only played a single game.

He spent the evening regrouping from what he considered a foul play. Circles of gray emerged under eyes and darkened each time he awoke, paced, stared out the window, and returned to bed.

Only after he repeated the ritual and made the decision on how to proceed the next day, did his body allow him a precious few hours of sleep.

Hoo, hoo, too-HOO.

***

The football team waited.

Blurry-eyed, Matt jogged in place for a few seconds outside his office before heading down the hallway. He added his traditional controlled breaths to assist him in getting back on task. He had to act as if his upside-down life had somehow righted itself.

He took his place in the center of the team's half circle and explained Hoochie's mental and physical advantage. The school had a history fortified with strong traditions and school spirit. Their team was more muscular, and they played more aggressively.

"Hoochie has climbed one class higher than us," Matt said. "This means they have a better record and have competed with more talented teams. We need to be at the top of our game if we're going to beat these guys."

Once he verbalized strategies to outwit their upcoming competitor, Matt's fervor for the game took over. Thoughts of the life-altering army correspondence receded into the background. Football had always provided relief that way, a reprieve from the outside world.

The boys seemed unimpressed. They either didn't comprehend the differences between Bakerton and East Chattahoochee, or they thought none of those things mattered.

"We can do this, Coach," Bo said. He raised his arm over his head and pointed forward, lowering it into an imaginary charge. "Kinda like we're David and Hoochie is Goliath."

"I like your optimism, Bo, and bring your slingshot to the game, but I'm worried you guys aren't listening. If you don't take this team seriously, you'll lose."

"The word *lose* ain't in our vocabulary no more," Bo said. "Hey, I reckon I'm learnin' somthin' after all. Vo-cab-u-laree. That was a word I knew, but sure as heck never used."

Matt heaved a sigh. He ordered Bo and Mulany to begin the updated drills and workouts. Muscles tensed, time clocks clicked, weights lifted.

"I love this game, Coach," Bo said, rubbing down the equipment after the boys had finished. "I'm already awake when *Reveille* sounds, can't wait for our day to start. Use'ta be I didn't give a crap about much. Now I really care 'bout somethin'."

"Bo, I . . ."

"What is it, Coach? You okay?"

"Fine, I'm fine," Matt said, pressing his lips together as he looked at the eager smile in front of him.

"You and me, Coach," Bo replied as he went out the door. "You and me can do anythin'."

Overwhelmed with the stinging urge to grab Bo and tell him their time together was almost over, Matt instead swallowed the lump in his throat and watched the boy almost skip down the hallway.

***

The following Friday in September was marked as a bye on the athletic calendar, so the team wouldn't play. As a surprise, the Tallahassee Businessmen's Association had purchased tickets for the coaches and football team to travel to Tallahassee on Saturday to see FSU play football against George Washington University. CHB rewarded boys rated as Ace or Pilot as well, buying tickets for them to join the outing.

Three days before the trip, Matt submitted the final bus list, which included fifty-three boys. The following morning, Tom sauntered into

Matt's office, roster in hand.

"Noticed Mulany's name, Matt."

"Sure."

"He can't go."

"I don't understand."

"You know the rules when it comes to public off-site visits."

Matt was baffled. "Excuse me? What are you talking about?"

"Come on, Matt, you do know Mulany was sentenced to CHB for some kind of manslaughter, don't you?"

"What?" Matt asked, unable to mask his sense of shock and disbelief.

"The boy was sent here for killing somebody, which means he's not allowed off campus for extracurricular activities. Are you telling me you didn't know?"

"I, I . . ."

"How is that possible?"

Matt had turned over every rock to uncover anything and everything about Bo. Why hadn't he been as thorough with Mulany, a kid entrusted with all kinds of sensitive information?

"I, I don't know, I . . . , I don't know how, why I . . . , Mulany's such a good kid. We've never had any problem with him, you know that. He's been an asset from the beginning. For God's sake, he travels with the team, Tom. What's the difference here?"

"Traveling as a supervised team member to a local school is one thing, but traveling to a public event as populated as a college stadium is quite another. Too many unknowns, too numerous temptations."

"But Tom, he's proven himself. He's dependable, hardworking."

"Doesn't matter."

Like Bo, sixteen-year-old Mulany had pushed to achieve good academic standing. Matt had assumed his improved grades, along with time served, was going to make him a candidate for early release.

"He told me he'll be discharged before Christmas," said Matt, "when he's seventeen."

"Every boy is discharged when they're seventeen. There's little chance he'll be going home. More probable he'll be transferred to ACI."

"Wait! There's no way! What can I do? Can't you do something?"

"A judge decides his fate from here."

Matt stared at Tom as if it was all a mistake.

"Did you know this the whole time, Tom?" Matt asked. "About

Mulany?"

"I probably got notified upon the boy's admission, but to be honest, if I had, I put it out of my mind. A boy's sentence isn't an issue until something like this happens."

"I feel like shit."

"Mulany knows he can't go to the game. I suspect everybody knows."

"Except me, apparently. But it's my job to give him the news. I'll take some time to talk to him while everyone's at the game."

"Folks fight for the opportunity to see the Seminoles."

"Already seen my share of FSU games, Tom. Rather spend time with Mulany. Maybe sneak over to see Betty."

"We've got plenty of takers for your ticket, but sure wish you'd go."

The team, scholars, and chaperones counted the minutes before they were to board the bus. The football team and faculty, including Tom and his wife, left the campus at quarter after four in two buses and a school car. For supper, they took a picnic of sandwiches, bananas, eggs, and cold drinks packed by the food service department.

Matt dragged himself down the hallway to the locker room. He gazed into the mirror and splashed cool water up onto his flushed face. He blinked back his disappointment and watched it drip from his chin. Both the water and his enthusiasm for the trip circled around the basin and disappeared down the drain. The harsh sting of assumption reflected off the mirror.

Matt chatted with Mulany before heading for The Country Club. The boy lamented about missing the game, but seemed to accept the rules.

Matt knew he would hear one enthusiastic comment after another tomorrow as the team members reported on their incredible day. The thought of his letter from Uncle Sam surfaced, but there was no way he would burst their bubble.

Was there ever going to be a right time?

***

Days of practice came and went, and the next Friday the team boarded the bus to East Chattahoochee High School where an intrigued crowd greeted the sharply dressed players.

Reports had come in after the first game that the Ospreys were no slouches. The Hoochie players had given up the thought they were going to play a bunch of low-life rednecks who didn't know their way around a football field. However, they still had trouble taking the new force at CHB seriously, because they had defeated the inmates so many times in past years.

Dressed like a proficient team and acting the part of the conqueror, the Ospreys strutted from the locker room onto the field. Like swashbuckling pirates, they carried themselves with confidence, almost defiance. A question rose in Matt's mind.

A false sense of security?

With the toss of a coin, the Ospreys drove to Hoochie's forty-yard line before turning the ball over. Alert play from the opposition denied Bo and the offensive team a touchdown three times. Castor held the CHB defense firm during the standoff.

Matt grabbed Tom's arm. "Break through!" he shouted. "Blitz Gonzales up the middle!" The team responded, and the Ospreys disrupted the play.

A bruising tackle by Bo, who had switched to defense, stopped East Chattahoochee on the fourth down at the fifteen-yard line. Within minutes, CHB's safety sustained a knee injury during the play. Dr. Graves ran on to the field, announcing the boy had to return to campus.

"Shit," Matt yelled. The first half ended 0–0.

In the locker room, Matt spoke to the offensive and defensive captains. Minutes later he spouted his words of wisdom, and the Ospreys ran back onto the field.

Time appeared to slow down the first moment the Ospreys got their hands on the ball. The hair on the necks of the fans stood as the ball thrown by CHB quarterback, David Bell, seemed to crawl its way into the sky, and then fall at the same snail's pace, into Bo's arms. He tucked the ball under his arm and sprinted downfield for a twenty-yard gain, pushing with all the speed his legs could give.

On the next play, Bo took a handoff from the quarterback on an off-tackle play and ran with the ball tucked in tight. Suddenly, a gasp sounded from the crowd.

Bo crashed to his knees, and then to the ground. Fear gripped Matt's throat and held on.

Bo . . .

Dr. Graves and the medical crew ran onto the field for a second time. The referee stopped the clock for an injury time-out.

"Huddle up!" Matt yelled to the remaining team members. "Stay focused," he demanded, the same time taking intermittent glances toward the boy and doctor on the field.

Matt turned his back to the scene across the gridiron. Everyone needed to concentrate on the next play, rather than on the seriousness of Bo's injuries.

Bo pushed his arms into the ground, trying to lift his body. Dr. Graves shoved a supporting arm under Bo's shoulder as the boy's legs began to buckle. After a few steps, Bo shook his head and separated from the doctor.

Walking off the field on his own, Bo looked toward his coach, and as if Matt's return gaze of concern gave him confidence, he straightened his stance as he reached the sideline.

Greetings and accolades from his cohorts were no doubt the cause of the smile inching across Bo's face. He seated himself on the bench. He looked toward Matt once more, and with this thumb and forefinger coming together, Bo gave Matt the "I'm okay" sign.

With newfound energy, Bell switched from quarterback to fullback and went through a gaping hole opened up by the offensive line. He sprinted down the field for a touchdown. Exhaustion blew from his nostrils.

The Osprey's try for the extra point failed. Bo insisted he had stabilized and begged Matt to put him back in the game. Dr. Graves ran him through a quick check-off procedure and gave the coach a nod.

East Chattahoochee returned the kickoff back to the fifty-yard line. On the first play from scrimmage, Bo sacked the quarterback for a twenty-yard loss and a fumble. CHB recovered the ball. Moments later, Bell, from his quarterback slot, threw a twenty-five-yard strike to Stalworth, who sprinted the remaining five yards with the aid of a key block. Touchdown! On the next play, Stalworth bolted around the left end and ran in for the extra point.

When the game was over, Bo had rushed for 161 yards on nineteen carries in a winning effort for the Ospreys, 13–0. The team slapped Stalworth and Bo on the backs until they almost tipped over.

The defensive team, with a willingness to hit hard, had turned the clear bright night into a nightmare for East Chattahoochee. At no time in the game, however, did Hoochie show signs of giving up. A stronger team had simply overpowered them.

"Even though our backs performed extremely well tonight," Matt said to the team in the locker room, "remember the game was won by both our offense *and* defense. And, of course, one hell of a sack by Bo, and one hell of a catch by Stalworth."

The boys cheered.

Matt turned toward Stalworth. "Maybe you should misbehave just enough to delay your discharge," he kidded. The boys cheered again.

For the past few hours, Matt had slipped between exhilaration and desperation, between hope and fear. Previous football games, especially those at FSU, had triggered strong emotions, but not like this.

The slamming sound of empty lockers echoed, and one by one, the Osprey team made their way to the bus. Matt leaned on the vehicle's fender, watching each boy lift his heavy legs to board. He nodded to every player as he boarded. He inhaled the night air, which assisted his tense shoulders to relax and drop into their normal position.

"Coach, can I talk with you a minute?" interrupted a strong voice. Matt recognized Hoochie's coach and moved with him away from the bus.

"You know, at most games like this, I'd be embarrassed being beaten by a hard-luck group of boys," the Hoochie coach began. "But this time, I tell you, that was one helluva game. Tell you something else, too. That tailback of yours, Beauregard, right? He's the best I've seen in a long, long time, and I hear he's only sixteen."

"Be seventeen this year."

"Well, he's going to make a hell of a ballplayer for somebody. I sure hope you keep him turned around, because he could be a great half-back when he gets out of your institution over there."

"Thanks." Matt smiled. Like a proud parent, he asked, "If you don't mind, would you tell that to Bo?"

With that, Matt whistled and Bo looked up. "Somebody here from the other team wanting to talk to you."

"'Bout what?"

"How should I know? Get over here."

Matt watched from a distance as the Hoochie coach and Bo talked and then shook hands. The day Matt had arrived on campus he was convinced the termination of his perfect career had ended the best times in his life. In July he had thought he could never feel right with the world again. Tonight proved it was possible to start over.

"Are you blushing?" Matt asked upon Bo's return.

"Aw, Coach, you know what he told me, don't you?"

"Yes, I do. There will be a lot of people outside of CHB looking at you with the same hopes I have."

"I feel like a million bucks, Coach."

"So do I, Bo. So do I."

CHAPTER 32

The CHB Ospreys combined an offense that operated like a precision machine with a hard tackling defense to overpower East Chattahoochee. The type of play displayed by these boys can only be described by one word: teamwork.

The article in the *Flying Osprey* reported the game with Hoochie at length, boosting the players' confidence. Matt used it as a repeated reminder about the importance of unity, hoping the positive sensation would springboard to the last Friday in September when they traveled to Anhinga Bay High School.

Matt countered Anhinga's reputation for terrific speed by walking through a series of new plays with the team. With no warning, the gym door flew open, bashing into the wall.

An immediate silence filled the room and Andrews stomped forward. His dark eyes flew from boy to boy, and he watched each one turn their eyes away or cower with their hands high up in front of their chests as if imagining the approaching pain.

"What do you want?" Matt asked, spitting the question toward the marine.

Andrews ignored him, continuing to advance, appearing to enjoy the panicked faces as he moved by.

"I'm running a practice here."

Still, the officer was silent. His fake smile curled with satisfaction in knowing he was in control. His gaze focused on Bo, and Matt stepped forward between them.

"I asked y . . . ,"

"They know what I want," Andrews interrupted, "don't you, boys?" No one moved as he continued his mock inspection.

"Get out!" Matt yelled, but it was too late. Andrews had already turned toward the exit.

In obvious defiance of the command to leave, the officer stopped his retreat and slowly turned around toward Matt. He made no move to advance, but instead lowered his head like a bull about to charge.

The boys' eyes widened.

Before Matt could make another move, the disciplinarian made his departure on his terms. The door slammed shut.

"Damn it!" Matt said low. All eyes centered on their coach. "Get back to work, boys. Don't let that man in."

But the damage was done. Despite Matt's efforts to distract the boys or push them to up their pace, Andrews' success in his mission remained in the forefront. The pungent smell of fear overrode the odor of sweat.

***

Matt's new plays did nothing to prepare the boys for the unwelcome reception that awaited them when they stepped onto the field.

"Hoods," "crooks," and "scum" were some of the names shouted at the CHB players. The rude Anhinga Bay crowd sat behind the Osprey bench, taunting the boys about where they came from and where they should stay.

The new psychological warfare of verbal harassment was a rough awakening.

Things deteriorated in the first quarter when the officials called back a touchdown because of an unwarranted penalty. Matt argued with the referees with no favorable result.

By halftime, after other penalties resulted in a loss of an additional fifty-five yards, a disgruntled team followed Matt into the locker room.

"Come on, Coach, these jerks are hittin' below the belt when the officials aren't watchin'. Even when the officials see it, they don't call it. It's not fair!"

"Let us keek a few butts," Gonzales complained. "If Anhinga plays dirty, why can't we?"

"Because," Matt said, "You guys have a record. Start any trouble, and you'll be back to Grub status or worse before the bus gets home."

Still, they persisted. "I'm gonna bash number 14," Bo mumbled. "He'll never know what hit him,"

"No, you're not."

"How 'bout an elbow to where the referee can't see?" Mulany asked.

"Stop it." He paused a moment. "Look, guys, toughen up. Bullies like these guys aren't unfamiliar. You know the type. They think they can rattle you, and it looks to me like they have. They're trying their best to bring you down to their level. It's how it is. So the question is, how will you handle it?"

"I know how I'd like to handle it," Bo muttered under his breath.

Matt cautioned Bo, then turned back to the group. "Face this," Matt said. "Close your ears and don't get thin-skinned on me. Do what you have to do, and do it by the book."

With an obvious lack of enthusiasm, Bo nodded. Another member pursed his lips, but he too gave an affirmative signal. Within seconds, the entire team indicated they would try it Matt's way.

After the team had hustled back onto the field, Matt raised his arms, bringing the boys together into a huddle. "Do it right," Matt said, "because you're better than them. Do it!"

"Do it!" the team repeated.

The Anhinga Bay team hammered hard. They muttered insults and slid in an unseen attack whenever possible, but the CHB team didn't take the bait. The crowd continued to harass the Ospreys, and the officials put a flag on any questionable play.

Despite the Ospreys doing their best, the boys suffered their first loss, 6–0.

Once on the bus, the number and volume of complaints increased. Anhinga Bay had dumped on them, bad. The ugliness of the day united the team, but the score made them bitter. They could call each other the worst possible names, but no outsider was getting that privilege. Talk of getting even surfaced.

Matt heard all he could. "You guys want to talk like this, fine, but don't do it in front of me. I'm not going to listen to crying about tonight's abuse. You stayed on top, regardless of the score. That's something that took guts and determination. Don't think about these losers, other than to thank them for teaching you how to cope with bullies. For God's sake, you're strong; you're the champs tonight!"

The boys calmed down from their frenzy, but there was no justice, and they knew it. Even so, no one could argue they had fought well and played with integrity.

They've got it, inner strength.

With this thought, Matt decided it was time. As the bus made the turn off Choctaw Avenue onto the campus, Matt stood and braced himself at the front. He asked everyone to remain seated. He had one more thing to tell them. The bus pulled to a stop and fell quiet as gym bags hit the floor.

"Tonight you survived tackles by a pack of bulldogs, and you came out on top. Remember that."

He shuffled his feet and repositioned himself. "Together you guys are a class act. I . . . uh . . ."

"What is it, Coach?" Bo asked. "What's the matter?"

"I've . . . I've got to tell you . . ." Matt took a deep breath.

"Just say it, Matt," Tom whispered as he leaned forward. Matt nodded.

"It's . . . Shit." Matt took a long breath. "I've received a letter from Uncle Sam and have to report for duty. For those of you who haven't been listening to the radio or watching TV, there are scary things going on in Vietnam, Cuba, and Berlin, too. It's my time to serve."

A cloak of dead air draped over the bus and made it difficult for Matt to breathe. The panicked faces, the dropped jaws, and other expressions of despair caused Matt to question the timing of his announcement.

"When Coach?" asked a lone voice from the back of the bus. "When are you leaving us?"

The words hit Matt with more force than the insults thrown earlier in the game. He fumbled for a comforting response. None came.

"End of October."

"You're not gonna be with us till the end of the season?" Bo asked in an unbelieving voice. Seeming unconvinced, he asked again. "You're leavin' before it's over?"

"Yes," Matt answered with hesitation. He stared at Bo with a pleading gaze. A portrait of hurt and disappointment stared back.

"I put my faith in you!"

Matt wanted to disappear, and it appeared Bo had mutual thoughts. The teen pushed to the front of the bus and shouted to the driver, "Open the damn door!"

No one spoke as the door folded to the side, and Bo rushed out. The boys rose one at a time, silently shuffling past Matt and stepping down off the bus. Matt sat unmoving, until Tom took a seat beside him.

"You okay? Need company on the way back to your cottage?"

"Not tonight, Tom," Matt answered, as he too grabbed his bag. *"You're leavin' before it's over?"* echoed in his head.

The night air was warm, and yet Matt's sweaty skin was cold. His legs felt like dead weight beneath him, and his rapid pulse caused him to lean against a lone pine. For a moment, he was afraid if he moved he would topple. Just like the world around him.

***

The following morning Matt made a phone call to Dr. Strickland. He arrived at the director's office, seeking approval to take Bo off campus. No need to explain. News of his departure had traveled fast.

His request granted, Matt searched for Bo. He found the teen sitting on the steps of his cottage. He wasn't sure if Bo would join him, or what he would say if he did.

"How about something to eat?" Matt asked as he approached the boy.

"Why?"

"I hear they're having a super special at the diner, and I'd sure like your company."

Bo lowered his head. He didn't say anything as he brushed a chameleon off the step. Puffs of white cumulus clouds shifted above.

"Not sure I wanna go anywhere with you."

"Not even for a thick, juicy, dripping, cheeseburger and grits?" Bo looked up.

"You tryin' to bribe me?"

"Is it working?"

Bo fidgeted about, pushing his hands up and down the top of his pants. "Guess so. Okay."

They walked in silence to the Ford Fairlane. Minutes later they parked in front of Hatcher's, the diner where both their lives had taken a turn.

Through the blurred chatter of local patrons, they found a booth. Matt grappled for the words to begin, but it was Bo who spoke first.

"I'm pissed, Coach. None of it means anything."

"Don't say that. You, the team, the effort . . . , they mean everything."

"What are we going to do? I mean, how are we going to play without you?"

Matt's hands quivered, and he held them tightly under the table. "Bo, let me tell you something. You can do anything without me, don't you know that? Sooner or later, you and I would have parted. You know that. It just came sooner than we expected."

"It's not fair. We worked so hard. It's gone."

Matt rubbed his arms and passed his fingers through his hair. Smoothing his hair back down, he looked into the disappointed face before him.

"It's not gone. It will never be gone. I'm proud of you, Bo. Your accomplishments and decisions over the past seven months have made a difference. The boys look up to you. And Bo, seeing you become . . . Well, you'll never know how much . . ."

"It was you, Coach," Bo interrupted. "You're the one who made stuff happen."

"Sure, I may have set the table, but you cooked the meal and ate it."

"Aw, Coach, you still have a funny way with words. Sometimes I still don't git what you're sayin'."

"Guess I'll have to learn how to speak more clearly. I don't want you to tune me out because my words tangle up."

"Don't worry, most times I figure out what you're tryin' to say, sometimes even before you finish sayin' it."

A half smile appeared on Matt's face. "Look, we have three more games together. Let's make them count. Let's play the best damn football games of the season."

"Can't you stay longer, Coach? Can't you ask permission or somethin'?"

"It doesn't work that way, Bo."

"Even if we win these next games, what happens after you're gone?"

"You and Coach Faber will be here."

"And when the season's over?"

"That's the neat thing. Another kind of game begins, and you pray that the one you finished playing makes you do a better job the next time around."

"You believe the stuff we do in football works outside this place, don't you, Coach?"

"Absolutely. It doesn't make a difference where you are. Every day you're in it. You make decisions based on what burns inside you. You choose whether to run or hold your ground."

"I dreamed of you being there when I finish high school. I mean, look at me. I'm almost an Ace, and I'll be goin' back home and graduatin', and you won't be there."

"Do you understand how important your graduation is? The value of a high school diploma is, well, immeasurable. Bo, it makes you a winner. You know that, don't you?"

"Yeah, you drilled that part into my head."

"Good."

It appeared Bo read between the lines to learn what Matt had known all along. Good players continue to play no matter what obstacles they need to overcome.

Leaving or staying, it was tough on both coach and boy. Bo didn't say another word on the way back to campus. Matt didn't expect he would.

Chapter 33

A sense of urgency swirled into campus on autumn's cooling breeze. With less than a month left as the school's coach, Matt pushed the boys hard in preparation for the first of three remaining games. The players responded by asking for more practice. Everyone wanted to win.

The first week in October, coaches and players boarded the bus for the two-hour ride south to Oyster City High School. By halftime, the Ospreys were leading by three touchdowns, and the trend continued into the fourth quarter. In the last minutes of the game, Bell took a hard hit and limped off the field, but not before the Ospreys bombarded the Bears 52–0. Dr. Graves promised Matt he would report back on Bell after a full evaluation.

The second weekend of October was another open date. Santo notified the coaches on both the South Side and North Side that their football teams would travel to Tallahassee. Matt loaded the Ospreys onto the bus to attend an FSU game, while the CHB Lions headed to Tallahassee to cheer for Florida Agricultural and Mechanical University (FAMU).

Matt again opted to stay behind. He sprinted to his car and headed for Betty's place before the buses had chugged out of sight.

"You're not the same person I met months ago," Betty said.

"I've aged a lot. Geesh, see any gray up here?" he asked, pointing to his head.

"Makes you more distinguished."

Betty's fingers lovingly touched his hair, while her other hand pushed a chilled Hamm's beer toward him. She tucked one leg underneath her as she took a seat on the sofa, and asked about Bo.

"He's at the Seminole game with the team. Tomorrow we'll continue our strategy for the battle with the Franklin Sharks."

"Always working on that winning football game, huh? Maybe things haven't really changed that much since your arrival after all."

Matt took a moment to reflect on his initial expectations of himself and the school. It seemed a lifetime ago.

"That's not exactly true. Winning the next two games is more important than ever, but . . ."

"But?"

"But . . . I see football through the eyes of these boys now, through Bo, and it's . . . well . . . , you were right the first time, he's changed everything."

"Looks like your dog is doing a pretty good job of hunting after all," Betty said with glossy rose-colored lips.

"Ha. He's had an impact on all of us, that's for sure."

"How's he taking it?" When Matt hesitated, she added, "Your leaving, I mean."

"Tough. He's tough."

Their beverages gone, the light in the room crept from an afternoon brightness to a reflected orange haze of sunset.

"I hope I've done something good for these boys," Matt said.

"You have, haven't you?"

"Yeah, I think so, but not without encouragement from one fine lady."

"My pleasure."

"No, it's been mine."

Matt extended his arm toward her and rose from the overstuffed chair. Tonight, boys and football games could wait. He fell onto the sofa, embracing both Betty and a fool's fantasy that holding on tight would increase their chance of seeing each other in the future.

***

"Did ya hear about the games, Coach?" Bo asked Matt during a workout session that following Sunday in the gym.

"Yeah, understand both FSU and FAMU were victorious."

"Got that right!" Bo exclaimed as he raised his hands in the air. "Touchdown!"

"Fun, huh?" Matt felt Bo's pleasure as it spread wide across the boy's face.

"The best!" the boy yelled. "They were unbelievable! We won 13–7! No wonder you loved playing for the garnet and gold. Go Seminoles!" As usual, the competitive action of football caused adrenaline to pump.

"Ready for the next game?" Matt asked.

"Might be our toughest game yet, Coach. We got 'bout the same number of wins, but there's a *biiiiig* difference."

"Yup, and this time I know what *you're* going to say before you say it: injuries."

Injuries had eliminated three important team players. One of Castor's hands turned out to be broken after the second game, and Mulany had been dazed in the last game and still had headaches. Most important, Bell, who had limped off the field at the end of the game with Oyster City, still had an unsteady gait. Dr. Graves had not given permission to play to any of them.

"I'll talk with the doctor again," Matt said, "but I'm pretty sure he won't budge. Find Tom. We need a new strategy."

"I got a new strategy, Coach, but it don't have nuthin' to do with the next game."

Matt heard the excitement in the boy's voice, and faced Bo's ear-to-ear grin. The boy held his photo pose until he could no longer remain still.

"I did it! I did it!" Bo yelled.

"Tell me!"

"I made Ace! I'll be gittin' out of the ninth grade. I go home!"

"Go home? You mean now?"

Matt now fully understood Bo's disappointment and anger upon hearing about his impending U.S. Army departure. He struggled to digest the news that Bo was scheduled to leave campus before the last game.

"When, Bo?"

"Any time after the forms come down, I guess. And I can't believe I'm saying this, but . . . ,"

"Saying what?"

"I don't wanna go home yet. Will you talk to 'em, Coach?"

"Come here, young man," Matt said, extending both hands. He grabbed Bo's hand between his and shook it with vigor. About to let go, Matt instead pulled Bo close, hugged him, and quickly pushed him back.

"Tell me more about this promotion."

"I'm one of seven Aces, you believe it? Never been seven at one time, I hear. We were worried they might not give all of us the rank up, but they did."

"Know how hard you worked to make this happen," Matt said in a heavy whisper. "Proud of you."

"Thanks, Coach. So how will you get permission for me to stay?"

Matt thought for a few moments before answering. "I'll stand behind you, but you need to ask for yourself."

Bo tilted his head in question, then his demeanor changed. He turned to the side, his sight moving from the posted football schedule clockwise around the familiar gym. "I love this place."

"I take it that lopsided smile means you'll do the asking?"

"Yeah."

"I'm liking this idea, Bo. With your classwork caught up, and permission to extend, you'll have more time with the team. I'm betting Santo will approve you sticking around for the next game."

"Not only the next game, Coach. I want to help win *every* game this season, even after you're gone."

Bo might be able to do for the team, what Matt wasn't able to. When did that transition take place?

"Let me know what Santo says," Matt said.

"Got it under control," Bo declared with a parting wave. He had always been a take-control kind of kid, and that hadn't changed one bit.

***

On that blustery October day, in front of the largest crowd of the season . . . it didn't happen. The CHB Ospreys lost their toughest game to the Franklin Sharks, 18–6.

"It may not be reflected on the scoreboard," Matt said in the locker room, "but each of you played well." Unlike the first loss, this time the boys appeared to believe their coach. Bo, not so much.

"I wanted to win, Coach," Bo moved toward Matt, a frown covering his face.

"We all did. It stinks, but we don't always get what we want."

"We worked so hard!"

"That's it, Bo!" Matt exclaimed. "You did! Every player worked hard!" Bo cocked his head.

"Working together is everything. Working hard, getting it done." Matt slapped the boy on the shoulder. "In one week we have our last game. Help me make the others understand there's more at stake than the score."

CHAPTER 34

The last October weekend, Matt rode the CHB bus for his farewell game. He clenched his fist in front of the team as he spoke, encouraging them to be tough.

"Make every play count," he yelled at the end of his pep talk, and threw his arm over his head, pointing toward the field.

"Put points on the board," Bo screamed to the offense as they ran toward the waiting crowd.

During the game, Matt stared out over the field and lived every play in slow motion. It was as if time allowed him one last look at what he had accomplished in this short tour of duty.

Each boy pushed with all his strength to make it happen. The quarterback focused on throwing the ball to the right player at the right time, and the defense held, out-running the opposing team and leaping into the air at the exact moment for an interception. The final score was a win, 25–18.

"If you stayed, Coach, we could win more," Gonzales said.

Matt winced at the sting of the boy's words. He tasted the guilt and pain as words tumbled from his mouth.

"You did it tonight," he said to the team. "And you can do it again. It took every one of you to make it happen. Every, single, one of you!"

Matt searched each boy's face as he boarded the bus. The broad grins and high-fives said it all. No longer football novices, these hard-luck kids had achieved a 4–2 record. Together they had made something un-predictable, almost magical, happen. This game showed them not only what was possible tonight, but also what was possible tomorrow.

Celebration, laughter, and singing resounded throughout the bus. The boys were on top, rehashing strategies and slamming their fists into their palms, reliving each winning play.

When "Soldier Boy" started playing on a portable radio, a loud voice yelled from the rear, "Turn that up!"

One boy after another chimed in, pointing their fingers at Matt and laughing. A few pushed their vocal cords to the limit. From there they crooned the first dozen verses of "A Hundred Bottles of Beer on the Wall," winding down to more subdued jubilation.

"Bet you're pleased to be leaving on a final victory," Tom said.

"No doubt about that. I'm enjoying this celebration as much as they are."

Ecstatic the moment the scoreboard reflected a win, Matt now set-tled into the warm pleasure of success. A sense of euphoria produced a tingle that lifted him upwards, and then eased him back onto his seat.

He sat sideways with his arm draped over the seat's back, his long legs sprawled into the aisle. The elation of the moment faded and a mel-ancholy descended. A part of him wanted to see a type of remorse, that in spite of the win, the boys were conscious of the inevitable upcoming void. But the boys seemed oblivious to anything but the victory.

After the bus driver downshifted and made the turn onto the gravel road of the main entrance, Bo moved to the front where Matt sat.

"Coach, before you climb off, could ya wait a minute? It's important."

The bus swung around in front of the gym, and one by one, the team members piled out. Only after Tom stepped off the bus did Bo grab his gear and turn toward Matt.

"Coach?"

"What is it, Bo?"

"I wanted me and you to be the last to leave. Will you take a short walk with me, you know, for the last time before we hit the gym?"

Matt bit down on his bottom lip, fighting back the emotion Bo's request evoked. "For the last time" laid heavy on his mind.

Slowing their pace to a crawl, they strolled through the campus.

They recalled their volatile relationship those first months, only now they could laugh about it.

"Man, I hated you from the moment I first saw you," Bo teased. "I thought you were the biggest phony I had ever met in my life. 'Mister Know It All.'"

"Oh yeah? I thought you were the most arrogant and stubborn kid I'd ever seen."

Laughing together, they strolled into the gym. The moment the door slammed behind them, a resounding cheer exploded from inside.

Matt jumped back, collapsing onto the bar of the door. His eyes fell on Tom, beaming in front of the crowd. Betty gave him a thumbs up from underneath the basketball hoop, and Santo stood at the half court, satisfaction covering his face. Staff members, including O'Hurley, Alan Jules, Bart, Gary Lissitar, and Mary Jo stood near a table covered with goodies. Dr. Graves waved from the corner. Folks from The Country Club, women from the garden club, and even parents of the players surrounded him.

Matt moved through the crowd, shaking hands, accepting well wishes. A lump formed in his throat as he soaked up the individual faces surrounding him. When Mulany shook his hand, he pulled the boy in for a hug.

Defiance had come from every angle in early spring, but those images were faded. His strongest memories would be of the crowd tonight. Gonzales laughing in front of him, Bell and Castor with their ties undone and their jackets slung over their shoulders, Bo silent, but plastered with a knowing smile.

He would miss these boys much more than they would ever miss him.

"Speech! Speech!" rang from the crowd. Arms and hands pushed Matt toward a makeshift podium.

"Okay, okay!" he conceded as the boys patted him on the back and eased a microphone into his hands. A hush fell on the crowd.

"I'm not sure what to say," Matt said softly. "I don't know where to start."

"Start at the beginning," Bart prompted.

"Thanks, Bart. That should be easy because it seems like last February was just yesterday. I remember playing the fool. 'Coaching can't be that hard,' I said to myself. A coach had been part of my life even before high school. All I had to do was apply what I had learned and I'd be a super coach of a super team." He paused. "Little did I know. I know now that the moment I thought I knew everything, I knew nothing."

Matt turned his head toward Tom. "Thanks especially to you, Coach Faber, for help with that lesson and many others. Matt casually saluted his cohort and friend. "I would have thrown in the towel on several occasions without your support." The crowd cheered.

"Looking back, my life as an FSU quarterback looks easy. If I had ever known the amount of work required for this job, I would have chickened out before I even started. Thanks to you guys, I have never been so frustrated, and yet so proud, in my entire life. Coaching is a lot harder than I ever imagined. I hope I did right by you."

Applause and cheering erupted, and several seconds passed before Matt continued.

"I focused on becoming a decent college football player since I can remember. I wanted to make it in the pros." Matt paused. "But hard as I tried, hard as I planned, things didn't quite work out." His eyes found Bo in the crowd. "Turns out, that's okay," he said, "better than okay."

Matt took a long breath and realized his hands were shaking. He rubbed them together and focused on the surrounding players. "I wouldn't trade this past year of my life for a lifetime of football. You won't understand that now, maybe never, but believe me it's true."

"Build on this team, the one we've built together. Take it with you, as I will take it with me. When life after CHB becomes difficult, re-member the haunting day at Anhinga Bay, and know you rose above it. Getting through that night means you can conquer anything."

"Have your goals, have your dreams," Matt said, "and follow them through." With a cracking voice, he lowered the volume and finished. "I'm gonna miss every one of you."

Applause erupted a final time.

Bo was the first to recover. "Turn on that stereo and play some music!"

"Here's a new song by Ray Charles, for you, Coach!" yelled Bell.

"Hit the Road, Jack" filled the air. The boys hummed or sang along as a few showed off their dance moves. Chatter increased as the crowd moved toward the food table.

"The boys planned this surprise party themselves, you know," said Tom when he finagled a moment alone with Matt. "They were the ones who elicited help from their families, and prodded me to approach ad-ministration for approval."

"They certainly kept this secret well."

"Oh, they're good at that." The two coaches laughed.

Easing himself through the dancing boys, Matt found Betty in the crowd. He slid his hand around her waist and pressed her to his side, leaning toward her ear.

"We okay?" he whispered. She tipped her head toward his shoulder.

"We said our goodbyes the other night." He squeezed her hand.

"Need a ride home?"

"Not tonight. Enjoy your party."

Matt made the rounds, thanking each person, shaking every boy's hand. He shared a customized word of wisdom with every player, wishing each boy the best upon his return home.

Clean-up was more a comforting labor than a chore, Matt and Tom locking the doors of the gym one more time together.

"Equipment ready for tomorrow?" asked Matt.

"It won't be the same."

"For either of us."

Matt gave Tom a parting wave on his way out the door. He stood for a moment as he grew accustomed to the dark. Within seconds the glow of a burning cigarette came into focus and he spotted a smug Andrews leaning against the brick wall, deeply inhaling the acrid fumes. Wanting to pass without a confrontation, he stepped forward, keeping the marine in his peripheral vision.

With a satisfied grin on his face, Andrews stepped from the shadows and gave a childish wave of his hand, silently saying: Bye-bye.

I'm leaving, and he's staying.

Refusing to acknowledge the man, Matt bit down on his tongue. The disciplinarian had not succeeded in his attempts to dominate him, but knowing that did little to ease his mind. He had not succeeded in his efforts to rid CHB of this man either.

Matt swallowed hard before turning to walk away, his stomach churning like a washing machine.

Had he done enough? Anger and guilt swelled inside when he thought about leaving the campus under the influence of this man. After several quick steps, the barred owl's rhythmical hoots interrupted his thoughts.

Hoo, hoo, too-HOO, Hoo, hoo, too-HOO, Hoo, hoo, too-HOO, ooo.

The message sounded like a repetition of "Who looks for yoou? Who looks for yoou? Who looks out for yoou-all?"

The hoots vibrated again through the forest. Once a racket, the owl's distinctive call soothed his mind.

Matt stared at the slight movement in the topmost branches of the massive pines. He had to let it go.

Hoo, hoo, too-HOO, I did what I could. I did what I could.

CHAPTER 35

At seven thirty the next morning, a red-eyed Matt faced Santo when he appeared at his gym office door.

"Whoa, rough night?"

"Restless night. Crazy dreams."

"A walk?"

They meandered around the campus, Santo praising Matt on what he had accomplished. The boys had come together as the team they both had hoped for. He told Matt that after he completed his tour of duty, his coaching job would be waiting for him.

The offer triggered an unexpected response. A sense of clarity rushed into Matt's head, accompanied by hot sweat from every pore in his body.

I will never be back.

He didn't share that with Santo, nor would he reveal his decision with Bo, Tom, or the team. He had given this job his best, but to play the game one must respect the rules, including the accepted whippings. He couldn't conceive of returning to face Andrews unless he had the authority to control the man.

Something else. If he returned, no Bo. The boy was one of a kind and they had formed an unexplainable bond. Without him, well . . .

And what if he couldn't help the next boy? Things would never be the same, nor should they. Perhaps coaching again wasn't meant to be.

"You've been a patient, understanding boss, Santo. I know we disagreed at times, but I couldn't have functioned without your support."

"I'd like it if you made it back at Christmas time for the boys' holiday efforts. As you know, it's quite the celebration."

"I have no idea where I'll be, but thanks for the invite. And Santo, may I ask a couple things of you?"

"What's that?"

"Will you continue to monitor the discipline?"

"You mean watch Andrews?"

Matt swallowed hard. "More than watching him. I'm asking that you have the name of every boy he wants to whip pass over your desk. Check the names. If any of my boys are on that list, look into the situation yourself."

"All right. I'll do that for you. You have my word on it. And?"

Matt extended a letter of praise and support for Mulany toward Santo. "Can you put this in his file and write up a positive official evaluation of the boy? He'll need every break possible. He's a good kid." The ensuing handshake confirmed both their deal and their respect for each other.

Cleaning out his office was Matt's last task of the day, and his impatience surfaced when the chores of packing and signing forms took longer than he intended. He glanced at the soiled and worn notebook on the desk. About to throw it in the trash can, an afterthought prompted him to press it to his chest. It held the secrets, strategies, and tactics of the last eight months, and it represented everything he and the boys had built together.

He gently flipped through the frayed pages and then, with two hands, lowered it into the one cardboard box he was taking with him. Grabbing the box and a gym bag, Matt left, hearing the metallic doors slam for the last time.

***

The trumpet's call of *Reveille* broke the morning's silence and announced the start of the overcast day. Already awake, Matt wiped the remnants of Burma shaving foam from his face and peered out his window. Anticipating the flow of boys from the cottages to the dining hall, he increased his pace.

He laid his hand on the leather game football, hoping to feel its comfort. The pigskin was cool to his touch. He stuffed it into the small, empty gym bag and threw it over his shoulder. Leaning toward the last, almost packed box, the faces of his mom and dad returned his gaze.

I gave it my all, Papa.

Tucking in the remaining items, Matt slid the lid in place and locked the door to Cottage C for the last time.

He stuffed the final load into the Ford Fairlane. Circling past Bo's cottage, he parked on the slight incline, pushing in the clutch to leave the car in gear. Matt straightened his stance and walked into the familiar building.

"Hey, Bart. Bo still here?"

"Right down the hall."

As Matt turned left toward the dorm area, Bart spoke again. "He's not the only one who's going to miss you, Matt."

"Thanks, Bart. I haven't forgotten that first day we met. My chest pounded. If anyone had ever told me the real scoop on these kids, how leaving would be the hardest thing I've ever done, well, I'd never have believed them."

Bart acknowledged the confession with a nod. He pointed down the hall.

Moving into the sleeping quarters, Matt approached the boy's back as he finished making his bed, pulling the sheets straight and tight.

Matt cleared his throat. "You could bounce a coin off that bed, my boy," he said softly.

Bo's face lit up. The two moved behind the cottage building to the playground and settled in next to the jungle bars.

Words unspoken, they sat together for several minutes. Matt didn't have a son, but he believed this must be what a father felt when saying good-bye.

"Got to leave," Matt whispered.

"Yeah, I know, Coach." Bo raised his face to the warm Florida sun peeking its way through the remaining mist of morning. "It's tough, what you're doing. I want you to know, though. Everybody should do somethin' for their country."

Bo's words reinforced the trust and honor between them.

"I wish we'd been born at a different place and time, Coach. I picture us cowboys, me and you, riding the range in the good ol' west. That wudd'a been somethin'."

"Partners."

"Yeah. Like that."

Bo shuffled his feet, inspecting the dirt around his shoes, and then lifted his head to the sky again. "I'm gonna miss you, Coach. I'll remember 'bout you being here, looking over my shoulder, helpin' me. I won't let you down. I won't let you down because . . . I lo . . . "

An all-encompassing pride, sadness, and affection squeezed hard at Matt's throat. His hand covered his pressed lips, and he sniffed the accumulating moisture in his nostrils. All he could manage was a feeble, "Time for me to go."

He took a small step to leave, but then hesitated. A hard squint pushed back the fluid in his eyes. He smiled at the boy who had found the way into his heart.

"Bo, I love you too," he stuttered. "I'll never forget you . . . for as long as I live."

As though thinking simultaneously, *what the hell,* they stepped forward and gave each other a long bear hug.

After a few seconds, Matt pushed back. He nodded at Bo and, wiping his wet cheek with the back of his arm, reached into his gym bag.

"One more time?"

"You bet." Bo ran into the cleared area beyond the playground.

Gripping his beloved game ball with both hands, Matt placed his fingers above the laces. He took a deep breath and positioned his body in a throwing stance.

"I don't need you anymore," he whispered to the ball. As he reached back, his left arm extended toward his target. He wound up and let the ball fly.

A panting Bo looked over his shoulder, jumped into the air, and reached high to catch an almost perfect spiral. A once-in-a-life connection. He leaned over, his breath rushing through his mouth. He examined the ball and raised his head toward his coach.

The boy's expression told Matt all he needed to know.

Matt waved, saluted, and turned toward his car. His hand shaking, he found the door, stumbled into the front seat, and turned the key. Trying to swallow the lump in his throat, he ground the gear into reverse and skidded out of his parking space.

With a quick shift from first to second, he lurched toward Colby

Hill's front entrance. The sound of crunching gravel disappeared as he made the turn onto the asphalt. Matt didn't look back. He didn't have to. He would never forget.

"Coach" Victor Charles Prinzi, 1936–1998

Victor Prinzi was a fifth-string quarterback at Florida State University when he first grabbed national attention. Lifelong friend and college roommate, actor Burt (Buddy) Reynolds, joined him in the backfield. Four years later, as a senior co-captain of the 1958 team, he guided the Seminoles to a 7–4 record and a berth in the Bluegrass Bowl.

After coaching at the Florida School for Boys in Marianna, Florida, Prinzi served in the military before joining the high school and college coaching ranks for twelve seasons. He joined Gene Deckeroff on FSU football broadcasts as a color analyst in the 1980s, filling in when play was not in progress. Providing background material, such as statistics, strategy, and injury reports for over seventeen years, he became one of the voices of Florida State football. During 1983–85, Vic became one of the "Voices of the Tampa Bay Bandits" of the USFL. Elected into the FSU Hall of Fame in 1988, he starred in pre-game segments called *Great Moments in Seminole History.*

Many remember Vic's successes on the Florida State football team. Football fans recognize his voice as a football color analyst. From this moment forward, he will be remembered for sharing his story that led to the creation of *Coach in Cottage C.*

Rosemary Ryan Imregi

Born and raised on Staten Island, New York, writing was always her passion. Her favorite assignments were essays or compositions and, as a teenager, she began submitting short stories to magazines. Ever pursuing the dream to write a novel, she attended Brookdale Community College and later wrote biographies in a monthly column for a local Florida newsletter. She has been writing ever since.

Today she resides in Florida with her husband, Anthony, and actively participates as a member of Florida Writers Associations. She completed her first work, *Coach in Cottage C,* with her co-author, J.R. Minard. She has individually published her second book, *Goodbye Danube*, a historical fiction novel based on a family of six who escaped Budapest during the 1956 Hungarian Uprising. Her third book is in progress.

J.R. Minard

Born in New York City and graduated from Wagner College on Staten Island, J.R. soon recognized the integral role teens were to play. Whether teaching in junior high and high school classrooms, or at home raising two daughters while working at Tallahassee Memorial Hospital, the importance of assisting young adults increasingly became the focus.

After completing a MA degree in adult education from Florida State University and working as a technical writer and trainer for a medical company, J.R. became part of the faculty at the Job Corps in Charles Town, West Virginia, and worked with RESA 8, a community program that provided educational programs and services. Today a portion of J.R.'s time is spent as a volunteer with the Patriotic Service Dogs that are trained at Lowell Correctional Institute for Women in Florida.

The determination to assist adolescents, the love of creative writing, a bond with a lifelong friend, and a chance encounter, all contributed to the debut novel, Coach in Cottage C.

ACKNOWLEDGMENTS

Rosemary Ryan Imregi

It has taken decades to complete *Coach in Cottage C*, mainly because I am the Yang to my co-author's Ying. Knowing and caring for each other, we complement each other through our opposite approach to writing. It has been a total joy to create a novel worthy of the years we explored the written world together.

I thank my husband, Tony, for his help and encouragement throughout this process. I'll love you forever. To my children, Ginger, Mathew, and Kelly, their spouses, and my grandchildren Sydney, Madelyn, Miles, Liam, and Logan, love you all.

J. R. Minard

I'm indebted to my family, especially my husband, for believing our story, and more important for believing in me. To my co-author, Rosemary Imregi, thank you for making our journey together one of everlasting friendship.

To our content editor, Heather Whitaker, who encouraged us to make every chapter, scene, paragraph, and line the best that it could be, thank you. Your workshops and the gracious folks who shared hours of their time every other week for over two years provided a never-ending learning experience and made me a better writer. A special thanks to James Noble, whose literary talent, sense of humor, and insights continue to amaze.

Our gratitude goes out to our first editor, Cecile Baker, and the Tallahassee critique members, Terry Lewis, Liz Jameson, Sam Staley, and Michael Whitehead, for sharing their wealth of knowledge. We owe a debt to the writers and readers of The Villages of Florida, and the Beta readers whose feedback opened our minds to correction and suggestion. You know who you are.

To our lawyer, William Wohlsifer, who took us over obstacles to ensure our manuscript made it into our readers' hands. Thank you to Sea Hill Press for bringing this story to life in the most professional way possible and for providing support going forward.

For more information on

Coach In
COTTAGE C

visit:

www.coachincottagec.com

Made in the USA
Monee, IL
16 January 2020

20399632R00150